i

# Dante's War

**John Kimmey**

Pocol Press
Punxsutawney, PA

POCOL PRESS
Published in the United States of America
by Pocol Press
320 Sutton Street
Punxsutawney, PA 15767
www.pocolpress.com

Publisher's Cataloguing-in-Publication

Names: Kimmey, John L., 1922-, author.
Title: Dante's war / John Kimmey.
Description: Punxsutawney, PA: Pocol Press, 2019.
Identifiers: LCCN 2019952632 | ISBN 978-1-929763-91-7
Subjects: LCSH World War, 1939-1945--Italy--Fiction. | Italy--History--
German occupation, 1943-1945--Fiction. | Spies--Fiction. | BISAC
FICTION / Historical | FICTION / Espionage
Classification: LCC PS3611 .I475 2019 | DDC 813.6--dc23


Library of Congress Control Number: 2019952632

## DISCLAIMER and ACKNOWLEDGEMENTS

The story and characters except for the general used historically are fictional, products of the authors imagination. Any resemblance to anyone living or dead is purely coincidental.

I want to thank Lynda Lamarre for her assistance with this novel.

# DEDICATION

For Jane

"Now let us descend into the blind world here below"

*Inferno* Canto IV

"Thence we issued out, again to see the stars."

*Inferno* Canto XXXIV

Chapter 1

I can't sleep. Lying on the cot under the mosquito netting waiting for dawn and thinking about the jump tonight. Hitch up the static line, snap the cotter pin in place. Exit head down with feet together and knees slightly bent. Assume a fetal position close to the ground and use the pull of the chute to raise up and run around it to collapse the billowing. If only I don't freeze and the damn thing opens. Hell, I've never done it at night before.

It's slowly getting light. My last day in this shabby old city by the sea. The church bell across the alley starts ringing. I go over to the window and look down at a line of girls in gray-striped cotton uniforms with their hair in pigtails marching through the front door singing. White-hooded nuns in brown habits follow, wooden crosses dangling from their waists like keys. Last night a couple of them were on the roof taking food from British soldiers who live in apartments behind the church. A legless blind beggar sits crumpled up against the wall at the corner, a fedora upside down beside him, cuddling a child in a dirty red dress. He'll be there all day like that.

Everyone in the apartment is dead to the world, including the two whores in the front room sprawled on the bare floor with army blankets covering all but their heads. Three G.I.s on cots with mosquito netting in two other rooms. There's no furniture. The hall reeks of vino. A rubber floats in the toilet bowl.

Back in the kitchen the scrawny maid who takes care of the place is chewing on a chunk of bread and picking little live silver fish off a newspaper and popping them in her mouth. The courtyard behind her echoes with radio blaring, people screaming, roosters crowing.

"*Buon giorno, Sergente. Mangi, mangi.*" She shows her two yellowish front teeth. "*Buono Americano. Fascisti no mangi, Fascisti finito. Molto contenta, molto contenta.*" She pats her belly bursting out of her half unbuttoned black dress. I kid her about being pregnant and then about being a Fascist, thinking of the first time I came to the apartment and she told me how when Allied planes bombed the harbor she ran out into the street lifting up her hands and crying, "*Americani, libertà.*"

After listening to her jabber for a while about how poor and hungry and unhappy she is, I walk down three flights to the dusky hallway where there's a picture of Christ holding a flowerpot with a cross-like plant. A beer can full of withered flowers sits on a platform in front of it. I slide open the heavy door and walk down the block past the

1

church and the beggar toward the university that resembles a fortress. A hunchbacked old woman in a long dress shuffles along the sandy, palm-lined paths of a park nearby, flies clustering around her eyes and along her nose, white fluid oozing out of her mouth. She moves from bench to bench placing a picture of the Virgin Mary on each person's knee and making the sign of the Cross.

I halt at the corner until a funeral procession crawls by, black-plumed ponies drawing a glass-domed cart holding a wooden coffin the size of a florist box. Girls in black gowns with veils proceed the cortège, bearded men in brown suits and two women in black follow. Continuing on, I pass butcher shops with fly-specked meat hanging in the windows, bakeries, jewelry stores full of cameos and medallions. A gypsy fortune teller carrying a brightly colored bird in a cage stops me. An epileptic is lying on the sidewalk, arms stiff in the air, bystanders gawking at him. A mother with one breast bared to the sun nursing a baby and balancing a laundry basket on her head at the same time looks longingly in my direction. Men dart in and out of street-corner urinals as if they were hurrying through subway turnstiles. God, what a country!

After breakfast in the mess hall with a bunch of OG's, operational groups that carry out raids, back from Tito's headquarters on the Island of Vis, I cross the street to the office building and take the lift to the third floor and the Message Center. It's a high-ceilinged room with French doors in back leading to a porch barb wired and a balcony in front facing the street. Five guys are sitting at tables coding and decoding messages on metal boards and graph paper. I watch a sergeant doing double transposition with a line from one of my sonnets. He's a stocky Harvard graduate with bristling iron gray hair. An Albanian, he was recruited to work with Hoxa's partisans but since he supported King Zog, they wouldn't have him, so he was transferred to Communications. He puts a message under a line of poetry numbering the letters and repeated letters beginning with a. Places the numbered columns horizontally in numerical sequence in another box. Next starting with column 1 he writes out five-letter groups for transmission. It's scrambling the plain text twice creating gibberish. The receiver unscrambles them twice in reverse and creates a clear text. Like reading a poem, first it's all nonsense, then the words become clear as a bell.

I ask him how he likes the sonnets for double transposition. He shrugs his shoulders and goes to fetch another message from the in-basket. Nobody here knows I wrote them. Lieutenant Lane swore me to secrecy back in the States. He had a terrific idea all right. I've composed several for missions and agents in Italy and Southern France, strictly Shakespearean and every line approximately ten syllables. He recruited

2

me at Dartmouth, his alma mater, because I won a prize my junior year for a sheaf of poems. But my rhyming days are over for the time being, sucked into this secret mission up north, God knows why. I suppose because I couldn't stand sitting in a Message Center the whole war when so many G.I.s were risking their lives. Then the general, who heard about my poetry, asked me to volunteer. And how do you refuse a general, especially when he flatters you about your writing.

I take the circular marble staircase around the lift to the SO office on the fourth floor, special operations dealing with the partisans, to see Major Rudd and Captain Marko. The major is tall and heavy-set and bushy browed with a bull neck. He taught me how to jump at Club des Pins in Algiers after I met him in radio school at Camp C outside Washington. It's hard to believe he went to Harvard, skied in Europe before the war, wildcatted in Oklahoma, served in the Merchant Marine for a year. He reminds me more of a wrestler than somebody who went to an Ivy League school. The captain reminds me of a barker at a carnival. He's a little wiry guy from New York with a receding hairline, pockmarked skin, bad teeth, always grinning. Just back from Rome he's telling the major about the situation in the Holy City. Directional Finders are spotting our agents when they transmit and knocking them off one by one. He has a great story about a benny who deliberately contracted VD so he could go to the hospital to send messages undetected and was caught by a nurse. He claims the CLNAI is poorly organized up north. They don't have many brigades operating in the Dolomites where we're going. But he's certain he can find all the men we need. He wasn't a union organizer at Gimbel's for nothing. And don't forget he led an attack on the Alcazar in Spain during the Civil War, killed seven Civil Guards with a Mauser. He knows these Fascist bastards. The major interrupts his spiel to remind him the object of Orange is not killing Krauts or Fascists. It's blocking the Brenner Pass and shortening the war.

"I know, I know, Bill. That's your baby. But I'm having fun too, don't forget. Paying back those Black Shirts for kicking us out of Spain. Just think we'll be the only Americans in the area. I hear SOE doesn't have anybody in the Cadore or Carnia right now, and even if they did they couldn't recruit. Nobody likes the Limeys. They're finished. Man, I can't wait." He rubs his thin little fingers together. "Like being in Spain in the Abraham Lincoln Brigade again. How about taking another look at the maps?"

The major unfolds them on the table, pointing out possible drop zones he considered, the Falzarego Pass near Cortina, the Fernazza Pass west of Cordeveole, Enemonzo on the Tagliamento River between

3

Ampezzo and Tolmezzo. He decided on the one near Belluno and notified Orange. BBC will broadcast the signal tonight.

"How long will it take us to get to the Brenner?" I ask in my usual naïve fashion, never knowing when to keep my mouth shut.

"Maybe a couple of weeks, Tony. Depends. It won't be too tough a job. The Monte Rosa Division is guarding it right now and they're weak. If we work fast, we can close a couple of key tunnels to coincide with the drive on Rome coming up, blow up a couple of bridges, knock out a few roads and rail lines. That should hurt them. It's the key route for supplying the German army."

We gaze with him at the 1:50,000 maps of Northern Italy showing roads, tunnels, bridges, hydroelectric plants, and railway tracks. Even cliffs, woods, orchards, churches, swamps, and canals are marked. I can't believe in less than twelve hours I could be up there. No more office buildings and crowded streets. No more G.I.s and orgies in the apartment, no more army regulations. Completely free. The sole connection with the outside world my radio and one of my sonnets. Like being at Dartmouth my freshmen year, deep in the woods away from everything and in love with "rocks, and stones, and trees." Boy, how I loved that place. I never went home Thanksgiving my freshman year. And only for a few days at Christmas.

After we finish studying the maps, the major says he'll see us in Brindisi this evening. He has to run down and check on supplies and make sure we're getting the aircraft General Twining over at 15th Air Force promised. Then the big guy is gone and I'm left alone with the captain.

"He thinks a lot of you," Marko turns to me. "Says you can send and receive twenty words a minute and code and decode faster than anybody he's ever seen." The grin and those small dark eyes make me uneasy.

"I think a lot of him, too. He's the only guy in this outfit except the general I'd follow anywhere." And I remember when he came back from Anzio in February thin and haggard-looking, his eyes under those heavy brows deep pits, his cheeks sunken. He had lost more than half his OG group, about forty men. The 1st and 3rd Battalions of the Rangers under Colonel Darby lost nearly everybody. Almost a thousand G.I.s. And half the 4th was wiped out. It was rough. The Krauts caught them in a crossfire in open ground near Cisterna. Mark VI tanks coming right up to their shallow ditches and ripping them to pieces. Prisoners were machine-gunned and bayoneted. And he spoke of them starting out for the town in the freezing mud so cocky singing, 'Pistol Packin' Mama.'

4

He told Donovan he'd never work with the army again. It was senseless slaughter.

"He's a good guy," Marko says. "Knows his stuff. But it's going to be a lot tougher up there than he thinks."

"How do you know? Been there?"

"No, but in Rome I talked to men who have. They say the bastards are hunting partisans everywhere. They have signs up warning of the bandits, '*Zona Infestata Delle Bande*'. You wound an animal a little you know, Tony, and he becomes doubly dangerous. And we're wounding the Krauts all over the country. Ever been in combat?"

"No."

"Ever seen a man killed?"

"No. Never killed one either."

"You're going to see a lot of that up there. Guys turn into rampaging animals when they smell blood. They end up killing just for the hell of it. I saw that happen in Barcelona when Franco's Moors poured in and started massacring women and children. You have to remember we're fighting fanatics trying to take over the world. And people everywhere are on our side in China, Russia, Poland, millions of people yearning to throw off the imperialist chains." His voice rises to the level of a political speech. His eyes pierce me.

"You're a communist, aren't you?"

"I'm interested in freeing mankind from slavery, Sergeant, getting rid of the bastards who control most of the land and money in the world. If that makes me a communist, so be it."

"There are a lot of those in OSS, aren't' there?"

"You mean Wall Street lawyers, financiers, heads of big companies. Oh, yeah, but we'll take care of them after the war. Until then we'll use them along with Ivy League professors, scientists, Washington diplomats."

"So, you're political, huh?"

"I wouldn't be human if I wasn't. Aren't you? Isn't everybody in one way or another?"

"Sort of. I've read books about it."

"Let me tell you, Sergeant, you will be after this is over. After you see what those sons of bitches are doing up north to the oppressed people of the world. You won't be able to stay out of politics."

"You mean I'll become a Red?"

"Or you won't be around long." He grins with his teeth. "Don't worry, I'll take care of you. Just stick close to me, Defreest. We'll fight the people's war up there together."

"I've read Snow's *Red Star Over China*."

5

"Great." He rubs his hands together. "That's a starter. Great book. He told the truth. If things work out up there, I'll take you to Yan'an when the war in Europe is over. We'll work with the 8th Route Army."

The little guy is practically spitting at me he's so excited. But, boy, those eyes are so cold and hard.

"You really think we'll be sent out there?"

"The general said when he recruited me if I did a good job, he'd ship me to China. We've already got a liaison mission with Mao's army, and he wants to expand it. Of course, it might mean living in caves and roughing it."

"Gosh, that would be great."

"But first we've got to prove ourselves."

"You mean going after the Brenner?"

"That and organizing partisans to slaughter the Nazis and liberate territory. Don't forget you're the key. Everything depends on your radio. It better be working." He faces me still grinning.

"And my sonnet. Don't forget that. Hope I can do it."

"You can. All you need is to believe in yourself like the major. The mission's been on his mind since the war began. You know how it came about, don't you?"

"He never told me. He doesn't talk much."

"He wrote the general a letter, and the old man invites him to Washington. I think he was training with the 10th Mountain Division in Colorado. Of course, Donovan's a sucker for the daredevil stuff. So he says, sure, go ahead, blow the fuckin' Brenner off the map. But first he goes with the OG's to Anzio. That was a mistake. Now me, I'm more interested in politics than sensational stuff. That's why the old man recruited me out of the infantry down in Fort Jackson. Said he needed somebody who spoke the language and could get along with the partisans, was in the Spanish Civil War. Well, see you around six. Don't be late. We're gonna have a ball up there, Sergeant. You'll see. A great team." He gives me a tap on the shoulder, grins, and disappears. Instead of calming down, I start shaking inside, my whole body tensing.

I stare down at a couple of OGs lounging under the awning across the street, their polished parachute boots, blue parachute insignias over the left blouse pocket. I wonder if any of them really belong to the Purple Gang in Philadelphia and go around the countryside throwing hand-grenades in farmhouses just for the hell of it and OSS has to pay for the deaths of the Eyeties. So many rumors about them. They whistle at girls parading by in short tight dresses, bare legs, and high-heeled cork shoes open at the painted toes, wiggling their big behinds.

6

I'm about to head for the street and the Red Cross building in the center of town to write some letters when the door opens. The general himself enters. I draw back too startled to salute. He saunters in and moves toward me smiling, a stocky figure in neatly pressed khakis, stars on each shoulder, ribbons galore on his chest, blue eyes, silver gray hair, ruddy checks. He shakes my hand hard.

"Came to say goodbye to my poet," he laughs. "Flying to England for the big show coming up, then on to the Far East. And I need to ask a favor. How about writing me one of your famous sonnets before you leave with the major so we can keep in touch privately? Give it to Lieutenant Dawson in the Message Center. He'll send it on to me."

"A code just between the two of us?"

"Like the one you wrote about the president's dog Fala I asked you to do back in Washington: 'Paint the doghouse white, hail the resident, / The country has a canine president.' He loved that ending. After he read it, he threw back his head the way he does with that cigarette holder in his hand and chuckled. He likes wit. Surprises too. Not long ago I went into the oval office with a .22 silencer Research and Development had created, fired a couple of shots into a sandbag I put in the corner while he was dictating a letter to Grace Tully. He never heard a thing. When she left, I handed him the pistol with my handkerchief wrapped around the hot barrel and he nearly hit the ceiling. Then he calmed down and said how wonderful it was, told me I was the only black Republican he'd let in his office with a gun. Probably the only one he'd let in with a poem on Fala too. You're some poet, son. Lieutenant Lane tells me you've written a couple of more sonnets for us." I bow my head. "Hell, we've got everything else in this agency, journalists, a movie star, a bank robber, policemen, stock brokers, even a wrestler. About time we had a poet."

"You want me to spy on the major and the captain?"

"I just want to know how things are going up there, how everybody's getting along."

"Won't they tell you in regular messages?"

"Not everything. I'm particularly interested in the captain, how he's behaving. I want to make sure he's working for us."

"And not the communists?"

"I don't care what a man believes, son, or what party he belongs to. But when he's under my command, I want him to go all out. I don't want him using OSS to spread his propaganda. You understand?"

"I think so."

"We've got a couple of others like him in SO. I knew I was taking a chance when I brought them into the organization. But they're doing good work I hear and causing no trouble. Trying to proselytize a little too much maybe. They after you yet?"

I shake my head.

"Those guys are certainly sending the best intelligence we're getting out of the north, don't you agree? You've been reading their stuff, haven't you, since you've been in Italy?"

"Oh, yes, sir. They're doing a tremendous job all right. They're really active."

"Let's hope the captain keeps it up, and I don't have Congress on my tail. So far I've been able to hold them off. It could hurt us using Reds. Especially if Drew Pearson gets a hold of the story and puts it in one of his *Washington Post* columns. So keep me informed. The president too." He winks at me, shakes me hand again, and strides out of the room before I can salute. I'm sweating all over.

I wonder if he's telling the truth about Roosevelt actually using my sonnet. Or if he's soft soaping me. And I fanaticize walking by the White House on the way to the USO Club on Lafayette Square one night when I was working in the Message Center in Washington and looking up at the light in the second story window imagining the president sitting in the Oval Office or in bed coding a message based on a line from the Fala sonnet. One of the "unacknowledged legislators of the world." What a bunch of bull, Percy Bysshe Shelley! But I love it. Great to be in touch with the general but out of this world with the president.

Chapter 2

After lunch I go for a walk through the ancient alleyways of the city that resemble the Casbah in Algiers. Tour St. Nicolas with its incredible Byzantine crypt downstairs, gold and silver plates depicting the Saint's life, oriental lamps twinkling away in the low vaulted ceiling. Then it's back to the main part of town where I meet a sailor who asks me where the nearest cat house is. I point with a smile back to the cathedral. British soldiers are everywhere, their thick rough uniforms and tough-lined faces a contrast to the G.I.s in khaki down from the airbase at Foggia. They ride around drunk in horse-drawn carriages, buying souvenirs by the bushel, having their picture taken, whistling at girls, even nuns. Like Dartmouth freshmen in Boston for their first Harvard game singing "Run, girls, run."

I reach the harbor and a palm-lined boulevard stretching from the ramshackle yacht club at the north end full of English subalterns to the modernistic building at the south end full of Air Force colonels sipping cocktails on the roof garden. Fishmongers stand by their stalls shouting and digging their hands into iced clams, frogs, and crabs. Men hawk boat rides. In the middle of the street a boy pulls a vegetable cart by leaping up, grabbing the two poles, letting the momentum carry him. An old man seems to be swallowing a live eel. Soft, big-bosomed bleached blondes bounce along. Soldiers of all descriptions pass by, Greeks in colorful skirts and dumpy Yugoslav girls in British battle dress with grenades dangling from their belts and hammer and sickle emblems on their caps, *carabinieri* with Napoleon hats and swords who look like movie extras. There are even a few monks in brown habits and leather sandals. Like a damn costume party.

When I get back to the empty apartment around four, I start packing my duffle bag and after that's finished sit down on the cot and take out my Dante. I found the *Divine Comedy* in the rubble of Bizerte when I arrived from the States during the Salerno landing last September. The Italian is on one page with the English opposite. I don't understand a lot of it, the allegory and allusions and people mentioned, but, boy, do the images hit home, the crazy characters and flea-bitten dogs, the lizards, frogs, and snakes. I'm up to this scene in the *Inferno* where these guys neither in hell nor out of it are running around naked in the dark chased by wasps and hornets stinging their faces, welts forming and blood and tears dripping to their feet where worms are devouring the mess. It's funny and weird but not too much funnier and weirder than some of the things I see happening around me every day. Although the poet is in the middle of his life, I can identify with him all right. I need someone like him to tell me where I'm heading and someone like good old Virgil, to keep me out of trouble and my mouth shut. Mauldin's cartoons of Willie and Joe in *The Stars and Stripes* can't compare.

At six o'clock I'm outside headquarters waiting for Marko to drive me to Brindisi. He appears and, wow, if a Russian officer isn't sitting in the weapons carrier with him. He has on black boots and red epaulettes, a bunch of ribbons covering his chest like the piece of a quilt. He's the tall, ramrod type, pockmarked cheeks, oriental eyes, cannonball head. His name is Ivan Slansky. He's a colonel. Marko says he's going along as an observer. He doesn't smile or even acknowledge me. I throw my bag in back, climb aboard, and we're off out Via Dalmizia, over the railroad tracks past an army depot and Air Force warehouses and down the coast road. The little whitewashed villages glow in the dusk, the boats, the nets drying on sea walls, the smell of wine and fish and roasting almonds filling the air. Communist slogans splash against buildings as if they're written in blood. Red flags hang from windows. Marko points them out to the colonel. He stares stone-faced. You'd think he would at least appear pleased seeing Stalin and Lenin and Russia in big colorful letters flashing everywhere. I know that's what I would do if I were riding in the Caucasus mountains and spotted Roosevelt's name smeared on barns and houses and Old Glory waving on flagpoles. Smiling away and cheering.

It's a warm evening. The sea is smooth. Streets and fields and olive groves are deserted. And I remember the Red Cross tour I took the other day into the interior to visit Alberobello. The towns we passed through to reach it looked biblical, oxen plowing, women clustering around a fountain in a square with gooseneck jugs, their black hair tied in back. Beggars sprawling in front of a cafe. Old men pulling wine carts followed by dusty dogs. A blindfolded mule stumbling around a well. Blacksmiths and wheel makers sweating away in shops. Then we came upon the settlement of *trulli*, pre-Christian houses shaped like beehives or teepees. Little white conical structures with a hole in the top for smoke and no mortar holding the cupola together. A single door and small square windows, an outside staircase. They're perched on a ridge overlooking wheat fields, remote from the rest of the world and time. The silence was overwhelming as if the whole populace had left centuries ago and their homes remained intact.

We reach the airport at eight. The major is at the dressing shed to greet us. He's already in his earth-brown strip-tease suit camouflaged with dark green spots. He's putting on his chute. Marko introduces the colonel.

"You have any objections to his going along to observe, Bill," he says. "I talked to the general this afternoon before he left. He approves."

I'm struggling into my suit and don't say a word, worried more about getting on my chute pack than anything but sort of longing to say let him come.

"Sorry," Bill says. "General Alexander's orders. The word got out. He can't come with us, not even as an observer. Donovan doesn't have the final say on this."

"I hear the Krauts are using troops from Turkestan to fight partisans. He could come in handy, talk to them, get information from prisoners, persuade them to surrender. The Nazis might think the Russians are parachuting people in and could panic."

"We can't do it, Marko! There's no way."

"He could be a hell of an asset. Don't forget the general wants good relations with the NKVD. Wasn't that why he went to Moscow with General Dean last Christmas to work out an exchange between US and Russian intelligence?"

"Okay, maybe he could help us. But I've got my orders."

"Who would know anyway until it's too late? Then they're not going to call him back. It would be impossible and embarrassing. Uncle Joe would have a fit. Come on, let him suit up. How about it, Bill?"

They face each other in the sallow light of the shed. The tall rugged-looking athlete who went to Harvard and the jerky little union organizer with a wry smile and gray pallor and a receding hairline who went to CCNY and fought in the Spanish Civil War. No doubt has been to Moscow and marched in May Day parades. After the war he could be fighting with the Communist Party to overthrow the Italian government.

"Can he blow bridges, mountain climb?"

"Done all of that. And he's in great condition. He's hiked hundreds of miles fighting with the partisans in his country. And he knows this kind of warfare as few people do. He'll be a great morale booster. They'll be seeing a real Russian up there for the first time. People followed him all over Bari the other day, the first Russian they've ever seen. Like a Pied Piper. He'll have the partisans eating out of his hand. So many will want to join us we won't know what to do with them all."

"Orders are orders."

"Since when has OSS ever operated strictly on orders? That's a crock of shit, Bill, and you know it. Come on, let him go. He doesn't

11

have to take part in any operations. And if he's a great success think of the praise you'll get from the Allies. From Stalin too."

"Has he ever parachuted?"

"Dozens of times. He's seen more action than you and me."

"I could be court-martialed when I get back."

"That's better than having the mission fail, isn't it? The colonel will make it succeed. Wait and see. He's never had an operation go bad on him."

The major looks away into a dark corner of a shed, then turns and faces Marko. "Okay, tell him to suit up. But if he chickens out at the last moment…"

"What?"

"He'll have to go back. Nobody goes on that plane who's not willing to see the job through."

So it's set. I'm glad and I'm not. I want the Russian to come along but hate to see the major back down, give in to the little guy, who makes me nervous. And in no time the colonel is slipping into his harness and adjusting his pack and we're a different team. A case officer helps me, especially with fitting the radio in a can on my chest so I can protect it with my arms when I hit the ground. He's a blond kid younger than I am. He cracks jokes, whistles, asks me how many times I've done it. At first I think he's talking about making it with a girl. He tells me not to worry about the chute opening. Ninety-nine times out of a hundred they do. The landing is the roughest part. He asks me where we're going. I tell him I think it's near Belluno in the Dolomites. He's been up there in the Cadore. The peaks are like spikes. You land on one, and it could split your ass in two.

At ten we're ready and waddle out to the plane dressed in heavy boots and padded helmets, straps under the arms and around the thighs. I feel like a man about to descend into a mine. It's hot as hell.

The B-24 sits there revving up with its red and green lights shining from the wings and belly. Bill says he wanted a B-17, it's slower and easier to jump from, but none were available. I gaze around at the sky. A full moon, the stars are blazing away like diamonds against black velvet. Clumsily we climb into the gloomy fuselage full of wooden boxes and wicker baskets twice the size of orange crates. The containers are in the bomb bay. I take a seat on a box between the major and the colonel. A tail-gunner sits high up behind us under a Plexiglas bubble.

"You okay, Tony," Bill says, looking closely at me.

"Just kind of warm and a little queasy. I have a weak stomach."

"When we hit 10,000 feet you'll cool off and feel better. It's the waiting that gets you."

We sit jammed into the interior nobody saying anything or seeming to be aware of anybody yet terribly self-conscious of not being alone. The engines speed up, the plane shutters, and we're taxiing along the runway faster and faster. We lift off, the wheels banging into place under us. Food shoots up my throat, and I have to gag myself to keep from puking. I cough. Bill pats me on the back, puts an arm around me, asks if I'm all right. It's going to be a rough ride.

He isn't kidding. After we level off, we start hitting air pockets and bumping up and down. The box shakes beneath me. Anti-aircraft guns pop away. The bomber dives and zigzags and bobs. I grab a bulkhead to keep from tumbling off the crate and look out the window. Orange colored flak is flashing everywhere. The colonel sits rigid beside me like a mummy. Marko mumbles in Russian to him and then breaks his concentration to ask who's meeting us. Bill says Ettore, leader of the Val Cordevole Brigade. Fires will be in an H or V pattern downwind. Flashlights will signal everything is okay. They don't have a Eureka. And I'm wondering if I'm really going to slip out of that hole on my own, or the dispatcher is going to have to push me. Maybe even take me back to Brindisi a Section Eight. It's a lot different from practicing in North Africa all right.

When we reach Belluno, the intercom rings and the dispatcher tells us to get ready. The flak sounds heavier. The plane shudders from the explosions. The tail-gunner lets loose with a pout-pout-pout, pout-pout-pout from his fifty-caliber machine gun. The old sergeant is confident we'll fly through the heavy stuff. No worse than usual except for a Messerschmitt hanging on our tail. Something about his tone and quiet manner is reassuring. Now I'm freezing my ass off instead of burning up. I can't stop shivering.

The buzzer rings again. The red light over the jump hole flashes. The sergeant opens the hatch. He and Bill push out boxes and baskets. Cylinders are already falling from the bomb bay. I can see through the opening fires glowing like matches in the dark and chutes floating down. What an eerie scene. Like Dante staring into the gloom of one of his circles and seeing the demons below like fireflies. The sergeant bellows above the roar of the engines to get ready, and Marko and the colonel inch toward the hole. He hooks up their static lines. They pull on them to test. Bill shouts in my ear that he hopes it's not a decoy. The Krauts are always setting up false fires to trap us.

The plane roars in for the second run at 2,000 feet and the red bulb comes on again. When it switches to green, Bill, Marko, and the colonel slip out, their chutes popping open like immense multi-colored blossoms in the moonlight. Now it's my turn. The pilot circles to make

13

another pass over the bonfire bigger and brighter than ever. The dispatcher across from me holds up the V sign smiling. I move to the opening and sit dangling my feet, checking the static line, trying to keep myself from staring down and getting dizzy. The buzzer rings. The red light flashes on again. He raises his right arm. I remain frozen. Like teetering on the edge of a bottomless black pit and praying for a net to break the fall. I can't see anyone on the ground, no flashlights, only hear the wind and the engines. The go light glows in the semi-darkness. The arm comes down. A voice shouts. Somebody gives me a shove, and I'm dropping into the darkness. The slip stream hits me, flips me over a couple of times, jarring every bone in my body. Certain I'm diving head first right into the ground.

The strap tightens with a jolt, the chute cracks open. A couple of shroud lines get tangled. I spin and fight them, dropping fast all the time. Parachutes dot the sky. And at last I am drifting down in the moonlight away from the fires. What an incredible sight, the hills, the peaks topped with snow, the woods, the rocks thrusting up closer and closer. Then for a second all is calm. I gaze around at the stars and realize I'm swinging suspended above the earth. What a terrific sensation. I don't want to land.

14

Chapter 3

I hit the ground with a crunch between two spikes of limestone and do a couple of somersaults down a gully toward some saplings. The chute drags me, but I scramble to my feet before I reach them. The ballooning canopy tugs at my body. I race around and deflate it, wriggle out of the harness, stand up, look around. No sign of the captain, the colonel, Bill, or the partisans.  Just this bleak, blank landscape, jagged and empty. In the distance the sound of the plane fading south. And for about twenty minutes I don't stir, rooted to the spot, thankful I'm down in one piece, nervous about where I am, feeling lonelier than I've ever felt in my life and not liking it the way I did in Hanover climbing Velvet Rocks and Bartlett Tower by myself  and leaving Richardson dorm to write poetry. Somebody said it would be like having sex for the first time. But, boy, Maggie was never like this at the Willard Hotel in Washington before I left for overseas.

"Hey, Tony," a voice calls to my right. It's Bill.

"Over here," I whisper and take out a flash and blink it a couple of times. He comes toward me out of the darkness.

"See the fires at the drop zone? Hear the gun fire?" I do. "The Krauts could have been waiting for us. A good thing we didn't land in the target area. We've got to get the hell out of here."

"See Marko and the colonel?" I ask.

"Not yet. But we can't stand around here waiting for them. You okay?"

"I scraped my face, bruised my back and legs."

"Walk?"

"Oh sure. Even run if I have to."

"First, you better bury your chute. Suit too."

So I struggle out of the strip-tease and dig a hole for it and the silk. Then we hunt for the others. Guns are firing close by. We head for a rock pile on a hill.

"Where do we go from there?"

"Hide somewhere. Look…" Not far away a huge fire is blazing into the night sky. "Our drop zone we missed. Germans must be around. In the morning they'll be out in force searching for us."

Two figures loom up not far away, and Bill calls out. It's the captain and the colonel. They rush forward and report they've just come from the drop area. It's filled with Germans. They had been waiting for us. We've got to leave the area fast.

Bill leads us to a hollow over the ridge, and we crouch under a rock ledge and wait for daylight, taking turns at guard duty. Nobody says he's tired or wants to sleep. And, gosh, I feel wider awake than I did in the plane. Every muscle taut as hell.

"What happened to the supplies?"

"God knows," Bill mutters. "Probably the Krauts got them. If we contact the partisans, maybe we can find out. I picked a rotten place to jump, didn't I? A good thing we didn't land where those bastards were or we'd be dead ducks."

"Is this the way it is in your country?" I turn to the colonel. Marko translates, and he grumbles something back in Russian. Marko's convinced somebody in Italian intelligence down in Brindisi informed on us. We've already lost a couple of joes who went by submarines to Venice because of leaks. He wants to know what kind of brigade this Ettore is leading. Bill tells him it's supposed to be a Garibaldi, which should satisfy him since they're usually full of communists.

"Jesus, you can't trust anybody up here," Marko spits out. "If the Krauts offer money for information, somebody's going to tell on us no matter whose side they're on. That's the way these Italians work over here. I know. I've been talking around."

"We've got to retrieve those boxes and containers," Bill says. "Everything's in them, maps, explosives, guns, ammo, a generator, batteries, headphones, food. How's the radio, Tony?"

"I don't think it got damaged. Feels intact."

"We better not try a contact. Might be a DF in the area. Then we could be cooked. As soon as it's daylight I'm going out to look for Ettore. He must be in the area. He knows about Orange and got the BBC signal we were coming. Set up the drop area. You guys stay put. I'll go look for him."

At the first speck of gray, he's out from under the rock ledge and over the hill. You can't hear him leave he's so quiet. We dig into our emergency K-rations. I notice the colonel is still in his Russian uniform. Marko keeps his on too. I thought they might go civilian in disguise. The two of them huddle together and talk in Russian. I watch them all the time, listening for footsteps, voices, motors. And I wonder if Bill never comes back will I be working for the Red Army up here? Then I'll have to sneak a message to the general via our private code. I wrote a sonnet on the trulli and gave it to Dawson before I left to send to him. He asked me what the hell they were, and I told him to read the lines, and he'll learn where Snow White and the Seven Dwarfs came from.

16

At nine Bill returns with a group of motley-looking partisans carrying a bunch of our containers and crates, some wearing Alpine hats and Italian uniforms, some in British battle dress. One even has on a parka he said a downed American flier gave him. Maybe took it off a dead body. A couple are in shabby civilian clothes. Almost all sprout Red stars on their hats and wear red scarves and carry weapons and shout "*Morte ai Fascisti, Libertá ai Popoli.*" Their guns don't look like much. Bill says they're old Italian Model 91 rifles and ineffective.

Ettore is their leader. He's stocky with a bushy mustache, long hair and small eyes. He's wearing a bandolier that reminds me of pictures of Poncho Villa. He says we have to get out of here fast. The *Tedeschi* are searching for us. He and his men had a battle with them. He knows a good hideout in Andrich, a small village up around Cencenighe in the Vallada community. It's a couple of day's journey. The hiking will be rough. We'll have to avoid roads, take to the hills. Bill asks Marko if he thinks he's up to it since he's the oldest and twisted his ankle in the drop. He nods. So does the colonel. We'll have to travel mainly at night and early morning while there's plenty of mist.

So we start out toward the peaks of the Dolomites that thrust straight up from the valley floor and look like castles, cathedrals, pyramids, fingers, and just about any pointed thing you can imagine. The sun turns them all different colors – blue, purple, gold, and red. It's awesome. Like looking through a kaleidoscope. I walk along gazing up and wondering if I'm able to climb those babies. Balch Hill and Moosilouke at Dartmouth are pimples in comparison. The scenery is breathtaking, streams cascading down out of rocks, steep wooded banks, old retaining walls and arches hanging on mountain sides so you get the feeling of being out in the wilderness and at the same time seeing the ruins of an old civilization.

Marko and the colonel mingle with the partisans. They're excited having a Russian along and gather around him like kids listening to bedtime stories as he talks about guerrilla days in the Caucasus mountains and Marko translates, probably embellishing like hell. Bill warns them not to talk too freely about the Russian being with us. So does Ettore. But I can see them getting steamed up and eager to go out and tell the world, hey, the Russians are coming, all's right with the war. Most are in their twenties like me, a few even look younger and appear as if they left home to escape conscription and have fun playing cowboys and Indians in the mountains. They give the colonel the clenched fists salute. Marko grins. Bill frowns. I laugh and sigh.

We stop around ten in a hay barn and camp there all day sleeping, cleaning our weapons, studying maps. Then we travel after dark, and the

17

next day spend our time in a cave and eat mushrooms and cold corn meal along with a couple of squirrels somebody shoots. Bill and Ettore talk off by themselves. I ask what's going on. He says he's planning drops, organizing a couple of battalions, setting up an intelligence network, discussing bridges to blow. A couple of other things too. But he doesn't mention what they are, and I'm worried he's got another mission on his mind aside from the attack on the Brenner Pass. Worried also about Marko and the colonel getting together with a couple of Red hotshots and talking in hushed voices. And I thought we'd be one big happy family up here, no secret confabs, no splitting up. Hell, isn't this kind of life supposed to generate comradeship?

On the third night we reach Andrich by skirting Agordo and sneaking up a valley to the west of the Cordevole. It's about a mile and a half above the Biois River and reminds me of a medieval settlement. The little stone cottage on the edge of the village we enter isn't much, but at least it's a roof over our heads and a bunk to sleep in. No sign of the Krauts or police or anybody else for that matter. Practically a deserted community.

"Our base for the Cadore," Bill says in the candlelight. "Okay, everybody?" Marko and the colonel nod. Ettore is silent. The partisans just gape at him.

"How long are we staying?" I blurt out.

"Until we're ready to hit the Brenner that's just over the Marmolada range to the north." Marko and the colonel and a couple of their Red fans eye each other. I look at the major. He doesn't notice. That's the trouble, he never seems to notice much so wrapped in the mission.

As we prepare for bed, he comes over and whispers he's leaving in the morning for Selva di Cadore below Cortina. Ettore told him about a group of ex-Alpine soldiers over there that are eager to be organized. We could use them at the Brenner. Marko will be in charge during his absence. I should watch him.

"I'm a little leery of those two guys, Tony. I never should have agreed to let Slansky come along. You can see what's going on."

"Yeah, morale is sky high."

" So sky high nobody will want to come down to earth to take orders from me when the time comes to make our move."

"Christ," I whisper, "do you think they could...?"

"Eliminate both of us if we get in their way? I'm not sure exactly what they're up to. But I've got a pretty damn good idea it's not what we're up to in Orange. Don't worry. They need your radio."

"And my sonnet."

18

"I forgot. You write it down?"

"In my head."

"Keep it there. Another thing. We've got to start working on something else as soon as I get back."

"What?"

"Can't tell you yet. I'll know more when I return. But it might make the Brenner job unnecessary."

"Gosh, that big?"

"Out of this world. Too good to be true. One of Donovan's big ideas."

The next morning he starts north with a couple of partisans. He's wearing paratroop boots and OD's, a parka and fur cap, carrying a carbine, rope slung over his shoulder, a pack on his back. The others look like midgets beside him. The snow-capped Marmolada range looms up ahead beautiful and forbidding. He has to skirt it to avoid the Nazis garrison at Alleghe.

Ettore takes off by himself and goes south. He doesn't say where he's headed, but I figure it must have something to do with Bill's mystery mission. Marko and the colonel are still asleep. And I'm more nervous and alone than I was jumping out of the B-24. Talk about being up in a Godforsaken country. This is like being dropped on the moon with no way of getting off.

## Chapter 4

Bill's gone almost a week. Marko and the colonel take daily trips. They don't say where they're going.  But they bring back tons of intelligence for me to transmit – identity of division shoulder patches, number of boxcars passing through the Brenner, bridges destroyed in Allied air raids. They even discover the headquarters of a Japanese Secret Service unit in the Hotel Corona in Cortina, west side of the town near the Falzarego Pass road. So all day and night I sit in my damp, cold room coding and decoding with lines from my sonnet and sending and receiving on the SSTR-1. Eating mostly C-rations, talking to a couple of shy giggling partisans who know a little broken English.

For relief I take short walks around the house and survey the country, not only the rock masses with their coral-like colors, but the whole Biois Valley a mile away – the cliffs, the pine-studded slopes, the swift clear water. I've never been in such sensational country, castles and villas on hilltops, terraced vineyards and green fields. Hamlets in valleys surrounded by meadows and sharp high peaks. Streams tumbling down over rocks, oxen pulling wooden plows, sometimes the dismal landscapes reminding me of the terrain in the *Inferno*. A lot different from the south, cleaner, rockier, colder. Many of the people are tall and blond. No beggars or half-naked kids as in Naples running after me yelling, "Wanna piece a ass, Joe? Fuck my sister, Joe?"

But I don't venture out often, and when I do I stay away from the native population. They're too damn curious about the uniform. Marko and the colonel are smart. They go around in civilian clothes, merge with the Italians in the towns and country. I have a feeling they're cooking up something. The captain keeps pumping me about other missions we've got in the Piedmont, Lake Como, Milan, Venice, Udine, Trieste. I shrug my shoulders, tell him I only know about a few. He wants me to ask for drops. Nobody but the major can do that. He gets mad and stomps out of the house. When he comes back, he doesn't speak to me.  Neither do any of the partisans. The tension builds from one day to the next. It sort of reminds me of the rooming house I lived in at Hanover my junior year where I kept to myself, and most of the guys thought I was some queer because I wrote poetry and wouldn't join the Outing Club or a fraternity and spent most of my time when not in class at the library and hiking alone.

20

It gets so bad I can hardly sleep in my tiny room, listening for somebody coming to threaten me. The .45 stays loaded under the pillow. My only consolation is that I'm the sole person who can operate the radio and who knows the code for Orange. And they recognize my "fist" down in Bari. Had it "fingerprinted" before I left. If anybody other than me takes over the key, everything will stop and Marko will be left stranded up here with no base support. Then the partisans will desert him left and right, and it'll be all over. Or that's what I think.

Bill returns one night looking beat. Not as bad as he did when he came back from Anzio but almost. A couple of ex-Alpine soldiers are with him sporting little beards and wearing long-peaked caps. He tells about leading them and a band of partisans in a raid on a German convoy near Enemonzo, west of Tomazzo where there's a big garrison of Turkestanians. The colonel should have been there to lure a few of them into the woods. The trick is called *"fare una comminata,"* taking a walk and is used all the time to dispose of local Fascists. After that was over, several hundred Nazis chased them up the steep gorges of the Tagliamento. He and his men found a couple of local trucks and got away and hid out in Ovasta, a shabby hamlet situated on a shelf overlooking the river and ringed by gigantic spears and flanks of the Alps. From there he went to check on the construction of the Alpine Line on the Austrian border around Val Visdende, a beautiful spot not too far from San Pietro Cadore. That's where they say the Germans are planning to make their last stand and maybe hold out for years. Coming back here, he almost ran into several hundred Nazis Alpenjaegers out hunting partisans in the Marmolada range. But he stayed at 7,000 feet, sometimes even climbing to 9,000 and ran into snow. It was a tough trip but worth it. He got a good idea of the kind of enemy and the kind of terrain he was up against.

"Oh, yeah, I forgot," he continues, "we blew out the railroad from Venice to Cortina and the electric line to Austria. Good practice for the Brenner. How are things back at the ranch?"

"Fine, fine, Bill," Marko says. "The colonel and I have been gathering intelligence and recruiting. How many messages have we sent, Tony?"

"Ten at least."

"You're overworking your sonnet."

"Don't worry I can use a line more than once. The reception's been great. I've been doing almost twenty-five words a minute. Base has been on time for every QXR."

"No sign of DF's?"

"Not so far."

21

"The word from the Nazi garrison at Alleghe," Marko says, "is that they don't know we're here yet. But they might soon. We'll need more drops. We've been recruiting pretty heavy and have a lot of men. They need food, ammo, *lire*, medical supplies, and weapons. They're getting discouraged."

"Okay, we'll set one up soon. But not around here. How about the Fernazza Pass? That's not too far. I think a little northeast. Ettore tells me it's a great place. We can hide in the pine forest. And there's a couple of *malga*s to stay in. I'll figure out the coordinates tomorrow and write out the message. When is your next contact, Tony?"

"Eight tomorrow morning."

"Good. We've got to start preparing for a few other things too. I talked to Ettore. He had a lot of success down south." He glances at Marko and the Russian in the candlelight. They look blank and don't say anything. The atmosphere tightens. There's a long silence. It's eleven o'clock. Bill says he better turn in, he's bushed.

So I take him to my room where there's an extra bunk, and he flops down after removing his boots. I can just make out the big head and the broad body in the darkness and think of what he's been through. Christ, I know I never could survive all that!

"What are those two bastards up to anyway?" he whispers.

"Search me. They go out every day now in uniform instead of civilian clothes, not afraid of being recognized as the Allies. I think they're organizing for the brigade."

"Like Gimbel's, huh?"

"A lot of recruits are drifting in."

"I noticed. The place is beginning to look like Red Square on May Day."

"They're not too interested in the Brenner operation."

"That's obvious. We might have to tackle that on our own, Tony. First, though, I'm visiting an old friend down in Belluno, Countess Gambini. I met her in Cortina in '38. We did a lot of skiing together."

"Anything else?"

"Use your imagination. We exchanged a few letters. Ettore's been to see her. She says she remembers me and is eager to renew old acquaintances. She's in contact with a Dr. Bauer, who's the Nazi Political Administrator of Belluno Province. He runs around in a green Alfa Romeo with a Gestapo bodyguard. I think she can help us."

"How?"

"Get us inside information about the Brenner Pass defenses. And a few other things."

"You going down to see her?"

"You bet. And you're coming with me. Ettore's got a truck with a huge open-ended lidless-like coffin turned upside down under a pile of logs. It's big enough for the two of us. We'll go early in the evening and be back by midnight."

"You trust her?"

"That's what I'm going to find out."

"Your age?"

"A little older. Maybe she's got a younger sister." He laughs. "Let's do it in a couple of days after I get my second wind. Don't mention it to the Red duo. They might want to go along or try to stop us."

He slips into his sleeping bag that came with the drop. I wander back to the main room. Everybody's hitting the hay. So I walk outside. It's a cool night, almost like fall. The mountains loom stark in every direction, shooting up from the valley floor like sheer rock walls, snow on a few peaks. This is some kind of remote world all right. Sort of like in *The Magic Mountain*. But I'm no Hans Castorp. I wonder what he'd be like in the *Inferno*. Stop and talk philosophy or medicine with every dead soul he met.

Bill waits three days until Bari confirms a new drop. Then early Sunday night we sneak out of the house to the mammoth truck, slide into the coffin, and take off for Belluno like two stiffs. Through Agordo and down the Cordeveole Valley. Hearing all the way motor bikes and trucks and at checkpoints guttural accents. We don't talk, not even a whisper. And it's creepy riding like two corpses to God knows where and imaging the river and rocky scenery outside. Some of the bumps shake my insides to death.

The countess's house sits on a hill all by itself, a big white square-looking villa with a glass front door. She's alone and expecting us, a tall, dark-haired fleshy woman in a print dress that shows off her breasts and hips. Very slow smiling as if she were sizing us up. Or at least Bill. He smiles back. But there's no hint of past intimacy. And I wonder if he ever thinks about women that way anymore, so caught up in this Brenner business. But, boy, she looks as if she might be interested in the good stuff. Any woman who puts on that much makeup and flashes that much of a sexy figure has more on her mind than just helping the Allies. Her place is showy, too, a marble hall with a chandelier, high-ceilinged white rooms with Orientals, a few Renaissance paintings. The biggest in blue and red shows a lot of half-naked guys and girls chasing a woman who looks scared to death of them, especially the wild man in the middle. She says it's a reproduction of *Baccus and Ariadne* by Titian who was born near here at Pieve di Cadore. Her first name is Teresa.

She's married now. Her husband is in Milano. She has no children. I'm curious listening to her talk with Bill about their time together at Cortina. How they took the aerial railway every morning from the Hotel Maioni to the Faloria ski slopes, climbed the Nuvolau to get an unmatched view of the Marmolada, shopped for jewelry and wood carvings by local artists. Then he asks Ettore and me to step out in the hall. He needs to talk to the countess privately. We do and a little later he calls us back. As we enter he's saying to her, "You tell this Nazi if he'll cooperate we'll see he's taken care of after the war. I have direct access to President Roosevelt through the general I work for."

She smiles at us in the sloe-eyed way of hers, sort of sneaky, flirty, and flaunting her attributes at the same time. It's as if she's toying with us.

"You do business with us, Bill." she says.

"Only the business we talked about."

"Oh, Bill, I love your country, your New York, your Chicago, your California, so lovely, so exciting. I go many times. We have good fun at Cortina, no?" She reaches over and pats his hand.

"So your husband is a Fascist, works for Mussolini?" Bill says. She nods.

"Very bad I know. I sorry. He only do it for *lire*. Hard times for us."

"We're having a drop in two days at the Fernazza Pass. See if your German friend can arrange for us to pick up the supplies without interference. Feel him out. If it works, then we'll go ahead with what we talked about. If not, then it's over. No deal."

"I do good. I talk to him. You stay? You have tea, cake. Maybe some wine?"

"We've got to get back."

"Where is that?" She looks at him closely.

"Military secret."

"If we have this arrangement, Bill, no secrets okay." She doesn't smile any more, just gives him a hard stare, moves her body slightly so it sort of ripples inside her dress. I'd have a hard-on being around her all the time. It seems Italian women are either too old and fat or too big in the bosom and tight in the crotch so you can't stop gazing at them and wondering if they aren't the sexiest and most natural acting people in the world. They don't leave much to the imagination. What you see is what there is.

"Okay, up in the Cordevole Valley."

"What town or place?"

"That's all I better say right now."

24

"*Sì, Sì, capisco*. You excuse, Bill, if I ask something of you for all I do."

"You mean how much do you want?"

"No *lire*. Citizenship in your country."

He gapes at her. So do I. Ettore grins. "You say your general is good friend of President Roosevelt. You ask him if I come to your country to live. He say yes I do what you want. A big thing you ask. I risk my life."

"Citizenship for your husband too?"

"He not leave Italia. Too many friends, works for *Fasciti*. No, I come to *America* myself, stay with you *possibile*. You not married, no." He nods. She looks intently at him. He starts to blush like a damn kid and doesn't know where to stick his eyes, afraid of looking where I bet he wants to. The first time I've ever seen him nervous. Sex could be on his mind after all despite the war and what he's been talking about with her. She's not the kind of woman if you've had anything with her in the past you don't forget and feel embarrassed meeting like this and her asking a favor.

"Whew," he breathes out loud. "Okay, I'll send your request as soon as I get back to camp. It'll take time for an answer. He's gone to England, and then flying to the Far East."

"I wait. A long war. You stay with me, no, meet Dr. Bauer. He come soon."

"I couldn't do that, Teresa. Not now. Sorry. Too much to do. But you work on him, will you and let me know?"

"*Si*, I work hard. We good friends. I know how to get what I want from him. *Tedeschi* like Italian women. We different from their *signorine*. And he is far from home. That makes a difference in war." She smiles at him with her long dark lashes.

Wow, I bet when she wiggles those hips, bounces that rear end up and down a few times, widens that cleavage, the Kraut comes crawling on all fours. If Bill stayed here he'd forget about the Brenner fast. And I've got to do the same thing. Put all this out of my mind. Can't be thinking of the countess or I'll be seeing her in bed the way I did Caroline Massey, that middle-aged divorcée from Richmond back in the Algiers Message Center with the frilly blouses and the big boobs peek-a-booing at me. Especially after the Christmas party at her house in the city where she stayed with the OSS women and where we danced to "In the Mood" on a record. And I was almost forgetting Maggie after drinking what was called "monkey milk." Becoming too aware of what I was missing in my short life.

We leave. She kisses me on the cheek, Bill on the lips. The perfume sticks to my skin. My thing stiffens. I hope the buttons hold. He acts as if he's saying goodbye to his sister. War affects the lower unit in strange ways.

"You think she's being honest with us," I whisper in the blackness of the fake coffin as we ride back up to the Cordevole. No sound of trucks or motorcycles or guttural voices this trip. It's after midnight.

"You mean do I trust her? I don't know. We'll find out when the drop comes off."

"I bet she'd love to spend the night with you."

"Hey, none of that stuff, Tony. We wouldn't last a day up here fooling around with women. Besides I had my share before the war."

"Enough to last the duration?"

"Almost. Though I suppose you can never have too much of a good thing."

"With her at Cortina?"

"We had our moments. She wasn't married then. It was nice. Now it's different. It's got to be. A lot's at stake, a lot more than I can tell you about right now."

"You mean the Brenner and shutting off the Kraut's supply lines aren't everything?"

"Only a small part. It's a big operation."

"You really sending a message to Donovan about her demands?"

"Why not? A small price to pay, isn't it, for shortening the war? Just think of the lives that could be saved. Maybe yours, maybe mine."

"I guess so. You told her a lot about us, didn't you?"

"Maybe too much. But I had to give her the drop zone, take the risk to test her for what's coming up. We can always fail to show if there are Krauts snooping around. Better to know whose side she is on now than to find out when it's too late."

"Are we going back?"

"You like to?"

"Sort of."

"To find out how she makes out with Dr. Bauer?"

"That too."

"It might be better to send Ettore again."

"She'd never accept a substitute for you after tonight. Her eyes were all over you."

"She might take you. She was giving you the once over too."

"I couldn't handle her. Too old for me."

"I'm not so sure I can either anymore." He laughs and hits me on the shoulder. And I wish it wasn't so damn dark in the make-shift coffin

26

so I could see the expression on his face. Imagine being buried before your time in something like this. Only Dante could think of something like that.

"What were you and the countess talking about anyway?" I can't help expressing what I should be repressing.

"Sorry, Tony," he turns serious. "I can't tell you yet. Wait a while. See how it turns out."

"It scares me you talking about a big operation. I thought the Brenner was supposed to be that."

"It scared me, too, when the general brought it up in Bari. He just sprang it on me, but I have a hunch he had it in mind when he bought my plan to block the Brenner."

"Yeah, and when he persuaded me to take up Morse Code, radio work, and go on this mission with you just because he liked poetry, wanted to have a special code for communicating with him alone, the president too."

"Yeah, he told me all about that. He thinks you're a genius."

"He doesn't know much about poetry. He's the genius, Wild Bill from the last war, Medal of Honor winner."

Marko is waiting for us. He wants to know where we've been. Bill tells him to pick up some information in Belluno and get a guarantee the Krauts won't bother our next drop. The little guy looks suspiciously at us. The colonel scowls. What have they been up to? Neither of them says. And I drop into bed after some C-rations more uneasy than ever. Up here in these mountains surrounded by Germans and uncertain of the Italians and dubious about the guys on our side. No matter what I've got to keep the SSTR-1 operating. And the good old Shakespearian fourteen liner delivering the intelligence. So far it's never failed me. No garbles or missing groups.

The drop is a terrific success. Three planes fly over the field and unload almost a hundred containers and crates right on target – food, medical supplies, ammo, Bren and Sten guns, carbines and Thompson sub-machine guns, batteries, a couple of hundred pounds of TNT and plastic explosives. It takes three trucks to bring everything back to Andrich. Bill is ecstatic. He keeps winking at me and shouting, "It worked, Tony, it worked! Now for the big one." He's like a damn kid. I never saw him so enthusiastic. All of the area turned out to help, people singing and laughing and not a Kraut in sight, and no rumors about any enemy nearby. He plans to drive to Belluno to see the countess, thank her, tell her he'll send the general her request. They're going ahead with the plan. He'll see she gets recognition for what she's doing.

Two days later we hear the area near the drop area has been attached by Nazi Alpenjaegers. A number of people in the village who participated in the drop have been shot, homes burned. Many have left, scared and grief-stricken.

Bill stands in the middle of the room towering over everybody, listening to the account of what happened translated by Ettore. "That bitch!" Bill spits out. "That Goddamn double-crossing bitch!" Marko glares at him. So does the Russian. "I'm going to Belluno and taking care of her and that Kraut lover of hers." He reveals where's he's been, whom he had met, what he had done.

"Better not, Bill," I say. "Let me go. Maybe she couldn't help it. Her Nazi friend either. It's the price they had to pay for what they were doing for you."

"No, I don't want you getting mixed up in this. Shit, we don't have to pay that kind of price!"

"Sometimes we have to, don't we? It's war."

"What the hell is going on anyway?" Marko confronts us.

"None of your damn business," Bill yells at the little guy. "We got taken, that's all."

"Lost your balls to a lousy broad, huh?" He snickers. "You poor dumb son of a bitch. I thought you had more sense than that. You could blow this whole mission."

"A blow job, huh?" I quip. "He knows that, Captain. He just thought he had a deal with her, that's all."

"A deal for what? Free sex?"

Bill stomps off to our room. There's a stunned silence. I hurry after him with a flash and find him sitting on his bunk, head in his hands crying. And for a moment I think about comforting him. But how do you comfort somebody's who's responsible for getting people killed? And I remember the townspeople gathering up the containers and crates in the Pass, hollering whenever they found something. Like an Easter egg hunt. I don't say a word but go over and shut the door, leave him to his darkness.

"He's taking it pretty hard," I say to Marko. "Better let him alone. He'll come out of it. He's tired."

"When the hell is he going to learn, you can't trust anybody up here? I don't care who they are - father, mother, wife, brother, grandfather. They look out for themselves first. Should be a good lesson to you, Tony."

I motion to Ettore and we walk outside.

"How about taking me to Belluno? Got something smaller than that logging truck?" He has, it's a Cencia. I could hide in the back under

28

a blanket. It would be faster. We could do it in a couple of hours. Hell, next they could be raiding this place. She could have told the Germans everything, who we are, what we're doing, approximately where we're staying. We've got to know where we stand with her, what she's up to. The major made a dumb mistake, took too big a risk."

"*Si, si*," he sputters. He spits out, "*Cagna, cagna.*"

"Maybe we expected too much of her and her friend."

He runs off down the road, and I duck back inside to wait for him. Marko and the colonel and the men are examining the new weapons and wiping the Cosmoline off, stacking up the cans of food, unwrapping plastic explosives.

"What's he up to anyway?" Marko comes over, pats me on the back, talks in a low confidential voice.

"I guess it's just a matter of getting what you pay for."

"He paid off some dame, and she screwed him?"

"He thought he had a deal with her about the drop and some other things. She just didn't live up to her part of the bargain."

"I told you he'd never make it up here. Guys like him are great facing bullets but like kids when facing a woman or a fast-talking salesman."

"How about me?"

"Lay off the dames and don't listen to any big talk. Distrust everything you hear and most of the people you meet. That's the only way to stay alive?"

I thank him for the advice and walk away, wondering how many dames he screwed and how many people lost their lives listening to his big talk.

## Chapter 5

It's a faster, wilder ride than the other night, crossing the Biois with its cliffs around Forno and roaring through the Val di Gares with its sheer steep sides thousands of feet high to Cencenighe. Then six miles to Agordo, taking a secondary road and avoiding the searchlights of the power station. The rest of the way down the Cordevole alongside the railroad tracks I'm curled up under the blanket. But sometimes I pop up to get a glimpse of the night scenery, the deep gorges and tunnels, the silhouetted old walls on the mountain sides, the great rocks in the river. By the time we arrive I'm stiff as a board. It's after one. The place is dark. Ettore goes to the glass door and rings the bell. A light turns on, and there is the countess in a white peignoir with that black hair flowing down her back, the fleshy slightly wrinkled face, no make-up. They talk a minute. I glance around and spot a Fiat but no Alfa Romeo. He beckons and I run to the villa.

She kisses me on the cheek and leads us into her living room with that riotous Titian hanging on the white wall, the high ceiling, the logs in the fireplace, the black leather couch and chairs.

"Where's Bill?" she sings out before sitting on the couch.

"Getting over the shock."

"Of what happened after the drop? *Si*, terrible, terrible. We do what we can, *Sergente*." She concentrates on me still standing, takes out a grayish-white cigarette from her pocket, lights it with a silver lighter. Ettore lingers by the door listening, looking around. "Dr. Bauer keep the Alpenjaegers from the area for a little while, suggest the drop in another area, another time. But he not stop them from punishing people who hurt *Tedeschi* when they find out. Happening all over Italia. It is war, *Sergente*. You come here to kill them. They do the same to you." She puffs on her cigarette, and the smoke melts into the air above me.

"He didn't tell them the people in the area helped in the drop?"

No, no, *Sergente*. He not do that. He good man. He tell them, make a mistake. Yesterday he arrange for the jailer in Belluno to release two of your airmen shot down. You find out I tell the truth. He help you. He like *Americani*. He not like Hitler, have to work for him. He has no choice."

"Like your husband working for Mussolini, huh?"

30

"That different. My husband not cultured man like Dr. Bauer. He teaches at the University of Berlin before the war. Distinguished professor of government."

"Does he want United States citizenship too?"

She smiles. "Ah, *Sergente*, we all come to your country if you let us, no? He never say that. Only no war crimes. He only doing his duty. He no criminal. This region is German now. He is administrator. Very *importante* job."

"How about the other things the major talked to you about?" Her face clouds.

"He tell you about them?"

"He just hints. Something big, isn't it?"

"*Sí*, very big, very dangerous. Dr. Bauer seeing people about it *domani* in Bolzano. He says he will get what Bill wants. You not trust us, *Sergente*?"

"We want to."

"You tell Bill to come back next week. I have everything ready. Maybe the war will be over soon and I go to *America*. You like tea, cake?" I glance over at Ettore. He nods. And I say fine and follow her to the kitchen while he stands guard in the hall with his Sten.

I watch her heat the water for the tea, cut the chocolate cake, and wondering where all the servants are. She turns slowly and puts a piece in my mouth laughing.

"*Sergente*, you stay *notte*? It late. I have room upstairs, bed, private bath. You look tired. Your friend too. You come a long way."

"No, we've got to get back. Bill will be wondering where we are."

"He serious, no? Not like the boy I know before the war in Cortina. We go skiing, hiking, drink wine, have good time." She grins. "Now the war, no good time."

"He's got a mission on his mind."

"You too, *Sergente*, you have mission?"

"Yeah, a big one. I wish I could tell you about it."

"Different from Bill's?" Her dark inquisitive eyes crawl all over me. She's standing too damn close for comfort so I can see her wet lips tremble, trace the outline of her breasts inside the sheer gown, the nipples prominent. God, I'm getting horny. I've got to leave. Maggie, Maggie, where the hell are you, girl?

"A lot different. Mine's strictly post-war stuff." I almost tell her I'm a poet and want to write a poem sort of like the *Divine Comedy*, but she'd laugh. And it is kind of farfetched, trying to do something like that at my age with my inexperience in everything from making love to women like her to making a great work like Dante's.

31

"You think he comes see me again after what happened?"

"Maybe when I explain. He's upset right now."

"You go back, tell him not my fault. Not the fault of Dr. Bauer. We do what we can. We on your side. We love America."

"Good. Well, we better go. I'll talk to Bill. Tell him what you said about the drop. *Grazie* for the cake and tea."

"I sorry, *Sergente*." She smiles, touches my arm. My thing perks up again. And I tell myself, kiddo, it's not your bedtime. Think of those poor people near the drop site you and Bill could have sent to an early grave. Yeah, and I'm thinking, too, of that soft scented body and watching those hands at her side, her painted toes wiggling in the sandals. Once again reminding me of Caroline Massey I had a drink and a dance with and longed for the kind of sex I had with Maggie back in Washington. Our drink was in a kitchen, too, wasn't? No dance this time. Everything normal in one way and abnormal in another. War's a situation, not life I read somewhere. I should stop moping in this guilty, melancholy mood, letting it transport me back to where I don't belong anymore. "*Sergente, Sergente,*" Ettore cries out rushing into the kitchen. "*Auto, auto!*" I step back and stare at her.

"This a trap?"

"No, nobody come."

"This Dr. Bauer and his Gestapo?"

"He go to Bolzano to help Bill."

I run to the front hall and look out. A green Alfa Romeo is parking beside our Cencia. A tall civilian with glasses is slowly getting out with a briefcase and striding toward the glass door. No one is with him.

"It's the Kraut,' I say. "Where can we hide?"

"You stay." She stands beside me. "You meet him. He tell you the truth about the drop."

I glance at Ettore. He shakes his head.

"We'll go out the back. Keep him busy. And don't tell him we were here. He'll be asking about the car. Make up something good."

"No, no, he know about Bill. It is *buono*, *Sergente*. He not hurt you."

There's a knock. She moves to the door. We hurry to the kitchen and out the back and around to the front.

"Think his bodyguard's down the road?" I say when we reach the car.

"*Possibile*. You have gun." He hands me the Sten. We jump in and take off down the drive lined with cypress to the gatehouse. I duck under the blanket in back and peer out. A military vehicle is parked at

32

the entrance. Ettore stops and two Germans standing beside it come toward him in their gray-green uniforms. The first enemy soldiers I've seen except for those Polish prisoners in a train station in North Africa laughing at us going to Italy while they're headed for camps in the States. One Kraut is stout and round-shouldered, the other shorter, leaner. Their faces in the headlights are smiling. I consider firing at them, then drop out of sight.

Ettore babbles away, and they're guffawing. He's probably telling them a dirty joke about the countess. I bet she's the subject of a lot of them around here. Then he starts up and we're off for the valley. No one is following. Teresa and the good-bad doctor maybe on our side after all. I throw off the blanket and sit up, unwinding, breathing easier. A checkpoint that wasn't there earlier looms ahead. Ettore says he's going to run it, get the Sten ready. He slows down as we approach the truck at the side of the road. A Kraut emerges with his hand in the air, a rifle slung over his shoulder nonchalantly. I lower the window and squeeze the trigger as we accelerate with a jolt. A couple of bullets ping against the metal. The guy hits the dirt. And I wonder if I killed him. He reminds me of a dead dog lying on the highway back home. The last sight of him is a scary one. Then the bastard jumps up like a ghost and starts firing wildly at us along with another Kraut.

Ettore swerves off the main road into a bumpy dirt one, and the little car rocks and rattles as if every screw were loose and the wheels were about to fall off. I'm holding onto the seat to keep from bouncing up through the roof. We come to the Canal del Mis, narrow and deep as hell with a limestone wall one side and a stream on the other. I can reach out and touch the rock we're blasting through. Then it's the Agordo Valley and around a garrison and the floodlights of the power station. Another detour at Cencenighe to avoid more barracks and lights and head up the Val di Gares and over the Biois to Celt and Sarchet and finally heading for Andrich, that bleak little settlement of stone houses and a solitary church huddling under the mountain ranges stretching like spiked fences cutting us off from the world.

"*Tedeschi* come," Ettore says. "*Subito*." He sits hunched over the wheel in the dark, sometimes driving without lights when we pass through villages. Everywhere those stark peaks pricking the stars overhead. The thunder of water rushing fills the air. Rock faces jut up out of the blackness.

Our place looks deserted as we drive up. A partisan guard steps out of the darkness to challenge us. We stop, emerge, and he marches toward us. Ettore yells something in Italian. A flashlight shines on us, and there are voices. A dog barks. Men appear with Stens and carbines

33

and those old fashioned 91 rifles. They recognize us, relax, and we walk into the house. Bill and Marko and the colonel are sitting by the fireplace, grim-faced, the candlelight playing over their faces.

"What the hell's going on?" Bill yells at me. I tell him.

"That was a stupid thing to do. You could get us all killed."

"I wanted to find out if she really betrayed us."

"And did she?"

"Hard to know. Suggested her friend lied about the drop area and the time. The Germans found out about it later."

"Sounds phony. Maybe I did make a mistake going down there to see her. But I just had to take that chance or everything would be over. Did she give you a message about it?"

"Only this Dr. Bauer is seeing some people in Bolzano, and she'd have the information you wanted next week."

"I wonder. She could be on the level, and this Nazi kept them away from the drop, and they found out later. Still we can't trust the two of them. We've got to move out of here fast. She could guess where we are, and they could come and wipe us out. Better pack up."

"Where to?" I say studying him. He's not looking at any of us, caught up in his own anguish over the whole affair. So damn sure of himself when he's in action and so full of self-doubt when he's with the countess and in a mess like this not knowing who to believe or what's going to happen.

"Fontanafredda, a basin in one of Monte Civetta's old glaciers. We could hole up there in a *magla* for a while. I scouted it last week. Good drop country. If only I was sure this Bauer was on our side and not playing games with us."

She insisted he couldn't prevent the incident after the drop. It was out of his hands. He had two of our pilots released from jail yesterday."

"That was decent of him if it's true. Shit, I swear I could trust her. She was so sincere when we talked, just like in '38. And the letters we exchanged were genuine. War, I guess, changes people. They do what they have to do to survive. The professor could have duped her and me as he did the Germans in order to make what we were working on succeeds."

"Is there a *Garabaldi* Brigade on Monte Civetta?" Marko asks out of the blue. He and the colonel are watching us, listening, quiet, detached, taking mental notes and trying to decipher Bill's double talk.

"Most of them are south of here. Too many Krauts around for large groups to operate. But Ettore says there might be some part of the Nino Nannetti Division. They've got a headquarters at Cesiomaggiora near Belluno. You thinking about leaving us, joining them, not doing the Brenner?" He scowls over at the little guy and the tall Russian.

"Afraid so, Bill. I never thought that was a good idea in the first place. And now you running down to Belluno to make some kind of fuckin' deal with this Fascist bitch and having people killed as a result. Tony and Ettore taking a trip to see her and jeopardizing the mission. You can't fight a war based on some sexy relationship with a woman."

"There could have been a mix-up." I'm not convinced she gave us away. She's an old friend. She could still end up helping us."

"The men don't believe that. They've heard of her and her Fascist husband and her sleeping with a Kraut bigwig."

"I'm still in command here, Marko. I'll make the decisions."

"You better be more careful who you trust. No more going off half-cocked and making a deal with a Fascist no matter how good she is in bed."

"We got supplies, didn't we?"

"At a price."

"I'm just as sorry about what happened. The chance you have to take. I'll make it up."

"You bringing those people back to life, rebuilding their houses?"

"Come on, let's get out of here, stop this Monday morning quarterbacking crap. Or we'll be digging our graves. I'll take the responsibility for what happened, but I'm not going around beating myself to death. The past is the past."

So the next day we gather our equipment and start off on the long trip to Monte Civetta across the Cordeveole. There are about fifty of us. Most of the heavy equipment, explosives and ammo and guns, we load in a couple of trucks and cars. We don't reach the *magla* until dawn. The place is a typical mountain hut, a small kitchen with rooms down and upstairs. No sign of any Krauts. The partisans spread out in tents made from parachutes they've collected after the last drop.

As soon as we settle in for a long stay, I string up an aerial and call the Guard Channel in Bari and send a message. Give our position and ask for an immediate drop. Bari confirms, and we're in business. At least I hope we are.

Then Bill takes me outside to ask again about the countess. Did I think it was a trap? What was Bauer doing there at that time of night? Was she inviting me to stay in order to have me caught with my pants down and pecker out? Or was it a purely friendly gesture.

"You think they gave us the drop to get in our good graces and get information out of us?"

"I don't want to, Tony. God, I don't want to. So much depends on her and her friend. They could provide us the defense set up at the Brenner, contact certain people who could help us in other things. And I don't want to give Marko the satisfaction of being right. He could take over the Orange mission. You heard him. He's on the verge of doing it already, him and that damn Russian. They could brand us as Fascist spies."

"What are you going to do about them? They've definitely got the partisans on their side. Did you notice there are more Red bandanas and fewer blue ones? The Christian Democrats must be changing their colors. Those two guys are out beating the bushes for recruits."

"I know, I know. I'm worried. And I've got a timetable. The drive on Rome should be starting soon, and we're supposed to coordinate our attacks on the Brenner with it. So we've got to head for the Pass or it'll be too late. And if Marko and his men won't come along, it's going to be tough to do much."

"Then your whole reason for being up here will be *finito*, huh?"

"The whole war you might say. Even my reason for living. You see, Tony," his voice softens and his big frame sags a little, "I've never done much with my life. Flunked out of Harvard my junior year, bummed around in a lot of odd jobs. Nothing ever satisfied me. Nothing ever worked, even one of the girls I went with turned me down. My father got disgusted. He's a pediatrician and wanted me to follow in his footsteps like my brother, who's now an obstetrician. My sister Anne is a nurse the way my mother was. Meet Bill the tramp. But there comes a time when you have to say to yourself, this is it. You're going to do something worthwhile or you're going to die trying. Your last chance. You're not getting any younger."

"And for you that's the Brenner, huh?"

"My brass ring up there just waiting for me to come and grab it. And I am, Christ, I am, Tony. No more lousy Anzios. I'm in control this time. So I've got to make it work and leave this life with at least one accomplishment. And if it's not the Brenner than this other thing that keeps haunting me and Donovan is counting on so much. He wants to show Roosevelt what he can do, like I want to show my father, and quiet the general's enemies in Washington who think OSS is a bunch of spoiled rich guys and crazies having fun playing war. Then, hell, who knows he might be thinking of running for president one day like he ran for governor in New York."

"Okay, when are we shoving off?"

"After another drop. I'll need you and a few volunteers and plenty of plastic explosives. We're going to bomb the shit out of the Brenner ."

36

"All twenty-one tunnels and sixty bridges?"

"As many as we can. You still with me, aren't you?"

"What do you think?"

"I know Ettore is."

"The place is guarded, isn't it?"

"Weakly guarded as I've said, but if we can get a map of the defenses and troop dispositions from Bauer, we'll be in good shape. And if we can't attack the Pass itself, there are always the feeder lines."

"Going to be tough, though."

"Tougher than I thought down in Bari. But we've got a great opportunity to shut down the war in Italy all by ourselves. Or at least shorten it. How many people ever get a chance to do something like that in their lifetime? We're going to show them, Tony, show them just how good and determined we are." He recalls the captain of the football team speaking at the Friday night rally before the Cornell game except there's no bonfire, band, cheer leaders, or fight songs. Just the vast and empty silence of the Dolomites.

I gaze around at them. We're way up here under the shadow of this 10,000-foot mountain and all these massive peaks. The forests and meadows below seem so green and picturesque. In the distance glimmer little white villages with their church towers. Boy, what a long way from the Hanover plain and the dear old Dartmouth wilderness.

The next day he strides off toward a rock face with overhangs carrying pitons and rope. He says he needs the exercise and the solitude. A true poet, more the born variety than the made. A funny guy all right. Sort of reminds me a little of Stan Marshall in my class. He was president of everything from Sigma Nu to Green Key, All American quarterback, destined to be Phi Beta Kappa. Then one moonlit night in March he drives into a snow bank on the White River Junction Road and puts a bullet through his head. The whole college is in shock for a week. No note or anything.

Everything returns to normal, the partisans lolling around, Marko and the colonel and a couple of Red bandanas going off somewhere without disclosing their destination. Ettore hands me a message they left to send. An announcement they want BBC to broadcast, three Cadore villages have been liberated by communists.

"Wait till Bill sees this," I say to him. "He'll hit the ceiling. You one of them?"

"No Party."

"Like me, huh? Though I admit once I had ideas in that direction, but I'm beginning to wonder about them now. Think someday the big Red banner will be flying over the Alps?"

"Only the Red Cross," he laughs. Then he goes up to lie in his bunk. I stay on the ground floor to wait for the major to come back from his exercise. He has his mountains, I have my Dante. Both probably will be around for a long time.

## Chapter 6

We wait a couple of days for the next drop, spending the time eating rolls for breakfast, coarse whole wheat bread and broth with meat or pasta for lunch, minestrone and cheese for supper. One partisan turns out to be a professional cook. Then there are always the C-rations. We sleep a lot and take turns doing guard duty, clean weapons, collect wood for the fires to signal the planes on the next drop. I pick up the *Inferno*, this time reading about Dante crossing a bridge accompanied by a squad of demons who stick out their tongues at a captain while he farts in their faces. Sort of like the Marx Brothers. They come upon these poor sinners lying in a ditch of boiling pitch like frogs with only their muzzles showing. All submerged but one. They hook him in the hair and haul him in like an otter dripping wet. Only in Italy could somebody write such gory and realistic stuff and be so weird and profound at the same time. Dante nails these characters and their sins and punishment as only he can. I start naming people I know back in the States and start chuckling over them and their wild stuff, Catclaw, Deadog, Crazyred. Make them into grotesque creatures the way he does.

Most of the talk is about communism taking over Italy after the war and linking up with Russia. Ettore is the only one who argues with Marko and the guys with the Red stars in their lapels. Bill, back from his exercise, sits dreaming when he's not cleaning his .45 and carbine, chopping wood, target practicing, scaling a rock face. I get "dit happy" sending and receiving four times a day, worried about the DF's triangulating me and the Krauts coming up the mountain after us. But the reception is good, and it feels great to be talking to Bari and sending messages via my sonnet. No match for Shakespeare, that's for sure. No dark lady that looms behind his. I should have written one about Maggie, my Wellesley Physic major. And no memorable lines like "When to the sessions of sweet silent thought/I summon up remembrance of things past," or "Like as the waves make towards the pebbled shore,/So do our minutes hasten to their end." I wonder if the general and the president ever use their sonnets, particularly the Fala one. Or if that was just a trick as I thought to flatter me into volunteering for this mission. When you write, you're a sucker for anybody who likes your style and thinks he can use you.

More Red kerchiefs drift into camp. We're up to at least a hundred, overflowing the huts in the area, forcing guys to sleep anywhere they can. Marko talks about bringing in five hundred. A lot of the new guys are in their twenties and thirties, escaping the roundup of Jews to be sent to concentration camps, avoiding the draft for TODT battalions building the Alpine Line. Some are former policemen, *carabinieri*, sailors, custom officials, forest rangers, firemen, and wear part of their uniforms along with trousers and jackets and coats from German, British, and Italian armies. What a motley sight, especially the hats, everything from plumed helmets and berets to gray caps like the French *kepi* and all highlighted by Red stars, some with feathers.

They're stirred up like freshmen at Dartmouth with green beany caps but instead of being eager to win football games going out and killing Fascists and Nazis, liberate villages. And in another way they recall the OG's in Bari, though not so savage and more political. Kind of simple and sentimental, too, singing sad songs at night. One I really like is "*La Montanar*a", the mountain girl, which melts me inside even more than "Lilli Marlene" that I used to hear the British singing at night behind the church down in Bari. A couple have relatives in the States, and I spend time telling them about Benny Goodman, central heating, and the World Series as well as great movies like Charlie Chaplin's *The Great Dictator* with Jack Oakie mocking Mussolini.

A drop comes the first night of the full moon. We hear the BBC "crack" from London, "Money in the bank," and light the fires in an H downwind at eleven. The planes appear an hour later. It's a beautiful sight, the moonlit sky filled with parachutes drifting down like multi-colored petals. The crates contain food and medical supplies, blankets and sleeping bags, maps and magazines, letters from home. In one of them Maggie tells me she's not working for Bell Labs in New Jersey anymore but for the government in New York. It's for an agency even more secret than OSS, and she's excited about living on 8th Street near the Village Barn, going to shows like *Oklahoma* and seeing in the Museum of Modern Art Picasso's portrait of Gertrude Stein and his explosive painting called *Guernica* about the Spanish Civil War. Can't wait for me to come home and we'll be married.

The containers are loaded with guns and ammo, explosives and radio equipment. We haul everything back to where we're staying, wipe the grease from the weapons, try out a couple of the guns with live ammo.

Marko and the colonel are beaming, going around announcing they ordered the stuff from Russia. US stands for *Unione Sovietica*. Bill curses under his breath but doesn't say anything. He tells me when we leave the whole brigade will become Red, take the name of an Italian Communist who fought in the Spanish Civil War. Part of a plot to set up a Red government in the region. He just hopes Bari will send a guy to replace him when he leaves who will keep Marko in line. He puts that in a message, but there's no direct reply.

"Hell," he mutters to me, "I don't give a shit who takes over up here after the war, but I sure hate it to be communists. Imagine, Tony, stretching their influence from the Urals to the Alps."

I don't say anything. He asks me if I'm sympathetic to them. In general, but not with Marko and the colonel. He has to admit, though, almost every scrap of intelligence we receive comes from their men. Christian Democrats, Liberals, and Socialists contribute little. It's a Red, Red world up here all right, even the peaks sometimes turn pink. The sunsets are awesome as if the rocks are switching colors right before your eyes, pink to terra cotta to gray to black.

One day Bill takes me and twenty partisans to Perarolo on the Piave River. He heard about a railway bridge he wants to knock out, a sort of rehearsal for the Brenner Pass mission. It's a thirty to forty-kilometer hike through rugged ranges, climbing hills, skirting Kraut and Fascist garrisons. Everyone is carrying a heavy load of explosives plus food, a sleeping bag, and a carbine.

The bridge is a high trestle over the river out in the middle of nowhere. He tells me and a young partisan to stand guard at each approach while he and the others get busy fitting charges under the girders at each end and in the middle, packing them in, wrapping the detonating cords around the stuff, connecting the three explosions so they all go off together. Then they attach detonating caps to the cord at each end and in the middle, put the fuses in place, go over everything carefully. I watch from the road amazed at the furious activity.

Finally, Bill hollers for me and the kid to duck behind a tree, and he and the gang light the fuses simultaneously and spring away. Hidden, we wait. Not for long. A terrific boom shakes the earth. The rails shoot skyward. It's a terrifying sight. Where there were tracks now there's only air and a mass of twisted girders and strips of iron dumped in the water.

"Looks like we've got our crew for the Brenner," Bill says to me when we gather together after the explosion. "These guys are pros. They follow instructions great. Now to get the hell out of here before the Krauts come running. They'll be offering a big reward for information about the bastards who did this."

"You've got the touch all right."

"The secret is having the fuses in the right places and packing the explosive material tight, putting it by the abutments. These Eyeties love it, don't they? Anything to make noise and cause a lot of commotion." I study them. Some are about my age, some older, some younger. Wonder how many graduated from high school or heard of the Boy Scouts. Instead of reading Shelley and Thomas Wolfe or learning to tie slip knots, build camp fires, give first aid, they're blowing bridges and sleeping on the side of a mountain with pistols and rifles. Most of them no doubt from poor families. Yet they act as if they're enjoying what they're doing while at the same time performing like professionals.

We spend the night in the woods, and the next day start the trek across the Cadore to base camp. No sign of the Krauts except for a small convoy snaking along the valley floor hundreds of feet below us. We stop at a village and have some wine, bread, and cheese at an outdoor café. Children swarm around us. The old people stand back and stare. A priest comes out of the church and talks in halting English. He's an old man and has been to America. Bill tells him to be quiet about our passing through. The *Tedeschi* could find out and burn houses, steal food, shoot a few people as a warning. He stares at us and says he knows all about that. Last week at Fondo two houses were destroyed and a family executed for sheltering partisans. "No *buono, Americano, Tedeschi* animals." He gestures with a finger, spits, and grimaces. I'm waiting for him to curse.

We leave, and as soon as we're outside the village Bill speeds up the hiking.

"What the hell's going on?" I shout after catching up.

"He's going to tell the first Kraut he sees we were there. He's scared out of his wits. Didn't you notice? And collect a reward for identifying the bridge bombers."

"A priest who's been to America?"

"You bet. He doesn't want any of his people executed. And he wants the reward money."

We trot behind him, and he swings off the road and we're climbing through the mountains again. I ask how come he knows these places so well. And he explains that he spent a lot of time in the Dolomites skiing, visiting towns and churches, noticing bridges, roads, tunnels. This is like a second home. He always wanted to come back. Why he wrote to Donovan about the Brenner mission.

That night we stay in a shepherd's hut, no straw or bunks or anything, hear the sound of trucks and motorcycles roaring down in the valley. I can't sleep and go outside and peer at the road twisting below. Every now and then strings of light flash by and a cannon booms.

"Think they've spotted us?" I come back to the hut where Bill has lit a candle. The guys are all awake and scared, sitting around clutching their guns, knees up.

42

"Maybe they know we're here, but won't come after us. Afraid of what happens when they leave the low ground and start roaming through these mountains. We could pick them off easily one by one. They wouldn't have a chance."

The next morning we climb even higher. But it's rough going. The partisans, despite being from the area, aren't used to so much steady, relentless hiking and such heights, wanting to stop every hour to catch their breath. It takes us two days and a half to reach Monte Civetta. And we're bushed. Even Bill looks weary stumbling up to an empty shed. The rest of us are dead on our feet. I'm blistered all over, my legs ache, my shoulders and arms hurt. God, I can't believe it was worth it for one lousy bridge that maybe didn't haul as much stuff as we thought. I dread the long hike to the Brenner and the bridges and tunnels he wants put out of commission. I can't see how I'll ever make it. Or how he'll ever do it. Bill's got to be out of his mind. Or maybe the general is for setting him up for such an impossible mission. Hard to imagine Clark or Alexander approved it. In fact, I'm convinced the big brass doesn't know a damn thing about what's happening up here. Even Donovan is ignorant. He comes over for the start of a big drive or a top secret mission, then boom back to Washington to get ready for the next opening night. Never stays around for the reviews. Just long enough to pat the actors and the director on the back and tell them what a great job they're doing. Keep it up. All the world's a stage.

The brigade has doubled in our absence, and right away Marko is clamoring for me to send a message to Bari for a mammoth drop. He needs tons of equipment. Everything that can be parachuted. Wishing they could land a tank or artillery. He's stirred up, gesticulating, spouting about all the men we're attracting and how they're itching for action.

Bill worries about informers. Whenever you take in so many men at once, it's hard to check everyone's credentials. Marko vouches for all of them. No spies, traitors, or bastards. They're good, brave men.

"Good Red men," Bill says.

"A few Socialists. They could be spies. We'll watch them. And we've got patrols out. Men down in the valley too."

"Girls also," Bill says.

"That's right. Bitches on bikes." He laughs. "They make the best couriers. We won't be surprised by a *rastrellamento*, don't worry. We'll have at least a day's notice to fight or scram."

"I hope so. But take it from me, Marko, these guys can lose heart fast. If too many men are killed in a raid and supplies get short they could panic and beat it home to momma and papa. Wait and see."

The captain's not impressed, and we climb to our room after supper and lie on a soft spot for the first time in days. Partisans are singing outside about that mountain "Lilli Marlene." The song sort of lulls me to sleep. Somehow I can't believe we'll ever get out of these mountains alive unless the war ends soon. More of the rotten pessimism I inherited from my Calvinist ancestors.

The next morning we hear a rumor that the Krauts down in Cencenighe know we're up here and are planning to attack the camp. But so far there's been no movement. They're supposed to be waiting for reinforcements from Alleghe. Then they're coming after us with a thousand men. Maybe use planes and tanks. Somebody's given our position away.

Everybody becomes jumpy. A spy in our midst. Bill debates with Marko whether to stay and wait for one more drop or break camp. Marko and the colonel are for hanging around as long as possible and picking up as many men and as much information as we can. In a week we could have a thousand up here, and the Krauts would have to waste a hell of a lot of bodies to drive us from the basin. It's a natural defense area.

Despite these arguments Bill is for pulling out right away. One of the guys who went with us to the Piave, Giorgio, has found a good spot with a couple of shelters over at Monte Pelmo, five miles away. It's higher and better protected. We could still use Fontanafredda for a drop field. He doubts the Krauts would look for us over there. And if they did we could keep moving higher and higher until they would have to have wings to reach us. Isn't that the guerilla strategy? You stay on the move, never fight a pitch battle? The Russian nods after Marko translates and agrees.

So we break camp that afternoon and head for Pelmo and Fiorentina. Two hours after we're gone we hear the Krauts appeared in force over the rim of the basin at Fontanafredda, saw no signs of life, and retreated. It'll probably only be a matter of days before they find us over here too. Where we'll go next nobody knows.

It's like playing a game of chess with the bastards, Bill thinks. You have to keep outguessing them and occupying squares they won't notice until it's too late. In the end we could run out of places on the board and maybe Knights and Queens and Kings too. Let's hope that's a long way off.

I set up the aerial on the roof of the new *magla* we end up in and begin sending as soon as I can, asking for another drop at a new zone nearby, giving coordinates. Also asking for bombing and strafing of enemy troop concentrations at Alleghe. Marko is all for collecting as big a force as he can and liberating some of the towns in the area. Not just small places like Alleghe but Pieve di Cadore, Ampezzo, and Talmezzo. And when we're strong enough hitting Cortina and declaring the whole Cadore except for Belluno a free state. Carnia, too.

"You mean a Red one," Bill says one night at our new base. "What you and the colonel have been working on. Fly in a commissar from Russia, proclaim Cortina the Moscow of the West and Piazza Roma the new Red Square."

Marko laughs, "You wait. After you leave things will change. You can have your Brenner. I bet you'll never get within ten miles of it. A sugar tit for a romantic ego. Not for me. Nor for most of the men. They say it's suicide." He smiles across the room at Bill. A candle sits in the middle. We're cutting bread and cheese and drinking wine.

"I know what I'm doing."

"I hope the hell you do. When are you leaving us?"

"Right after the next drop."

"Then I'll be in charge."

"Unless Bari sends a replacement for me."

"You requested somebody?"

"Yes."

"Why you...!" Marko glares over at the major. "I'm the one who should be in command when you leave. If Bari sends somebody, he won't last long."

"You'll take care of him?"

"The men won't accept him."

"Especially if he's a Wall Street lawyer or an Ivy League asshole."

"You know the kind of people Donovan selects to head these things."

"I ought to."

"I don't mean you, Bill. You're an exception."

"Not really. I went to Exeter, Harvard. I've never done any work I didn't want to. I've travelled all over. You're a union organizer. You know what it means to go hungry and unemployed. Fought in Spain. I'm a capitalist playboy in your eyes, somebody who never grew up and deserves to be executed when the revolution comes. Though let me tell you, Captain, you too, Colonel, I can out-hike, out ski, out-climb, and out-shoot anybody in this camp. Out fuck anybody too." He laughs in that boyish, ironic way of his.

"You're a Byronic Bakunin."

45

"The 19<sup>th</sup> century Russian revolutionist, friend of Turgenev and Herzen. See, I know something about your world. Not just Marx and Lenin."

"Not much, Bill. You're too…"

"You mean none of your comrades will follow me to the Brenner Pass. They'd rather stay here and fight for the people under you?"

"Why don't you reconsider? Give up that nonsense. You can't shut down the place with a few guys. You'd need a division."

"So you don't want me to leave, huh? Afraid the officer who's coming to take my place won't be so friendly?"

"We're working together good. We've got a great brigade here."

"Sorry, I'm not interested in political warfare, and that's what this partisan stuff is turning into mainly. I've got my own little war to fight."

"And you're taking the sergeant here to fight it with you?"

"Right. Any objections?"

"No way, Bill. He stays, the radio too, until we have another operator. You're not leaving me up the creek without any communications. I'd be a dead duck. No chance of a drop, no way to send intelligence. I'd lose the whole Goddamn brigade."

"Tony stays with me and that's that. I'd be dead in a couple of days without him."

" Don't forget my sonnet," I pipe up. "It's keeping you guys afloat." They gape across the table at me, wondering where the hell that outburst came from.

"That's another thing," Marko says. "This damn code stuff. "Only the sergeant here knows it."

"The new operator will bring in different codes. Maybe one-time pads. They're quicker and easier and break-proof."

"But not as much fun," I interrupt.

"The sergeant stays here, Bill." He stares over at me. "He understands us."

"I understand the major too," I say.

"You're not going with him. I'm taking over."

"You kicking me out?" Bill glares at him.

"I'm just telling you the way things are going to be from now on once you're gone, The men are taking orders from me. If you stick around, you could be doing the same thing."

"You can't do that," I shout at him. "The major's the head of the mission. Wait until the general hears about this."

"Shut your Goddamn trap, kid!"

"Don't talk to him like that," Bill snaps.

"I'll talk to him and to you, too, any damn way I please. Nobody's stopping me."

For a couple of minutes they look at each other as if they're about to draw their .45's and shoot it out right then and there. The colonel sits beside Marko like a Sphinx. His black boots, pock-marked face, red epaulettes make him a forbidding figure. As if he's Ivan the Terrible and Peter the Great rolled in one. A sign from him, I bet, and we're goners. Marko seems to wait for it along with the partisans. When it doesn't come, everything seems to fizzle out, and the men drift off and Bill and I get up and stroll around the camp. The wind is blowing. The mountains ring us like barb wire.

"We gotta get out of here, Tony. And soon. The bastards are going to finish me off. I can feel it. We'll wait a few days, and then make a run for it. So get your stuff together. After the last drop and your last contact one evening I'll give the signal, and when everybody's at supper we'll take off. I know some good trails. They'll never catch us."

"Just you and me going to the Brenner? How about Ettore and Giorgio and the guys who went with us to blow the bridge on the Piave. You'll need them. Round up some others."

"Plans have changed. We're not going there. I sent Ettore down to see the countess again, and he just came back with some good news."

"What is it?"

"I can't tell you yet. Too early. Wait till we get there. Damn it, I never should have let that Russian come with us. He's complicating things. Marko would never threaten what he's been doing if he didn't have the colonel and all these guys loyal to him."

"Why did you consent to let him come?"

"I thought he would help. He's a pro. Knows this business."

"So do you. Been at Anzio."

"Not like the two of them. They've been through this."

"You sure the countess and her Nazi are on the level?"

"They better be or we and the general and a lot of other people are in for it."

" So this is the mystery mission, huh?"

"Right."

"And it doesn't have anything to do with the Brenner business?"

"That was to make them think we could be going there."

"You mean the Krauts?"

"Marko and his friends too. An alternative in case the big one doesn't work out. But it has. The countess confirmed it to Ettore. Now we better hit the hay. I don't think they'll murder us in the straw tonight." He laughs. I'm shaking.

47

The next few days everything is tense in camp, even after a successful drop. Nobody speaks to us, and they're watching our movements as if we are some kind of spies. Mainly Marko. He checks the messages I send to be sure I'm not pulling a fast one, even going over the boxes and the columns of letters in my double transposition. When I'm finished with it one day, Bill gives me the signal. We're heading out. Get your stuff packed including the radio. Nobody sees me. I sneak out to the end of the camp carrying everything in a knapsack, k-rations, bedroll, and Dante. Stick the radio in a small splash proof container. Batteries, crystals, headphones, aerial in another case. Hide it all in the bushes. The .45 I carry in the open like everyone else. Bill also walks around carrying his carbine.

Around five when the sun sets behind the pink peaks we make our break. The partisans are lining up for supper outside a tent. Marko and the colonel are busy talking to a girl partisan courier from Alleghe. We stroll casually away from the *magla*, meet in the woods, grab what we had hidden, and take off down a meandering trail to the Boite River and the Ampezzo Valley. Our first stop is Cortina. Thank God, it gets dark fast up here. Bill doubts anybody will risk coming after us through these passes and ravines. The footing is too dangerous at night. One misstep and you're a goner. The drops are hundreds of feet, and groping along behind him, barely holding on to his shirt, and gazing down into the darkness, I get dizzy just thinking about the abysses below. Like walking a tightrope.

We camp above the river around two, make a small fire, eat salami, and devour chunks of bread and cheese. Every twig that creaks, every breeze that sweeps through the trees arouses us. We don't talk, just listen. The air is black and cold. Like late October back in Hanover. Massive jagged peaks line the horizon. Bill whispers that sometimes there's snow at these elevations this early. I ask if he's worried what Marko will do now."

"He'll be glad to get rid of me. Now he can start setting up his Red state without any interference."

"But he doesn't have any radio or operator with a code."

"That could be a problem."

"He's such a tricky son of bitch. I won't feel safe till we're out of the Cadore."

"Don't worry. We'll be all right. We'll travel only after dark to be on the safe side."

"I hope I can keep up. You know this country. I don't have your energy. Gosh, how do you keep going? You never seem to get tired?

48

"That's what my father always said. I couldn't sit still long enough to accomplish anything. He sat still and became rich. My brother will too. They're the student type."

"And your sister?"

"Yeah, good old Anne. I found out in the last batch of letters she's engaged to a MD. Wouldn't you know? Runs in the family. None of that good life for me. I hated school, reading all that psychology, economic, sociology junk. Except I did like the poetry, Housman, Rupert Brooke, Hardy, Frost. Couldn't take Elliot. Too damn dull."

"Ever read Dante?"

"Just heard of him. No, this is my kind of life. This is where I belong, up here fighting my kind of war. I wish it would snow and we had skis. The slopes around Cortina are terrific. Some of them straight down, take your breath away. The Marmolada has the fastest trails in the world. You whizz along like you're flying. You ski up at Dartmouth much?"

"A little. But I never tried Suicide Six."

"Yeah, that's some slope."

"How about the Brenner? Any good skiing around there?"

"Some great trails around Merano nearby. But we're not headed in that direction, Tony."

"Where are we headed? Can't you tell me now?"

"Okay. First to Cortina, then to the Falzarego Pass, follow the Dolomite Road to Costalunga. From there we cut over to Bolzano."

"Bolzano? What's there?"

"SS Headquarters for all of Italy."

"Where the countess's Nazi friend was supposed to go and get some information for you?"

"And where we're going to see a wolf about some sheep. Donovan's plan is clicking."

"Christ, Bill, what's going on? What plan?"

"You'll see when we get there."

"Aren't there a lot of Germans in Cortina?"

"Yeah, troops convalescing and a large force guarding them. But I have friends who will help, give us food and a chance to rest up before taking off. They were great to me when I was there a few years ago."

"I hope they're still around."

It's a freezing night even with the fire and the sleeping bag, and I spend most of it staring at the coals and thinking about the SS. Everywhere the peaks of the Cadore are piercing the sky brilliant with stars. And the wind rushing and the river roaring. A strange kind of wild peace excites the air. I try to write in my head a poem about the scene.

49

But all I can come up with are images from the *Inferno*. Thieves fusing their bodies and a six-legged lizard fastening itself to a human form until both are one and their colors melt together like the brown on a burning page changing from white to black.

Funny, though Dante wasn't overly concerned about war, there's a tremendous feeling for it in his work better than in the work of most poets I've read, even Whitman and Wilfred Owen. Maybe that's the way to do it. Ram home the horrible and the outrageous, surprise with the ordinary. Merge all kinds of farfetched stuff with the people and things you know about first hand. Keep your nose to what's going on or what has been going on. Make words come alive, bite, scratch, kick. But you've got to be more than a realist. You've got to persuade and provoke, mix up the past and the present. And that's what he does, and I have to do someday if I ever get out of this deadliest of places to be right now.

Chapter 7

The next day I contact Bari via the Guard Channel and inform SO that the major and I are headed for Bolzano and ask for another QRX for a response and instructions. The message from the south is clear. What the hell is going on? Why Bolzano? Why not the Brenner Pass? What happened to Orange? Where's Marko? Shall we send him a drop?

"Good, Christ," Bill explodes. "They're more interested in him and his damn Reds than they are in ending the war. Nothing from the general, huh?"

I tell him no, and we begin a slow nighttime journey up the Ampezzo Valley, dodging Kraut convoys, sneaking around hamlets, darting past candlelit farmhouses and barking dogs. Around three I'm pooped and insist we rest. I'm not used to this uphill hiking. My feet are killing me. My arms and legs are tired. The pack on my back is growing heavier and heavier. Darkness makes it slow going. I have visions of taking a wrong step and dropping into oblivion. And to think we might have another week or more of this grind.

We reach the outskirts of Cortina at dawn two days later. A light mist is falling. The sun resembles a communion wafer. A typical Tyrolean city with squares, a bell tower, and broad streets. The teeth-like Tofana Mountains in the west tower over the pine woods and the meadows. Bill says it looks the way it did in '38, only no snow and more buildings and ski runs and cable cars and certainly more Germans. He bets they're welcomed like scorpions after the devastation they caused during the last war. Big battles were fought close by, a key one up north on Monte Piana. Over a thousand solders buried in the town cemetery.

He talks about going to a beautiful little church near the Boite river. He met the priest, Father Vincent, there six years ago, and they became good friends. He's a skier and mountain climber. He'll hide us, give us meals, provide us with a guide, maybe find a car. I'm skeptical. He could be dead or departed or working for the Krauts.

Bill dismisses my fears. The Father was in his thirties then and loved America, had relatives in the States. It's as if Bill has become so caught up in this new mission he's not thinking about the dangers facing him. So we sneak along the river to a clump of pines opposite the church. No one anywhere. We listen for vehicles, watch for soldiers to appear, wait ten to fifteen minutes. Then we dash across the open space to the front door, duck in, glance around.

The place is empty. The light green marble walls and floor give off a soft glow in the dusk. I look up and there's a skeleton with sparkling gems on the bony fingers and a painting of St. Peter crucified upside down. The figures are scary. The silence is eerie. I feel like getting out of there in a hurry. I've never been in a church that had so many sinister looking objects. Bill gazes around smiling, taking in the familiar sights and acting as if this is home and he can't wait to meet his old friend, the skiing priest.

"We'll hide in the Confessional and wait until Father Vincent or somebody shows up for Mass. You can take his side and hear some of my dirty little secrets through the screen.

"Suppose he isn't the one you're expecting and the one who shows up doesn't know him."

"I'll mention his name to whoever comes, and he'll take care of us. I never met an Italian who didn't like Americans more than Germans."

We start for the booth on the right side in the corner, our footsteps echoing. The door behind us flies open and four partisans wearing those peaked Alpine hats and Red scarves and carrying Sten guns rush in yelling, "*Tedeschi, Tedeschi!*" I recognize the big guy in the middle with the mustache. He's Volpe. He motions me out. I race for the door. Bill trips behind me, his carbine clattering on the marble. He lets out a yelp. I turn around and confront the burly partisan blocking my path. He shoves me though the door. I fight to go back and help Bill lying on the floor shouting after me, "Go on, Tony, go on. Tell the general to cancel Sun Up." He's holding his right leg and grimacing like a basketball player who's fallen charging the basket. His face is white. The sight cuts through me.

"We can't leave him," I holler. Two men yank me across the open space to the trees, push me down on the pine needles just as a truck drives up. A bunch of Krauts jump out with rifles and bang into the church. Bill starts screaming horribly, his voice piercing the air. A few minutes later they're dragging him through the door dazed, his face bloody, his pants ripped at the crotch, his balls hanging out. One solider is jabbing the butt of a rifle into his back.

I jump up to run out of the woods ready to start firing my .45, not giving a damn what happens. But before I can take a step and pull the trigger, Volpe knocks me down, snatches the gun away. I raise up to cry out. He turns and jams a fist in my mouth. I gape at him, teeth hurting, swallowing blood. He's shaking his head and cursing. Two partisans hold me, wrenching my arms behind my back. I'm eating pine straw.

"They're goin' to kill him," I whisper. "Christ, they're goin' to kill him! We've got to do something."

"No *buono*, no *buono*," Volpe says. And I lie there watching the Krauts tossing Bill into the truck, remembering those torture devices I heard about in Bari from the OG's, the electrodes, the vices, the hot pokers. I should have stayed with him no matter what. Maybe the six of us could have out fought them. Anything would be better than leaving him like this.

The truck roars off and it's quiet again. The church stands spectral-like in the misty fall-like morning. The sun is burning through the haze. I'm shivering like hell.

The partisans release me, and I get up gradually and eye them.

"Radio?" Volpe says.

"In my knapsack. Other stuff too. I put it on my back under the bedroll. He smiles.

"Have you been following us all the time?"

"*Si,* no want *Tedeschi* capture you."

"Protecting us, huh?"

"*Buono* protection, no?"

"You did a great job protecting the major."

"He fall, hurt bad. Niente." He throws up his hands. I look at him in disbelief. He acts so damn innocent, so damn indifferent. He could he have alerted the Krauts? Betrayed us?

As we start down the Ampezzo Valley back toward Monte Pelmo, I ask if they aren't afraid that the major will break under questioning and give them away. They shrug their shoulders, shake their heads. They are confident he will never tell where the brigade is or what they're doing. A brave man, *patriottico*. And I have to admit they have a point. But then I think of what the poor guy is going to suffer the next couple of days. Volpe wants to know what this Sun Up is. I never heard of it before. Maybe the Brenner Pass operation. He's not convinced. Neither am I. Why the hell did he want to go to Bolzano for anyway? And who is this wolf he was going to see some sheep about?

It doesn't take us long to reach Monte Pelmo. Most of the way we travel at night by truck using dim lights and driving so slowly I could walk faster. Gazing at the treacherous peaks Bill and I struggled through in the dark, wondering how we ever made it. And how in the hell were these guys able to follow us? Unless they guessed where we were headed. And why were they after us? Thank God, at least I had that time with him. I remember a letter he gave to a priest one morning to mail. It was to his father. He let me read it. The ending struck home: "I don't know if I'll ever get out of these mountains, Dad. So I'll say goodbye just in case. I haven't been much of a success according to the world's standards. And I know I've disappointed you by not becoming a doctor like you and Sam. But you can't say I haven't done a lot of things and had a lot of fun. Maybe that's what it's all about. Thanks for the life. It's been a short but exciting one. So long, Bill."

We reach camp the next morning. I can hardly walk, blistered and sore and weary. All I can think of is Bill and the letter and the note I better write to Maggie before my time comes. A message to the general, too, about Sun Up. He should know what's going on before it's too late. Because I can tell by the attitude of the partisans toward me that I'm not going to last much longer up here if they ever find an operator to take my place.

"I'm sorry about Bill," Marko greets me. "He shouldn't have left on account of our differences. We could have worked them out. His big mistake was getting involved with that Fascist countess. You know he sent Ettore down to talk to her again. They had something going. I bet any money he told her he was going to Cortina as part of some plan they had."

"That's your story."

"It's the truth, Tony. I hear you were almost trapped in the church and Volpe rescued you. He could have rescued Bill, too, except he fell and injured his ankle and there wasn't time."

"Or he was tripped up."

"Nonsense. Nobody pushed him. What are you talking about?" He acts more flustered than angry.

"You sent those men to bring me back here and to get rid of him."

"You're crazy. I never did any such a thing. We were wondering where you guys were going, not wanting you to get in any trouble when we discovered you beat it. But I realize what you've been through. You really liked him, didn't you?"

"Like an older brother."

"I was fond of him too. A great guy. If only he hadn't been so foolish. He should have known what that whore would do to him. Think she was tied up in this Sun Up mission?"

I don't say anything.

"Now I have a message I want you to send to Bari along with a request for a drop. And I want it sent straight. Nothing added or changed. Nothing about this tripped up business. Thank God, you didn't drop the radio."

"And if I refuse?"

"You have no choice, Sergeant. It explains the major's capture and lists supplies we need. Maybe before you code it you should get some rest. It's a long one. Still remember your little sonnet?" He snickers. Somehow that gets me almost more than anything else. Silly, isn't it? Losing Bill, feeling guilty as hell, raging inside against these bastards who I'm sure did him in, yet hurt by a slighting reference to a trivial poem I wrote.

I go up to the loft in the *magla* with a partisan at my side and drop off to sleep until noon. The rest of the day I work coding and sending the message about Bill's fate, explaining to Marko what I'm doing, even telling him what the numbers at the beginning and the letters at the end of the message mean. But not telling him I reversed the "a" and "n" in the first "and" mentioned. The signal to indicate I'm being forced to send with a gun at my head. After I finish, I wait around for the evening contact, thinking about inserting a message to Donovan inside the next one I send without Marko noticing, who's been careful watching me writing the double transposition. But I give up hoping they got the word that Bill's been captured and he wanted me to inform the general to cancel Sun Up. He'd be suspicious if I used the special code between us.

"We wait now," Marko says. "When we get the drop, we'll go Kraut hunting, liberate towns, take over the whole area from Belluno to Cortina, stop all military traffic. They'll have to come after us with a division."

The message we receive the next day is vague. No planes available for the drop. More information wanted about the Alpine Line. Where is the 10th Panzer Division? I hand Marko the decoded text. He tears it up and stamps his foot, pounds the air with a fit, and curses.

"You added something to that message, Sergeant. You gave them your version of what happened to the major. I know you did."

"You read what I sent."

"I don't trust that code of yours. The line you used, it could have a double meaning, 'I love you too much to love you at all.' What the hell does that mean? You and your Goddamn poetry! I wish we had simpler codes. You took it out of your head too. How do I know if it's what we've been using? It could have been a planned signal."

"You have to trust me and the poetry I guess. I'm the only operator Bari will accept stuff from right now."

"We've got to have that drop damn it!"

"How about a replacement for me?"

"Christ, Sergeant, if I ever find out you double-crossed me. If I find out you pulled a fast one on me…"

"You mean a double transposition. What'll you do?"

"Your life won't be worth shit. Tie you to one of those wire cables they use for bringing wood down these mountains, send you

55

hurling to the bottom to be smashed to bits. Or maybe just turn you over to the Gestapo. Which reminds me, I heard this afternoon Bill didn't talk. They beat the shit out of him."

"Is he dead?"

"We don't know."

"If he dies, Marko, I'll…"

"You'll do nothing. The general will see he gets the Medal of Honor and is buried in Arlington. His family will talk about how brave he was to give his life for his country. And if you go the same way, he'll say you died for poetry, make you a posthumous poet laureate." He guffaws. "The Shelley of the Dolomites."

I'm kept inside away from everybody for some reason. And Marko hovers around me at every contact in order to watch me send and receive, code and decode. He wants me to keep urging Bari to hurry the drop. He expects an attack on the base at any time. And I keep reversing the letters on the first "and". The little guy doesn't catch on as he watches me transpose the columns in the boxes until the code groups emerge to send. Or maybe he has dyslexia. Besides, I can see the procedure puzzles him just as another line does: "I reach ahead for what I left behind." He asks me what the hell that one means. I tell him nothing like most poetry. It just sounds good, rhymes, and has ten syllables. He scowls. He's got more important things to think about than a stupid line of poetry.

So do I. How do I get out of here alive. I can sense everybody sort of ganging up on me, everybody except Giorgio, one of the partisans who went with the major to blow the bridge at Perarolo. Even the other guys on the mission don't talk, hardly acknowledge I'm around. Ettore has gone back to Andrich. It's one thing to be here surrounded by the enemy and another to be surrounded by friends who are almost as hostile.

Once on the way to the latrine I spot Giorgio. He comes up to say hello, kind of shy and simple. The guard shoves him away. But he gives me a cigarette and the tough-acting kid lets him stand around while I take a crap in the ditch.

"*Tedeschi*," I whisper. "*Domani. Subito, subito.*" He looks at me bewildered. He can't figure out what I mean. When it dawns on him his eyes get big. I nod tight-lipped, shrug my shoulders. I say in a very low voice, "*Morte ai comunisti.*" He half smiles and shuffles off. And I wonder if he will do it. Talk about Marko betraying the major. This could bring me a court-martial and every other damn thing you could think of. And if the colonel is killed or captured I could have Stalin demanding my scalp. What the hell's the matter with me? So wrought up about Bill's fate I'm not thinking straight.

Meanwhile I keep sending plea after plea for another drop in the beginning of each message inverting the two letters. Marko threatens to disband the brigade, suspend all intelligence gathering if he doesn't get a drop soon. There could be noise from the Russian. The colonel could tell his government quite a story. The men are hungry and depressed. Some are seriously ill with dysentery, influenza. He sets a deadline, five days. If there's no drop by then, he's heading for Yugoslavia with Colonel Slansky. The hell with Orange and OSS.

The answer comes back the same. Be patient. Supplies are packed and ready to go. As soon as planes are available the operation is on. They've appealed to the general to use his influence with Twining. But he is in Burma now at Detachment 101.

"Another lousy excuse," Marko says after I decode the message. "They're sitting down there on their fat asses eating steak, sucking cunt, and letting us rot up here. The capitalist bastards. Why did I agree to join this organization? I should have known what would happen working with Wall Street pimps."

"What are you going to do with me if you decide to leave?"

"Let the Krauts take care of you." He chuckles. "Don't worry, Tony. Where we go our little poet goes. You won't suffer like the major. By the way, I heard they hung him down in Belluno. From a steam pipe in a cellar. A doctor certified it was a heart attack. They buried him in an unmarked grave. He never should have tried to make a deal with them."

"A deal with them?"

"Volpe found out about this so called Sun Up. A friend of his from Belluno who brought the news about Bill gave him the story. He wasn't going to blow the Brenner. Just a cover. Going to make a deal with the Nazis in Balzono. That's what all the countess stuff was about. And that's where the two of you were headed when they caught up with you. Lucky we rescued you. It was a dumb idea. I never thought the major was that gullible. Innocent maybe but not stupid."

"Why would they torture him then, kill him?"

"He wouldn't talk. Or maybe they were just using him, didn't need him anymore."

"That's going to be your excuse for abandoning him in Cortina?"

"Not my excuse. The truth."

"He never told me anything like that."

"He told you to cancel Sun Up, didn't he?"

"He never told me what it was."

"I heard he and Donovan were fixing it so that when the German Army retreats up north they won't destroy any factories. The Allies will go easy on them with the bombing and the war crimes. A deal cooked up in Wall Street between him and his banker friends and the fat cat industrialists here. Who says there isn't an international capitalist conspiracy?"

"That's a crock of shit," I say.

Later on the way to the latrine I look around for Giorgio. He's nowhere. And I have this funny feeling I did something terrible. A lot of those guys could die if the Krauts attack us. It was idiotic. But I couldn't help myself, damn it, not after Cortina and seeing those Krauts carrying Bill out of the church and hearing about his torture and feeling more and more Marko was responsible for his capture. Now he's gone. Still maybe I shouldn't have hinted the way I did. I hope Giorgio just got tired and left like so many partisans do after a while because there's no fighting or women and camp life gets dull and difficult with little food and no action.

Anyway I lie around and read more Dante. I'm up to this man they're crucifying on the ground with three stakes in his body. It's so everybody can be better off. And I think of Ivan in *The Brothers Karamazov* returning his ticket because he couldn't accept a baby being tortured for the good of all. Nice of those guys to think of something like that, though I bet neither one would like to be in that man's or baby's place.

Marko comes to see me that night. He's in a jaunty mood. We're leaving in the morning. We've been here too long. The Krauts might have heard about our location. Or they might have squeezed something out of Bill. I ask if I'm still going along.

"You've got the radio and the codes."

"Your salvation, huh?"

"A poet to my rescue," he mocks and goes out.

I go to bed and listen to the partisans singing outside, remembering Bill and the mountain girl song he loved so much. Tears come to my eyes recalling our last conversations about skiing and rock climbing, Hardy, Housman and Frost. Gosh, he could quote reams of their stuff. And the great stories he had about wildcatting days in Texas and Oklahoma, sailing with the Merchant Marines in the Far East. What a waste! What a lot of bastards in the world.

A faint cracking sound outside mixed with the wind rushing through the trees breaks the calm. I ask the guard to take me to the latrine quick. I have to go pretty bad. Beat the storm. I don't want to stink up the place. "*Puzzo, puzzo.*" He laughs and we start together for the ditch.

That's when the first shots erupt. The whole area suddenly explodes. Flares burst overhead lighting up the ground, tracers streak through the sky. Everybody is shouting, screaming, tearing around, firing into the darkness. I run back to the *magla*, grab a Sten and my knapsack but no radio, dash out headed in the opposite direction from the heavy action. Marko and the colonel rush into the battle yelling for their men to take cover, set up a Bren gun. Most of them are not paying attention. They just want to get the hell out of here, running for their lives. Bodies flying everywhere through the lurid light. Moans from guys who are hit and probably dying. Like a stampede in a burning theatre. I curse myself for suggesting to Giorgio to inform on us, which I'm sure he never did. But I'm too busy fleeing myself to worry anymore. I've got to get out this place alive and not end up shoveled into an unmarked grave.

The Krauts are swarming over the camp. Their searchlights catching clusters of men fleeing everywhere. Their guns slam into them, ripping bodies to pieces. Partisans are falling all around me. I trip over dark forms. Any second I expect to be hit.

A hand reaches up and grabs my shoulder. I'm about to swing around and fire at the shape when I recognize Giorgio.

"You bring *Tedeschi?*"

"No, no *impossibile*. Not do what you say. No *buono*. They come. You follow. I know way to go."

He darts past me, and I trot behind along a stream bed and then through woods into an open field. We climb over a bunch of rocks, jump off a ledge to a path below. I wrench my ankle but get up and hobble on. He's just a blur in the distance, and I keep scrabbling as hard as I can to catch up, the breathing getting tougher, until I collapse under a tree and see him dash on and disappear over a hill. He rushes back. The fire is growing dimmer but the sky is still lit up with tracers and shells going off. The sounds ricochet through the ravine.

"*Avanti, avanti,*" I shout. "*Fatica, fatica.*"

"I carry you. Get on my back."

"You can't do that."

"I big, tall." He stoops down to help me up. I struggle to climb on top of him dropping the Sten, keeping my bag. And away he gallops. It's wild. Like we used to do years ago as kids pretending we were knights dueling on horseback. Or like the Centaurs in Dante running along a bank shooting arrows at shrieking war mongers and tyrants who try to rise too high out of the river of boiling blood. I can't understand

59

how he keeps his balance. The ground is rocky as hell. Holes everywhere. The path drops sharply. I'm hanging on tight as if I've got my hand around a horse's neck. He's puffing too, plunging deeper and deeper into the dark. The noise of the guns fade. He stops in a clump of trees, puts me down, and we collapse together on a grassy plot, panting, not saying a word, our bodies touching. Overhead the stars blaze away so near it seems yet so far away. The horizon bristles with jagged peaks. It's as if we were on another planet, and a scary silence is humming all around us. The throbbing in my ankle subsides. Then we get up and start walking together, I still limping but able to keep up. *"Buono"*, Giorgio says finally after we've gone a few miles.

*"Sí, buono, molto buono."* I touch his hand. *"Grazie, grazie. Molto grazie."* He laughs shyly. I'm almost too weak to talk. "Think we're okay here?"

*"Si, Sergente, Va bene. Tedeschi* not find us."

"Where are we anyway?"

"Valle di Zoldo. We go to Longarone on the Piave, Paiinaz, Fugina, Dont Forno."

I listen to the music of the names mingling with the rush of the river, the sighing of the wind. What a fabulous spot to vacation. Pine trees and mountains and the sound of water nearby. No one around. Just the two of us.

"What do we do there?"

*"Amici."*

*"Partigiani?"*

*"Si. No comunisti."*

*"Buono. Comunisti* shit." He snorts in agreement. "They'll be looking for us now along with the Krauts. Accuse me of bringing the bastards. Maybe we better head back to Andrich, stay with Ettore."

*"Capitano* find us at Andrich."

"Yeah, that would be the first place he'd look."

"Go *sud*, Firenze, Roma."

"You mean through the lines?"

*"Si, Sergente."*

"In this uniform? Are you *pazzo*, Giorgio? Maybe I'll be stuck up here until the whole thing is over, not get to deliver the major's message. I've got to find a radio or I'm doomed. Know what that means, doomed? *Kaput, finito."*

*"Si, Si."*

"It's an American phenomenon. Comes from listening too long to old preachers talk about sin and death."

"Belluno. We go Belluno."

60

"Are you out of your mind? No *buono*. Not down there again, not after what happened to the major. Christ, no! Maybe the countess did do him in the way Marko said."

"Ettore go see her. He say she help you."

"She pretended she would once. I doubt it now."

He becomes silent. But the more I consider it the more I wonder if maybe he's right after all. She and Bill seemed to be working on something big together. But not what Marko believed. Hell, despite the drop and the reprisal and Bill's execution she could be on the level. Bauer too. It definitely made Bill decide to head for Bolzano and SS Headquarters. They could be involved in this Sun Up mission but couldn't help him after he was captured and interrogated any more than they could prevent what happened after the drop. Unless the countess did inform the Germans Bill was going to Cortina. But why would she do that and why would they treat him like that?

I grow tired of speculating about what to do next and fall asleep with Giorgio sitting there peering out into the darkness. No master. But a good Injun. I bet Dante could have used him as a scout. Maybe he wouldn't have been so scared and bewildered in the "dark wood" of the *Inferno*.

Chapter 8

We start out on empty stomachs just before daylight. It's rough going climbing down to the river until we reach the main road. Then it's listening all the time for traffic and ducking behind rocks and lying flat in ditches whenever we hear a motor. Only one convoy passes, a TODT battalion made up mostly of Italians with a couple of German officers. They remind me of a chain gang. Red-starred partisans we have to watch out for too. News travels fast. So we don't stop at any houses and skulk around villages like Forno, the capital of the valley. Looking back to the northwest, we can see the three peaks of Monte Pelmo jutting into the clouds like fingers. Mountains huddle against the horizon in every direction. They make you feel so damn small. And as we walk along I recite my sonnet for Orange to keep myself pumped up. Somewhere in this country at this moment somebody on a mission I wrote for could be using one of my lines and puzzling over the meaning. At least they're good for something. Immortal they're not. Then, hell, neither am I, even though I like to think so and can't get used to the idea I'm about to lose it all.

A long day, and after a while I get tired of the scenery, the strangely shaped peaks, water spilling down through the rocks, the vineyards and wheat fields, the apple and pear and peach orchids, the odd looking wooden houses perched on hillsides with balconies and outside stairs. Church towers dominate the little old towns among the slopes hovering over them. Giorgio acts proud and happy as if he were showing me his hometown. Like a big kid beaming, singing, skipping stones over the water. And I wonder about handing over my life to such a young guide. No Virgil. Still I can't help becoming fond of him. Recalls a little of a Robin Hood character with his peaked Alpine hat pushed back on his head. Instead of a Sten a bow and arrow slung over his shoulder. He laughs at my worrying all the time about the *Tedeschi* and *comunisti* and offers to exchange clothes. He would like to wear my uniform, be *Americano*.

We stop at a house he's positive is safe. An old woman, Anna Rocca, lives alone, stout, morose, mumbling to herself, a mustache under her great nose. Giorgio kids her, and she brightens up and feeds us a bowl of broth mixed with meat, bread and cheese. We drink wine. Everything tastes great. I can't get over the huge stone fireplace with a dais and wooden bench on three sides and an iron chain and hook dangling from the chimney for cooking. The blaze from the wood evokes ski lodges in Vermont. Giorgio says Anna is a friend of his mother. Her brother is in America. She'd never give us away. Her cousins are Christian Democrats. Besides, she understands partisan warfare. All the women around here do. They hate the *Tedeschi*.

We leave after two hours and make our way along the Maè River toward the Piave, Giorgio pointing out fig trees as we near Longarone. We arrive at dusk just as the sun is sinking and the peaks are turning those brilliant coral colors. We don't venture inside the town opposite a gorge. Instead he takes me to a cabin back in the hills. His family and their friends use it sometimes for hiking trips. There's a grand view of the Piave Valley and Monte Toc to the other side of the river. He wants me to stay here while he goes to see his brother. Maybe he'll try to get in touch with the countess. Belluno is only ten kilometers away.

"Find out first if she's alone. If she is we won't stay, just pick up some food, maybe a couple of guns. Tell her not to say we come."

"*Si, si, Sergente. Buono, buono.* I go."

"Does your brother have a radio I could use to contact Bari?"

"Radio? I see."

"Radio to send messages with. The dot-dash type, earphones." I do a pantomime with my hands. "What does he do anyway?"

"Engineer. Builds roads."

"Then he won't know anything about radios. Or maybe he will. My father's one, too, works for the state and is building sets all the time in the cellar as a hobby. Tell him the radio could bring good things, food, cigarettes, clothes. All free. Planes come and drop everything with parachutes. Just like Christmas."

"You do this, *Sergente*?"

"Maybe. After we visit the countess."

"I go. Anybody come, you hide." He points to a trapdoor under the rug. He pushes back a board to reveal a dark hole and then closes it. "I come back *notte*."

He lights out down the hill, and I watch him from the doorway disappear into the night. If he doesn't return I'm sunk. And if he can't find a radio I can use I might as well be dead. Like a poet with no audience, no one to communicate with, no messages to send. A sundial in a grave. Or like Dad down in the cellar at his workbench putting together radios that never work.

More and more I'm beginning to wonder what the hell Sun Up is all about. A deal with the Germans as Marko claims. And he knew it and that is why he got so damn mad and told Volpe to take care of Bill. He would have gotten rid of me, too, except for the radio and my codes.

It's a windy night. After twelve there's a thunderstorm that scares the daylights out of me. I picture the cabin blowing away or blazing up as the streaks sizzle down the sky and pitchfork right into the hillside. Giorgio never shows, even after the fireworks. It gets to be later and later, and I'm sitting in the dark staring out the window listening to drops plopping off the roof now the gusts have subsided. Boards creak. Rivulets run off fast gurgling away.

Suddenly voices are coming up the path. I contemplate hiding under the floorboards underground-man style. But not enough time. So I turn out the oil lamp, crouch in a corner, waiting for the knock.

"*Sergente*, Giorgio, Giorgio, *subito*, *subito*." He raps hard. I run over and unlatch the door, and he and another dark figure rush in. He lights the oil lamp on the table and introduces me to Victor Marsella, a friend from Longarone. He couldn't see his brother. Partisans are watching the house. Victor says they suspect Giorgio was the one who tipped off the *Tedeschi* about the brigade on Mount Pelmo, and I was the one who told him to do it. We were seen talking together a couple of days before the raid. The story is that the major and I were secretly working for the Germans to destroy the partisan movement, and that's why I went to see the countess and her Kraut boyfriend.

"Captain Marko hinted at all that and spread it. A capitalist plot to keep the factories intact when the German army retreats. But why would the SS or the Gestapo torture and kill the major? Nothing makes any sense. Marko is just spreading lies about Bill and me so he can build his own Red empire up here and save face about losing his brigade."

"They come after us, *Sergente*. We go."

"Belluno?"

"*Si, si,* countess."

"God, I don't know now, Giorgio." He looks at me. "But maybe it's our only chance if she's on our side. If she isn't though it's *finito*."

"Victor says we go Belluno. He know people there. We stay with them. Not stay here. A reward for us, *molti, molti lire.* *Fascisti*, Nazis, *partigiani*, they look for us. They shoot us. No *buono*."

"They know about this place?"

"They ask in Longarone. They find out *subito*. We go see the countess."

"Okay, but, hell, Giorgio, you don't need to stay with me. I'm the one they want, not you."

I study his animated horse face in the glow of the oil lamp, the hands and arms moving. A lot more nervous than he was a day ago. Victor stands beside him, a squat, blank guy with a bushy mustache, still as a stump. He's older, calmer. There's something almost lifeless about him except for the bright blue eyes staring at him. He's carrying a 9mm sub-machine pistol.

"Giorgio with you. We see countess. She help us."

"How?"

"Give us car, *lire, Tedeschi* pass. We go *sud* to Allies. No *buono qui, Sergente*, no *buono. Finito, finito.*"

"How about your friend here? He feel the same way?"

"He no come with us. Countess not know him. Victor, *buono, multo* buono." He puts an arm around the stubby, silent, glum little guy. He grins at Giorgio and gives him his pistol.

I'm still skeptical but agree. Christ, to come up here to fight these bastards and then find yourself asking them for help.

We start down the hill toward the river. It's a cloudy night, no moon. Except for the sound of water, quiet everywhere. When we reach the bottom of the slope and look back up the hillside, we see the cabin on fire, flames shooting up. There's an explosion.

We hurry on down the dirt road and then stop and listen. Nobody is coming after us. So we head south following the Piave, sometimes on the highway, sometimes on trails through the woods, sometimes climbing above the valley floor and walking the edge of a cliff gazing down at a waterfall and the rocks and logs floating by, the river widening, growing louder. Giorgio talks about a big dam nearby and points to lights brightening the sky to the east.

All the time I'm worrying about the countess. Hell, why wouldn't whoever is after us be waiting at her villa just as much as they would be waiting for Giorgio here? And she failed us on that drop business. At least it seems as if she did. Then there's Dr. Bauer. No, Jesus, I can't go to that villa despite what Giorgio suggests. He's just a poor naïve guy who has lived his whole life in these mountains and doesn't know what's going on. I can't let him trap me.

But I think of the alternative, roaming around this country with him, no radio, no friends, no transportation, no gun. My uniform giving me away plus my speech, my looks except I'm kind of dark. We'd never make it to the Allied lines. And the countess seemed genuinely interested in going to America. She and Bauer must be pretty deep into whatever deal Bill was working on. She wouldn't betray me, not at this late date and not about Bill going to Cortina. She'd have too much to lose, especially with her husband working for Il Duce. She could have her head shaved after the war like a whore collaborating with the Krauts. And that's not her style.

But what do I know? Poets are supposed to be the dumbest people in the world about practical things. The trouble is all I go by are guys like Dante, and they're always sending up mixed signals.

We stop at a crossroads, not a house anywhere. It's four kilometers from Belluno. Ahead lies the town perched high on what looks like a rocky spur. The lights are dim.

Victor says he has to leave us, return to Longarone. We should be all right now. He tells us friends to look up in case we need them, street and phone numbers. I take them down. Then he and Giorgio embrace. I shake the glum little guy's hand and urge the two of them to leave me. I can manage by myself if they can point me the way to the countess's house. They laugh. And I suppose it's crazy. I can't speak the language, don't know where the hell I am, hunted by everybody, and I think about going off alone. A sitting duck in this uniform. No one to turn to but a woman shacked up with a Nazi. How insane can that be?

So Victor vanishes, but Giorgio stays, and we sneak into the town that looks out over the Piave. It's seems deserted. We pass a monumental gateway and enter a piazza lined with Renaissance buildings, a fountain in the middle topped by a religious statue. Next there is a square with a church and a campanile and a couple of palazzos with arches and balconies. A fine rain begins falling. The misty lights, the shadows, the massive old structures around the square evoke a ghoulish atmosphere. Walking cautiously down a big open street that resembles a platform, we gaze off in the direction of the river and the valley.

"You know where the countess lives?" I say.

"*Si, si, Sergente*. Villa Maria. *Due, tre chilometri*. Victor tell me."

"Well, let's take a look then. And if nobody is around pay her a visit, see what she's up to. Hate to interrupt her beauty rest." He glances at me as if he doesn't understand.

Outside of town we head down a dirt road and come to the familiar gatehouse. Then it's up the steep drive lined with cypress. At the top stands the villa and to the right a small chapel. Behind it a tennis court. What a fantastic view of the city blinking away through the mist. Only one car is parked in the drive, a Fiat. No sign of the Alfa Romeo.

I approach the glass door and peer into the wide hallway with the black and white marble floor. A faintly lit crystal chandelier hangs down. Giorgio goes behind a tree. Before he does he points to a vehicle to the right almost out of sight. It's Bauer's car."We go, *Sergente*," he whispers. "*No, buono, no buono*."

"Check around and see if there is a bodyguard." He runs off and returns.

66

"*Niente, Niente.*" He shrugs his shoulders.

"The bastard is probably up in bed with her." Giorgio giggles softly, reminding me for a second of Maggie. Think I should go in and interrupt *coito*?" He laughs.

"*Amante* no like, *Sergente.*"

"I know. But we don't have a hell of a lot of choices."

"We go *sud.*"

"How far would we get? You ever been out of the Dolomites?"

"Milano, Venezia."

"We'd never make it. Not without their help. You stay out here. If there's any trouble run. Go back to Longarone. Don't worry about me."

"No, no, stay with you." He sticks a hand grenade in my face.

"Jesus, where did you get that? Whatever you do don't throw it or we'll have the whole German garrison in Belluno up here."

I advance again to the door, ring the bell, knock. At first no one comes, then the countess slowly descends the broad staircase in a sweeping blue dressing gown, her tinted black hair flowing down her back, looking sleepy and annoyed. I had forgotten what a hefty sexy woman she is with that sensuous face, those big breasts, thick neck. The kind of sexuality older women exude in their twilight years before brightness falls from the air and dust closes the dimming eyes. Another reminder of Caroline Massey back in Algiers and the kitchen scene with her at that Christmas party when we were both high and then later dancing. Only she was better preserved and not so saggy.

"Oh, *Sergente!*" she cries out in a hushed, almost hysterical voice as she opens the glass door. "Where is Bill?"

"Dead. Didn't you hear? The Gestapo tortured him, then hung him from steam pipes in a cellar."

"No, oh, my God, no!" She puts her hands over her face. Tears come. "That dear boy. No, no. Did he talk?" Her voice abruptly changes. She stares at me.

"Talk? About what? I don't know. I don't think so. Better ask your friend upstairs."

"If he did we are in much danger, me, Kurt, you, General Wolff."

"General Wolff?"

"Head of the SS in Italy. In Bolzano. Bill going to meet him."

"Meet him? What for?"

"Not tell you. Bad, very bad."

"Kind of funny your friend never told you what happened to him, isn't it? And you two being so close. Some communication."

67

"I have to think of myself first, *Sergente*," a tall, thin man with glasses wearing a bathrobe speaks from the middle of the stairs. The countess glances around.

"Kurt, why not you tell about Bill?"

"Afraid it would upset you. If the plan failed, remember what would happen to us. General Wolff warned of the consequences. It had to be just between the three of us and the one in Bern."

"You should have at least told me tonight before…"

"And spoil our good time." He smiles.

"You *Tedeschi*," she mutters. "You are all alike. You think of nothing else."

"I do not have him captured, not order his death."

"You are the Administrator of the Belluno Region."

"It was the Gestapo. I could not stop them or it would have given everything away. Neither could General Wolff. The Gestapo would become suspicious and report it to the Fuehrer, who could order *sippenhaft*, the elimination of the whole family if one member commits a crime. And it would be considered a crime. We are lucky he not talk."

"You could have found some way to save him."

"Airmen, partisans, I arrange not to die. Not spies in uniform. Hitler's orders. They must be executed. No exceptions."

"So what's going to happen to us?"

"To you nothing. But the *Sergente*…" He takes a Luger out of his pocket.

"No, Kurt, no," The countess muffles a cry. "He not know the plan."

"He knows enough. General Wolff's life is in danger, his family too. General Kesselring's too. Mine, yours. If he is captured he could talk. And to think this could have been the end of the war here. We could have saved thousands of lives. And we will. But I cannot let him leave. Sorry, Teresa. Too much depends on it. There have to be sacrifices."

"People who say that never know sacrifice." She glances at him and then runs up the stairs past him. A door slams.

"Christ!" I say. "Bill and you and the countess were going to…"

"That's right, *Sergente* end the war in Italy. We surrender to your army. No more fighting. Now it is too late and the communists take over. Your partisans, they destroy our chances. Now we all live under the Russians." He laughs in a hollow way. And I wonder what the hell is so funny.

"How were you planning to do all this?"

"Military secret."

68

"So that was Sun Up, now Sun Down."

"Better than blowing those tunnels and bridges in the Brenner Pass."

"You knew about that?"

"We know much about your OSS, *Sergente*. We have spies."

"Get me a radio. Let me send a message to General Donovan of OSS. I have his private code, and he has one with Roosevelt. He'll do something. He's the one who thought up the whole thing anyway, wasn't he?"

"General Wolff gave me orders to do away with anyone who found out about the plan before everything was ready and the Fuehrer found out."

"So you had the major killed so he wouldn't talk after he was captured without you knowing about it. If he did  it could give away your plan.." He looks steadily down at me grinning. A smooth bastard if there ever was one. "And I'm next."

"Sorry, *Sergente*. We counted on you, you and your major. You were going to send your message from Bolzano to Caserta that would stop the war. General Wolff had spoken to General Kesselring. There was agreement if everything went according to plan the German Army in Italy would lay down their arms in a couple of days. Your General Clark, the British generals Alexander and General Montgomery would be contacted."

"I can still help. All I need is a radio."

"Your major was the only person General Wolff would see. He went to Switzerland to talk to OSS and they agreed. But someone tipped off the Gestapo in Cortina about him by mistake."

"Allen Dulles in Bern, you mean, huh? Couldn't somebody be brought up here from Caserta? If General Donovan knew about all this he would act fast. I know he would. He would send someone in Bill's place."

"Too much time. Too many risks. It is better this way for General Wolff and your general. They will not get hurt."

"Hurt? How?"

"Your general could be court-martialed. And my general in Bolzano, he could be executed, his family, too, as I said. He takes a great chance after the July attempt on the Fuehrer's life."

"It's that big, huh?"

"Very big, *Sergente*."

"Then I guess I better get the hell out of here quick. See if I can find a radio." I make a move toward the door.

"Halt," he roars. "We go out back. Do it far away, not upset the countess. Not feeling well." He strides slowly down the stairs, the pistol pointing at my gut. I want to reach for the .45 in my holster. It's not there. He stops a couple of feet away. It's hard to think of him as a killer with those glasses and that bathrobe, the bony frame, the long thin fingers. The more I look at him the more he resembles an English professor at Dartmouth I had for Romantic Poetry.

"I'll give you General Donovan's private code if you let me go. As I said he uses it with President Roosevelt."

"You know their codes?"

"I wrote them. They're based on my poems. You can get in touch with both of them. Wouldn't that accomplish a lot more than shooting me?"

"You have them with you?"

"That's right. I always carry them."

"Show me."

'They're in my head. I can recite a line you could use. Send the message to Bari. I know the frequencies. All I need is a radio."

"What is this, *Sergente*? Codes are in books. They are numbers. I never hear of poems as codes. You stall for time, as you Americans say in movies."

"It's double transposition. Ever hear of it? We use sonnets."

"No time for poetry. You have no radio. It is late. We go in yard and down to pond."

"If you could get a radio I could send the message. They know my 'fist' down in Bari. Nobody can duplicate it either."

"You talk too much. Go to the dining room on right, open doors. They lead to the yard. I turn on the light."

"You have quite a good life here, don't you?" I say.

"The countess and I understand each other. We enjoy each other's company."

"You know I told some partisans I was coming. After the war you could get in trouble. You could be tried as a war criminal."

"A long way off. Before then I be hero for stopping the war if I make deal with the Allies. I help them, they help me. Go now. No more talk. You make the countess feel bad."

I turn and walk toward the right of the stairs into the dining room. He shuffles close behind in his slippers, switching on the light and the one outside. I can almost feel the gun pressing into my back.

A slight noise on the landing. I stop and turn my head slightly. The countess appears with a small pistol in her hand. It looks like a Beretta.

70

"Kurt, no, no!" He glances up at her.

"Go back to bed. This is for you, for all of us, for the end of the war." He speaks with a deep, hard German accent.

"He will not say a word about this."

"They capture him, make him talk. We are executed like those officers after the bomb plot on the Fuehrer's life."

"He could help us. Go to Bolzano like Bill. Not give up the plan."

"You just want American citizenship."

"You want to be a hero. We take him with us to Bolzano, talk to General Wolff. Please, Kurt. He contact Caserta, send messages for us. Americans will help us when the war is over."

"Don't be a fool, Teresa. He cannot help us. I find another way to get in touch with Caserta. The Americans will still help us. They not find his body. I hide it."

"He is only a boy."

"So are thousands of boys dying all over the world. Go back to bed."

She hangs there holding the gun. He points his Luger at her for a second, his mouth set, body stiff. There's a sharp silence, then a fierce clatter of bullets. Bauer slumps down, the Luger falling to the floor with a bang. Giorgio is standing in the front doorway grinning, Victor's machine pistol in his hand, the hand grenade hanging on his belt. The countess appears on the stairs and looks down at the crumpled figure, her eyes bulging, stock still. Blood is splattered all over the marble, sprayed on the wall like graffiti. I walk over to feel the body. It's rigid, cold.

"Mama Mia, Mama Mia, what have you done?" she shrieks. "What have you done? He is head of the Belluno Region for *Tedeschi*."

"And your *amante*."

"No, no, we are friends. It is because of plan we know each other, we have relationship. I am married. No, no. And it would be good. Kurt would find a way to make everything work without Bill. He knows General Wolff, General Kesselring. Now there is no one. We leave *subito*."

"Does anybody know he's here?"

"Everybody, Gestapo, Wehrmacht, SS. Not kill him. Only warn him."

"He was going to shoot you."

"*No, no, Sergente. Non capisci.* He never do that. Never. He depends on me to help him. Now I get dressed, go with you."

"With me?

71

"I no stay. Not safe. They come in the morning. If they  not find him, they question me. I am arrested. They shoot me. You not know *Tedeschi*. You take me to *partigiani*."

"Partisans? Hell, they're after me and Giorgio here too. They think we told the Krauts where their camp was, informed on them. They'd knock us off before the Krauts would. They hear about you."

"Oh, no, that is bad. Then we go *sud* to *Americani*.  The only way."

"How?"

"I have car."

"They'll stop you."

"They know me. I have pass. Not stop me. You bury him. I clean up the blood. No one come till morning. We have five, maybe six hours. Good, no?"

"Where will we bury him?"

"In the pond. Take the path, go by the rabbit hutches. You see it. When you come back, we go."

Giorgio and I carry the bloody, bony body out of the house to the yard. He is heavier than he looks. A long way in the dark past a garden shed to the cages and then down a hill to the pond where there's a small dam and across the way a windowless stone building, a foundry maybe. Giorgio uses his flashlight. Pine trees and shrubbery border the path. The area is like a park. We grope along, stopping every now and then to catch our breath. It takes a couple of healthy swings to heave the corpse into the water loaded with stones. When we return, I call the countess. She doesn't answer. I race upstairs and search all the rooms. She's gone. Back down in the hall, I notice blood still staining the floor and walls.

"The bitch!" I mutter into the air. "We've got to beat it, Giorgio, or we're *finito*."

"We go?"

"*Si. Subito, subito*." We run through the front door to the drive. The Alfa Romeo still sits there. The Fiat is missing. Everything is quiet. Only a slight breeze stirs in the trees. No sound of a car motor.

"She took off as soon as we left. Probably notified the Krauts partisans attacked the villa. Now they'll be gunning for us with a vengeance. We killed one of their big shots. Sometimes you wonder, Giorgio, who's on your side. Maybe just the two of us are left with no one." He stares at me uncomprehending once more.

We start down the road to the gatehouse. An engine roars towards us, headlights bobbing up and down. We jump behind a cypress. Four Kraut officers flash by in an open car followed by a truckload of soldiers.  Giorgio wants to throw his hand grenade at them. His arm swings back. I restrain him. It will take them awhile before they fish the body out of the pond if they ever do and pick up our trail. Maybe we've got a couple of hours before all hell breaks loose.

Chapter 9

We dash down through the woods to the Belluno road. Another truck full of soldiers rumbles by. Dogs are yapping in the back. We've got to find a stream, pond, or river quick to jump in and lose the trail. And I think again about heading for the Cordeveole Valley and hiding out at Andrich. But Giorgio says no, too risky to go back there. And if the countess has alerted General Wolff, the SS hounds could be barking at our heels no matter where we went. I still can't believe the major was planning to end the war in Italy. The idea boggles the mind. And my poems could have helped make it possible. Maybe poets do rule the world after all. Except Dante would never proclaim anything so farfetched. Or at least I can't image he would. Too much engaged in the moral and the spiritual life of mankind and the mess people have made of it.

I keep brooding on the "So Long" letter Bill wrote to his father. I should be sending one to Maggie with a few poems to remember me by. Mom and Dad would never understand, a highway engineer who works for the state and a country girl from Berne in the Helderbergs who now belongs to a high-class bridge club. I love them both, but my being in OSS is as mysterious to them as my writing poetry. They wanted me to go to Tuck after Dartmouth and become a business man. How could I make a living writing poems? Well, folks, the old verses are keeping me alive and our side winning. Poetry must be good for something other than wishing happy birthday and love you on Valentine's Day.

No time to stop. Plunging through the trees and over a couple of hills and crossing water and following the Piave southeast. Somehow we have to sneak through the lines and reach Dante's old hometown. It's our only hope. Gosh, if I ever needed a radio it's now. My lines for Orange rattle around in my head clamoring to be used along with those I wrote for the general. But what the hell good are they if I have nothing to transmit them with? Talk about sitting down and contemplating your navel. One thing I've learned up here, there's no point going anywhere unless you can communicate. Being without a radio is like being without a life jacket in a sinking boat.

At daybreak we're still moving south and not stopping, not even for something to eat, only to drink water and piss. And it seems the farther we travel the more Krauts there are, especially in the villages. Somehow we manage to avoid them. We don't talk to anyone or stay in cabins, barns, haylofts, or *maglas*. We dart across open fields, hide in woods, in ditches hearing vehicles coming. A nerve wracking feeling. Not just wanted as enemies but for murder and the whole countryside alerted to watch for us.

The first inkling we get we're being chased is the next day down near Feltre, an old town with ramparts and a Palladian-like castle on a hill. We're following the Piave and the big broad green valley on our way to the Veneto plain when an airplane without markings flies low and strafes us. We dive in a ditch and the hotshot pilot zooms off to report an American uniform. After that we climb up out of the valley into the hills higher and higher. A line of troops is strung out below acting like a posse except they've got trucks and motorcycles. We continue moving up and up until we lose sight of them at twilight.

The following day we run into a Garibaldi group we can't avoid. They're headed north to Agordo. I tell them the partisan brigade we were with up on Mount Civetta was wiped out, and we're trying to reach Firenze and want to know where the front is. They act suspicious. We don't have a radio. They never heard of our leader. The commander is a red-faced, black-haired, blustering tough guy who calls himself Burrasco. He quizzes me relentlessly through Giorgio, and I invent a lot of junk about places we've been and battles we've fought and communist brigades we've been with. Then I tell him I'm in OSS and a radio operator. He's impressed. He says he has a radio, an SSTR-I that OSS dropped to his group, but the operator was killed in a *rastrellamento* and nobody can contact the base down south. They need weapons and food badly. It's the Eagle Mission. I never heard of it. Anyway I explain I'll use my code and try to reach Bari. He acts excited. I'm just the man he's been looking for. Apparently he doesn't know anything about Marko's 22$^{nd}$ Garibaldi Brigade. Which makes me breathe easier.

Reception should be good. We're on a slope of Monte Grappa full of shell holes left over from World War I, occupying one of those lonely little familiar mountain huts. The set isn't in the best condition, the key a little damaged, the batteries run down, the aerial in need of repair, but the headset and crystals are okay. After a lot of tinkering I get it going and scribble out a drop message using Orange call letters. I conclude with the coordinates of the field from a map Burrasco shows me, and end by saying I'm on my way south to reach OSS headquarters and mention what's going on up here. Everybody and his brother is after me. I hope I make it. Lots of info. And after fifteen minutes of trying to raise somebody on the Guard Channel and finding the base operator in the static and losing him and finding him again, I punch out the message in groups of five letters via the Morse Code. I only have to repeat it twice, which isn't bad considering the condition of the radio and the atmosphere and my uncertainty about the frequencies.

The next day an answer comes back at the right time. A drop is in the works. Date and time later. I'm to return to Bari right away, by sea if possible. It's easier. I tell Burrasco I'm leaving in the morning with Giorgio. He acts sad. He wants me to stay. He likes the way I finger the key and is amazed how I can take the code line right out of my head and unscramble the message in boxes on paper. The operator for Eagle used pads. He didn't draw boxes or use poetry. He wrote under letters on tissue paper. I tell him that's the difference between a technician and a poet. Pads are made by IBM machines, poems by fools like me. He doesn't *capisco* but acts as if he does and smiles. At least he's impressed, more impressed with my poetry than anyone has ever been before.

Then he changes his mood and starts shouting at me. Giorgio says he demands that I stay and send messages to get more drops. Besides, he likes me. I'm his *"poeta mio."* And suddenly he's laughing and putting an arm around me. I tell him OSS will send an operator to replace me. He doesn't have to worry. And I promise to remain until the guy arrives.

A week later the drop is right on target, twenty containers, thirty-five boxes, but no operator. We trudge back from the field after gathering up the equipment and rubbing out the fires. Over fifty men and women are involved. It's another one of those fabulous sights up here, the bonfires blazing in a H pattern, the sound of the planes growing louder and louder, a flashlight signal and the parachutes drifting down in the moonlight like colored balloons and kites. Everybody running around and shouting at each discovered treasure. Back at the hut they start drinking, singing, laughing. For a moment I forget the Krauts out hunting for me, forget the journey south, lose myself in the gang of partisans clustered around a fire with their Red stars and scarves flashing in the flames, their clenched fists hurled at the night sky. Like the football rallies in Hanover on Friday night and Coach Blaik from West Point saying, "Dartmouth men are tough." Yeah, when they're drunk. Boy, some life. As long as I've got my poetry and Dante to keep me warm, what the hell.

I can't get over how lucky I've been with the sonnet. Like having a rabbit's foot or a pack of Tarot cards. The men hover around watching me code and decode and marvel at where the code is coming from. Like savages once marveled at how fire popped out of a match, a bullet out of a gun, a picture out of a camera. I point to my head and my heart.

76

What's that line about looking in your soul to write? They giggle. To them it's like I'm rubbing a magic lamp and making sense out of a jumble of letters. And they do. Food and guns fall out of the heavens like manna. Who says poetry doesn't work? The difference for these guys between starving and singing.

And I start believing in the miracle myself in a way. It's not just communicating, it's saving lives, creating hope, changing the desolate landscape of war for the time being into something radiant and unforgettable. I might make it through the lines after all if we get enough of these drops and Burrasco releases me. But I'm beginning to doubt he will. He realizes with my code and the radio he's got supplies coming to sustain his men, help him survive the winter approaching, maintain his power. No matter how much I plead for my replacement in the messages none arrives. Bari keeps telling me, come home, little black sheep, come home to Bo-Peep. It's all over for you up there. But I can't until they send an operator. And they don't and I'm stuck. I plunge back into Dante and read about this wild boar of a man in a snake pit having an epileptic fit raging against God and these slithering reptiles swarming over him tying up his balls. What a terrific scene. I begin to feel tight down there myself.

Everything is going smoothly until one night Marko and a handful of his men drift into camp looking beat. They lost almost all of the brigade during the last attack and have been walking and hiding for days, hungry, low on ammo, weary. Colonel Slansky is the only one who appears sturdy on his feet. He's still wearing those black boots, sporting those red epaulettes and medals, unsmiling as ever. The inscrutable sourpuss.

I stay out of sight for the first couple of hours. But eventually Marko hears about me, and I'm back listening to his ravings about my collaboration with the enemy, giving away the position of the brigade. I even betrayed the major, led him into a trap at Cortina. The guy has lost his marbles. He yells, waves his arms, pulls a pistol threatening to avenge the deaths of all the brave men he lost. They have to restrain him.

Burrasco confronts me. And all I can say is that I didn't inform the Germans about the brigade's location. Giorgio killed Bauer at Belluno after he was going to shoot me. And the countess could have put the Krauts on our tail. So what kind of collaboration is that? But Marko keeps roaring back, accusing me of spying on the brigade. It becomes a real face-to-face showdown between the only two Americans in camp. And, wow, do I holler my head off. But he hollers louder and in their language so most of the men look pissed off at me.

"Rank still counts up here, Sergeant. Don't forget it."

"Rank never counted in OSS, and you know it. I'm free to go wherever I want, do what I want. I'm on a special mission for the general, the same as the major was."

"What mission? To make that lousy deal with the Krauts we heard about."

"I can't say."

"Answer or I'll have you shot. I'm your commanding officer."

"You mean you're the Gestapo now. This your idea of partisan justice?"

"What do you think? Either you tell us what you're up to, why you went to see the countess again, what's her connection with the major and the Nazis, or I'm ordering you shot tomorrow, you and your buddy here."

"Partisan justice, huh? I can't tell you anything because I don't know anything. It's all very confusing."

"You're lying, you little son of a bitch!" His face reddens. He thrusts a finger at me.

"Only the major and the countess really know."

"Baloney. You were in on it, you and Bill and the Fascist cunt and her pimp. Trying to pull a fast one on us, destroy the partisan movement up here, the whole CLNAI. And in the name of anti-communism. Save the north for the capitalists like Parilli and Olivetti. Shut us out. And the best way to do that is to cut off supplies to Red brigades, keep the capitalists in power. The Krauts don't blow up the factories when they retreat, and the partisans don't crap all over them. Isn't that the deal, Sergeant? This isn't a war against the Nazis, it's against Russia and communists, the only real friends the people in this country ever had. The rich are afraid of them."

"I don't know anything about politics. All I know is your men could have saved the major at Cortina. You wanted to get rid of him so he couldn't prevent you from taking over the country up here."

"That's all you've got to say?"

"Yes, and I am reporting it to the general when I get back."

"You're not going anywhere soon."

"You stopping me?"

"Unless you confess what the major was up besides what we've heard and put it in writing. Colonel Slansky is also interested. If you were collaborating with the enemy, he wants to report it to his government. He's Stalin's personal envoy here, in case you didn't know."

"Yeah, I bet."

"By tomorrow morning, Sergeant. Or else." He points the finger closer to me.

"Or else what?"

"I'll leave that to your poetic imagination." He guffaws and stamps out of the shed.

A long cold night. Autumn definitely is breathing down our necks, and just behind it at our backs you can feel winter creeping in. It could be worse than up at Hanover where the snow is on the ground from November through March and the temperature falls to 30 below. I've got to tell him about the peace plot, yet if I do, Christ, imagine how Stalin would react. The German divisions here could be sent to fight against his forces. Then I bet he wants the war to continue until the Russians reach the heart of Europe and he can take over. And with the colonel around and maybe in contact with a commie mission and Tito in Yugoslavia the whole thing could blow up with a bang. Uncle Joe would cause a terrific stink with Roosevelt and Churchill and Donovan would be out on his ass. Jesus, how did I ever get into this mess?

All sorts of gloomy prospects whirl around in my head. The grimmest is my own. No chance this time to get help from anywhere. Taken out and shot for collaboration with the enemy, a double agent. And I think of Dostoevsky's fake execution in St. Petersburg, the hair of a friend next to him turning white and everybody kissing each other madly, his whole life passing before him in seconds as the firing squad gets ready to do their duty.

Just before daybreak I ask to see Marko. The ragged peaks of the Dolomites hovering in the distance are beginning to brighten. He comes limping in, sleepy and cranky, and sits down at the table. The candlelight shows the creases on his face. He looks more tired than I've ever seen him. The strain is beginning to tell. Too old for this kind of life. I feel sorry for him. He's had a hard time, labor organizer in the Depression, volunteer in Spain, now partisan warfare.

"You have your confession ready, Sergeant?" He laughs.

"I'll make a deal with you."

"No deal."

"My codes for my life."

"You mean that stinkin' little sonnet you wrote for us?"

"Not that one but the others I've written for missions. Tell you where they're located, their frequencies, stuff like that. I've briefed a lot of those guys when I was in Caserta and Bari. Then you and the colonel can read every damn message they're sending. Give you an idea where OSS missions are located and what they're doing." He looks as if he's swallowing it."How many are you talking about?"

79

"Maybe three or four. Then I have a code for Donovan and Roosevelt."

"You made up a code for them?"

"That's right, the Fala sonnet."

"The Fala sonnet?"

"The president's dog. I wrote a poem about it."

"Jesus Christ, what next in this organization? How do I know you're telling the truth?"

"I could try to intercept a message and decode it for you. Remember once you wanted me to tell the colonel all about our codes, how our communication system works. Well, here I am giving you everything I know."

"I'll see."

"At least this way you get something since I don't know anything about the other."

"You keep all those poems in your head?"

"Right. I wrote them, didn't I? I have a good memory. Frequencies too."

"I'll think about it. Let you know in an hour or so."

"I could send a message from another mission in their code on the Guard Channel saying you've joined us. Wait for the reply. That would prove something."

"It might."

He gets up from the table and walks out of the hut. I sit there staring at the candle dimmer in daylight, wondering if he really believes me and I could do it.

I don't move waiting for him to return. The noise of guys snoring upstairs is grating. So is the sound of those moving around outside. I suppose it would take me a couple of hours or so to remember all the lines, recall where each sonnet went. Trade my life for a bunch of poems. What a nutty idea. To think it would someday come down to this. Sidney Cox, my writing teacher, and Robert Frost up at Dartmouth, would tear their hair out at my writing what amounts to silly limericks. None of the poems are any good by their standards. Maybe not even by Edgar Guest's. Yet the trite little things could save my neck. And I'm depending on writing the genuine thing after the war once I get out of here.

The wick grows smaller, the flame paler. The sky becomes brighter and brighter. I gaze out the window at the snowy peaks thrusting up against the horizon. They remind me of prison walls and picture postcards at the same time. And I thought when I signed up for OSS I had it made. No infantry and frontline duty, no KP. Spend the war deciphering messages about somebody else's misfortunes. How the hell did I ever volunteer for this madness?

Boy, who says poetry is for the birds? Maybe not Milton in *Paradise Lost* or Wordsworth in *The Prelude*. But my doggerel does. Hey, Auden, you should be here to write an elegy In Memory of Anthony B. Defreest. The nightmare is on all right, and the dogs of Europe are barking their mangy heads off. I wonder if you'd be telling me to sing of "human unsuccess/In a rapture of distress." That sounded so profound once. Anything with a paradox or irony did. Not anymore. What I need are a couple of straight lines out of *The Book of Common Prayer* to buoy me up. How about the bishop laying his hands on me during Conformation and asking the Lord to defend his child forever.

The morning is becoming sunnier. A partisan guard is leaning against the door with his Sten gun and bandolier. He's smoking a cigarette and watching me. Younger than I am. No doubt never went to college. Maybe can't even read or write. I stand up and move to the window. He stirs. I turn and smile. The candle is guttering. I tell myself I can't possibly hand Marko and the Russians those codes or information about missions. Yet I have this terrible fear of being gone forever. Talk about the "rapture of distress." Holy Moses, I gotta get the hell out of here. I can't choose. I just can't.

I pray for a Kraut attack like last time without really meaning it. But none is coming. A hollow stillness hangs in the air. I strain to listen. I could hand over fake codes except for one and then use it to send a real message and get an acceptable reply that would satisfy Marko. That would only compromise a single mission. But, no, I'd feel that one on my conscience. Maybe even tell about Sun Up. No, I couldn't do that.

A group of partisans gather outside with rifles. They peer in at me and grin as if they know what I'm going through. The bastards!

"It's time," Marko appears in the door. The colonel towers over him. "We accept your offer. Start writing down those codes. Then we'll pick one for a test contact to see if it works. If it does, you're safe. If not kaput." He slashes his throat with a finger, grinning.

"Like Russian roulette, huh?"

"Colonel Slansky says those codes may come in handy getting extra drops, finding out where missions are. The more food and guns the better. It's going to be a tough winter if the Allies don't get any farther and we're stuck up here. I brought you paper and pencil. Give complete identity for each mission in addition to the codes and the radio stuff."

He walks over to the table and plunks down a tablet and a couple of pencils.

"Can I have something to eat first?"

81

"Sure. We've got bread and cheese and a little wine. Help your memory?"

"I hope so. I'll try to remember everything."

"You better. And don't forget Fala." He laughs.

"You don't want much."

"After what you did to us at Pelmo you're getting off easy. You should be shot for that. We lost a lot of good men, not counting prisoners."

"I had nothing to do with it I told you."

"Just like the major had nothing to do with those who were shot after that drop the countess and her lover were supposed to guarantee there would be no interference. And, Christ, how many were lost after that fiasco?"

I sit at the table. The candle is a pool of wax. I glance up at him and the Russian.

"You have two hours. We'll try a contract at noon on the Guard Channel using one of the codes you come up with. If we get a response you're okay."

"Then what will you do with me?"

"Keep you glued to the radio asking for more and more drops."

"What happens when the war is over?"

"I wouldn't worry about that."

"You mean I won't make it."

"Your problem is staying alive today. So get busy. We'll be back. Meanwhile the firing squad is outside in case you change your mind or try to fool us. They've never shot an American before."

"Always a first time for everything, huh?"

"Don't be a wise guy. Start writing. Breakfast will be coming up."

He and the colonel leave, and a man brings in a plate of cheese and bread and a canteen full of water of instead of wine. I devour everything in sight while staring at the gray-lined paper, feeling alone. The place is empty except for the guard.

All of a sudden my mind goes blank. I can't remember anything, even lines from the sonnet for Orange. And I can't think of any fake stuff either. I pound the table jiggling the canteen and the plate. The guard comes over pointing his pistol at me, acting surly. I slap out a drum roll on the wooden surface with my hands and smile at him. My old days playing drums with the Rhythm Cadets at the Boys' Academy come back to me. He relaxes, intrigued by the rhythm and the scat singing I start in time with the beat. The whole room rocks.

Chapter 10

I stand up, still rapping away against the wood, moving my body, tapping my feet, spitting out jive talk. Then I stop and urge him to try. He leans over and puts his hands on the table. Just as he's about to bang out a solid beat and simulate my mumbo jumbo I chop him on the back of the neck with the edge of my right hand, a clean hard blow. He chokes, makes a gurgling sound, grasps his throat, and slumps to the floor. He looks dead, but he's still gasping to breathe. I grab his Sten on the floor, gather ammo out of his pockets, grab my knapsack with the Dante, and rush to the door.

"*Assistenza, assistenza.*" I cry out, pointing inside as three men come barreling past followed by four others. They cluster around the body yelling and cursing and gesticulating. I walk steadily away, searching for Marko. He's nowhere. Partisans are standing around in small groups jabbering, eating, cleaning weapons. I don't see the firing squad. No one pays any attention to me. At the edge of the clearing I duck into the woods, and glance back. Someone is shouting, "*Americano, Americano!*" Men are dashing around firing guns wildly. I look for Giorgio. He's nowhere. So I turn and dart through the pines not knowing where the hell I'm headed, only sure it's in a different direction from the way I came.

So far nobody is following. I beat it away from the area as fast as I can, tripping a couple of times, almost losing the Sten, bursting through bushes. Now they could shoot Giorgio. I should have thought of that before I took off. At least there aren't any dogs on my trail. But after an hour I can hear footsteps growing closer. Why didn't I stay and write down what Marko wanted, even if most of it would be fake. Lucky that Marine sergeant back in Club des Pins taught me that chop shot in combat class when he said, "We'll make professional killers out of you college kids yet." He didn't think I'd ever last behind the lines. I didn't have the killer instinct. But I'm sure I didn't kill that kid, just knocked him out.

No time to worry about such stuff. It's either get to the coast and find a boat and hug the shore sailing south or be picked up and shot. Simple as that. I couldn't give away those codes. I put too much of myself into them as lousy as they are. Any more than I could betray a secret to the enemy no matter how fierce the pressure. Or could I?

83

Reading Dante gives me hope I'll get out of here someday no matter how bad things get. Christ, I could be among those guys in the *Inferno* who've done all those horrible things and are wallowing in pitch and blood and shit. Yet I know I'm not and never will be just as I never could describe such grotesque self-laceration so vividly. Still thinking about the freaky sinners in the different circles makes me wonder what I'm capable of and where I'm headed. Like I'm on the rim of one grotesque circle after another getting ready to mingle with the dead and witness the sins they've committed and haunted by what's in the future for me.

So I'm heading south not too confident I'll make it back to Bari. Almost certain I won't. Pessimistic as always. It insulates the shock of disappointment, keeps the demons suppressed. Maybe that's what it is all about, running from something you can't escape yet jogging on as if you can. Thinking of Dante and what he went through in his poem and in his life, knowing he's for all eternity, I'm just for the wastepaper basket.

They give up by afternoon. At least I don't hear any more footsteps or see anybody behind me cutting across the meadow. I'm so pooped and hungry anyway I can hardly think straight. And if I find an empty stretch of woods on the road to Vittoria Veneto I'll crawl into a ditch, cover myself up with leaves and branches, and immediately fall asleep.

In the middle of the night the ground shakes as if there's an earthquake. I jump up to see trucks and motorcycles and tanks roaring by shadowy against the night sky like gigantic shapes on a newsreel screen, those low-cut Kraut helmets bobbing up and down. After they pass I climb out of the ditch and start traveling south again. I must be over a hundred miles to the coast near Ravenna. And I have only the Sten, an empty holster, little *lire*, Dante, and this uniform that's beginning to stink like garbage. The paratroop boots are wearing thin. No food. Few civilians seem to be around, and there are no signs of American or British soldiers or even partisans. Maybe the war's over and everybody is celebrating. I haven't had any news since the announcement of D Day in June. I don't even know what day it is or week or month.

The first farmhouse I come to I knock on the door and ask for something to eat. I'm an American pilot shot down over Belluno. The old man and wife are friendly enough but shake their heads and tell me there are no Allies in the area. *Tutti Tedeschi*. *Amercani* in the skies. They point up and act out bombing raids, covering their heads and imitating the noises, falling down, simulating pain. Then they feed me, mostly pasta and tea. And I get to sleep in a bunk bed full of straw. In the morning they point me towards Vittorio Veneto, *molti, molti chilometri*. And I set out.

It's a long, lonely walk and by the next night I'm circling the city, part ancient buildings and part run down factories like so many places in Italy. Sometimes you don't know which is which. An old palace could be a sweatshop or a bicycle plant or a museum. Like the one OSS occupies at that palace above Caserta. In one part girls are working at silk looms in a huge damp storage room with dusty cobwebs in the windows and in the other G.I.s, WACs, and civilian women from the States are walking down gilded hallways peeped at by cherubs and decoding messages in rooms with flower-decorated blue ceilings. A big cobblestoned courtyard with a statute of Ferdinand IV in front of a battery of broken windows that separates the two sections. What a moldy, magnificent place for a headquarters.

Signs for Conegliano, Treviso, and Venezia appear up ahead. The mountains fade way in the distance. It's all rolling hills now topped by villas and castles, great meadows, rivers, stretches of cultivated fields and vineyards, and walled towns. I stop at a barn for the night and feast on the bread and cheese the farmer's wife gives me. Aching all over and brooding on how much longer I can keep up this endless hiking or where I can hide or whom I can trust to help me out of this tangled web of mystery and mayhem. One thing is certain, I've got to shed my uniform to survive, become a homeless native.

The next morning I meet a bunch of teenagers on a country road. They cry out, "*Americano,*"

"*Americano*" and come running after me. There are at least four of them. Others pop out of houses and vineyards and green fields where peasants are working. The women look like they're wrapped up in layers of rags, their heads swathed in a bands. They rise up off their knees and stare at the stranger going by as if they were characters out of the Bible. And I feel like some battered old turtle crawling past. I wave. They stand still, a hand up to shade their eyes.

"*Dove Americani, partigiani?*" I shout at the kids. They're touching the Sten gun. Scruffily dressed but not as bad as the *scugnizzi* in Naples. At least they have shoes. And no begging and obscenities, just an excited curiosity. Treviso I gather is thirty or more kilometers. No, they don't know of any *Americani* in the area. They belong to a partisans group nearby that raids German convoys. Kill *molti, molti, Tedeschi*. I look at them. They talk as if they're trying to impress me. So far I haven't seen anybody as young among the partisan bands.

85

"Radio?" I say and act out putting on headphones and keying dots and dashes, making noises with my mouth. They don't' understand and take me to a village close by. Old people are sitting on benches around a fountain in the square facing a church. As soon as they spot me, they begin smiling, waving their arms. Within minutes it seems the whole town turns out to witness the arrival of the *Americano*. It feels good after being hunted for so long. Like I'm some millionaire or Martian.

"*Parla inglese?*" I say to the group staring at me.

"*Si, si inglese,*" one woman emerges from the crowd. She's short and stout with a fat oily face, graying hair, a long brown dress. She's Maria Paselli.

"I need to go to the coast, Ravenna, Rimini. I am *pilota*. I was shot down. *Tedeschi* after me. I need a boat to go south to the Allies. *Capeesh?*"

"*Si, Capitano.*"

"And I need clothes, shoes, food. Sleep."

"*Si, capisco.*"

"These kids really partisans?" I point to the gang who brought me here.

"*Poco,*" she smiles. "*Tedeschi* come, shoot, run. A game with them."

"Any around here?"

"Treviso, *molti, molti soldati. Bombe, molte, molte bombe.* You no go there. *Male, Americano.*"

"Does anyone have a car, truck, motorbike?"

"*Si,* I find. Take you *casa.* You *mangia.* Give you clothes. Everything good, nice, *va bene.* You have *lire?*"

"*Molti.*" I dig in my pocket and take out a few bills. The crowd smiles. I hand them over. She reaches up and kisses me on the cheek. A couple of other women standing nearby do the same thing, and I hand them money too. Gosh, I've never felt so much like the rich American passing out goodies to indigent peasants. Several men shuffle forward, and I hand them cigarettes.

"Radio? Send dot-dash?"

"No. Listen BBC."

"Have you seen any *Americani* around here?"

"Near Padua. *Partigiani.* You go there?"

"On the way to the coast. Will anybody take me?"

"I find somebody. You come." And she grabs my hand and leads me through the square and down a cobblestone street to a whitewashed house. I bend down passing through a low doorway and enter a dimly lit room filled with holy pictures. Cabbage, garlic, wine, and charcoal odors fill the air. A short thin man with bags under his eyes and a grayish-white stubble gets off a chair and hobbles forward to greet me.

"*Buonasera, Capitano.* Good day, huh? Sun, sky, all goo, fine, nice, okay. Me *Americano.*" Taking out a wallet, he shows me a snapshot of himself at Coney Island. "1918, Mr. Wilson. Goo, huh?"

"Very good."

"Me live New York, *Capitano.* Me tailor. My brother he Chicago, he tailor. My wife, bambino, Mamma come back 1936. No goo, huh? No goo, *Capitano. Il Duce Fascisti.*"

"That's right. You should have stayed in New York."

"Ah, *si,* America goo, fine, nice, okay. This place no goo, this place *cacca.* America *mangi* every day. Ten dollar a day. This place one day *mangi,* ten day no work, no *mangi.* Oh, America goo, fine, nice. This place Goddamn!"

He waves his arms in my face. "No work, no *lire.* Thirty-five *lire,* please, *Capitano.*" He starts counting with his fingers in Italian, shoving them nearer and nearer my face, peering at me like a tailor through the eye of a needle. "My mamma sick. She ninety-nine. No coffee for my mamma."

"Where is she now?"

"Oh, America, nice, goo, fine." He pauses and lowers his voice. "*Capitano, scusate, sigaretta?*"

"*Si.*" I hand him one and some *lire.* "Bad for you. I don't smoke."

"No smoke. Good, make you strong." He moves off into the room putting the *sigaretta* in his mouth unlit.

Neighbors are crowding the doorway and peering in at us through the window. Maria flies over and shoos them away and takes me to a small low-beamed room with a tiny window, hands me a shirt and pants, sweater and cap, a short coat. She even finds socks and a pair of heavy shoes that fit pretty good with some paper stuffed in the toes. I face myself in the mirror, and, gosh, if I don't resemble a damn native, dark complexion, brown eyes, black hair, scraggly beard. The first time I've been in civilian clothes in over a year or more. I feel funny.

The supper is great, all the wine and pasta I can swill down. Everybody is talking to me at once about the war and America, the wife, the husband, the two boys. It's as if I understand everything they're throwing at me. I'm in bed by nine, scarcely able to stay awake. It feels good to be lying on a mattress again and having a pillow and blanket and not worrying about the Germans and the partisans hunting for me. My first taste of true Italian life. A long way from Dante country. I can't ever remember him stopping somewhere to eat a meal and sleep, change clothes, peeing and crapping.  Just going around in circles with the damned.

"*Capitano*, *Capitano*!" the little roly-poly woman hangs over me, breathing in my face. "You go *pronto*. *Polizia*. Someone say you here." I sit up startled. She's holding a candle. I notice the clock on the table clicking. One-fifteen.

"Oh, Christ, I knew it was too good to last!" And the memory of the major being dragged out of the church in Cortina flashes through my mind, stories about his torture and hanging. Quickly I dress in the civilian clothes flung on the chair along with the coat, grab the Sten and the knapsack. The yellow flame trembles in the damp air. No sign of the tailor or the kids, no noises from outside.

"Do they know I'm in your house?"

"They get *lire* for telling *polizia* about *Americano*."

"Any car, truck, motorcycle?"

"I take you."

"Where's your family?"

"They sleep. You give me more *lire*, no?"

"*Si*, here." I hand her a couple of bills.

"*Grazie, grazie*." I look at her wondering if she's going to deliver me to the police herself. There's a hurried conspiratorial air about her, a sort of eagerness to push me out of the house fast. Her tightened face full of deep lines.

We hurry out the back into an alley where a small truck is waiting.

"Giuseppe," she says to me, pointing to the man behind the wheel. "He take you Padua. He know the way. No one stop you. *Buono*."

"Gosh, *grazie, molto grazie*," I say again and hug her, believing she is telling the truth yet at the same time hesitating, my stomach churning like mad.

I climb in beside the driver. He's older than I first thought, smaller, clipped moustache, hunched shoulders. He's wearing a thread-bare overcoat too big for him.

"Padua?" I say.

"*Si, Americano buono*."

"*Polizia?*"

"No *polizia*, no *Fascisti*." He starts up. I wave goodbye to the stubby woman standing in the alley. Her husband glides up beside her, the glow of a *sigaretta* barely visible. She can't be sending me into a trap. Everybody here is anti-German and anti-Fascist, pro American. She fed me, gave me clothes. I gave her *lire*. Yet I recall what Marko said about these people even though she doesn't seem to be one of them, generous, friendly, likes Americans.

Out on the main street and rattling across the square I hold the Sten on my lap. No lights anywhere. It's like a ghost town. Nobody is stirring. Only the splash of the fountain echoing against the walls, the thunder of the engine breaking the silence. The cobblestones are rough, and the old guy is traveling fast.

"*Lento, Lento,*" I cry out, grabbing his shoulder. He doesn't hear. I shake him, shout in his ear. He's trembling, breathing hard. Abruptly he stops, cuts off the motor, and bolts out of the cab. I sit there in the middle of the piazza stunned with the scrape of his footsteps fading and the water splashing, the sound ricocheting. Headlights blaze into the darkness lighting up the old stones.

"*Americano, Americano,*" a voice whispers loudly from a doorway. I glanced around, raising my gun ready to fire. I can't see anybody. I think about driving on across the square except I don't know where the road to Padua is. And if I get out and run I'm a target. So I sit waiting, gripping the Sten. The whole thing could be a trick. The voice calls again, tenser, louder. It's coming from the direction of the church. But nobody is over there. So I slide behind the wheel, fumble for the starter. The motor scratches to life, and I depress the clutch, shove the gear into first. The truck jerks forward toward the opening across the way hoping it leads out into the country.

Two bodies jump into the headlight beams, waving frantically. I slam on the brakes, grab the Sten off the seat ready to fire. It's the damn kids I met yesterday. They come running toward me with those old model 91 Italian rifles.

"*Fascisti, poliziotti, Fascisti, poliziotti!*" they shout in high-pitched tones.

"You mean they're waiting for me outside of town?" I shut off the lights and motor. "Is it a trap?" They babble something.

"Padua?" I say. "You drive me to Padua?" I put my hands on the wheel.

"*Si, si,*" they mumble. And I open the door on the driver's side and move over and they hop in, the tall one first, the shorter and stouter one second. He's driving.

"Mario," he says.

"Alfredo," the one next to me whispers. I reach out and shake their hands.

"Tony. Maria Paselli *non buono*, huh?" I ask.

"*Buono,*" they sing out together.

"Giuseppe *non buono,*" the fat kid mutters.

89

"*Andare. Va bene?*" They laugh at my pronunciation, and Mario starts the motor but turns off the headlights. And we shoot across the square. Only instead of bumping along to the other side of town, he swerves around and enters an alley behind the church.

"Padua?" I say.

"*Si,*" he shouts above the roar of the motor. They burst into a laugh and jabber together. We stop at a house. "*Momento.*" Mario pops out and knocks on the door and returns to the driver's seat, and pretty soon two kids appear and jump in the back. They have rifles with them. He drives to another house and another until the truck is loaded. And we're off into the country on a dirt road, headlights blazing away. The kids in back begin singing. Good God, it's like being on a bus of high school football players headed for a game and pepped up. I glance around to see if anyone is following. Only the hills back there and the little dark town. All around us fields and vineyards, the damp fresh smell of the night. A lot more humid down here than up in the Dolomites and no great peaks jutting into the night sky like bayonets outlined against the horizon. At least I've got my own partisans to protect me. Now all I need is a radio, and I could be in the mission business in a big way.

Without any warning the singing in the back switches to yelling. And I look around and the kids are waving their hands frantically and pointing. Not far behind a car is rushing toward us, its lights shining brighter and bigger.

"*Fascisti, poliziotti?*" I say.

*Si,*" Mario mutters. He steps on the gas and hunches over the wheel. The truck shakes so much it seems ready to fly apart. After careening around a curve, he slows down and stops sharply on the side of the road. Everybody leaps out as if by signal, some going across the way, some staying. I remain with Mario and Alfredo. As the pursuer races into the turn, tires screeching, the kids open fire. The vehicle swerves and rams into trees, crumbles, bursts into flames. An officer jumps out screaming, his arms in the air like torches, his hair lit up. Mario shouts at him, and he falls to the ground and rolls over. The flames eat away at his hands and face until they're red, black, and blotchy. The smell is awful. Christ, I can imagine the charred bodies inside that inferno. Before I rush to rescue him, there's an explosion. We dive for the ditch. Then another, this one louder and more flames.

The gang swarms back onto the road to ring the wreck burning away, raising their rifles and shouting, "*Morte ai Fascisti, libertà ai Popoli.*" The Red battle cry. The officer continues to smoke on the road like rubbish in a dump. The kids yell and fire into the air while watching him act if he were some kind of triumphant sacrifice they're both awed

90

by and jubilant about. Then they turn to me. But I don't join in the celebration sickened by that poor guy smoldering on the ground, horrified by what I've just witnessed. And what about the others in the car? For some reason the kids consider me their leader who planned the whole thing. I tell them Mario is II Duce. He sticks out his chin and chest in mock fashion and they laugh. I also tell them I have to go to Padua where there are Americans and then to the coast to get a boat to reach the Allies at Bari. They don't act interested in that, especially Mario. He's smiling away hardly listening, a cocky, cheerful teenager if I ever saw one.

We take off leaving the wreck still burning in the road. The stench clings to my clothes like a bonfire of leaves in the fall. I can't get out of my mind the sight of that officer on fire with arms up squealing for help and then rolling over and over while these maniacs are laughing, shouting, firing into the air. We stop at daybreak outside a small town and hide in the forest. Mario sends a couple of his gang ahead to locate the police station. I protest. No more attacks on *Fascisti*, no more crazy killings. We could have the *Tedeschi* after us. And they would come with tanks and machine guns this time. We wouldn't have a chance. If they want to fight, they should join a regular partisan brigade. No more of this wild racing from village to village shooting up a couple of helpless policemen. It's senseless. They're not the ones carrying on the war. They have family and are only doing their job.

Mario listens to me fumbling through my crude Italian, nodding, smiling, not understanding much of what I'm trying to say, ignoring my scowling. The next thing I know half the group is gone. And they don't come back until after dark. They bring cans of petrol along with pistols and rifles and bottles for making Molotov cocktails. Lots of food, too, loaves of bread, cheese, pasta. And they have a great time eating and chatting around a fire like Boy Scouts camping out. I ask where everything came from, and they say the people gave it to them. They support the *partigiani*.

"You mean you got it from the police," I say.

"*Morte ai poliziotti.*" And I gather maybe they killed one or two and routed others. I'm dubious about starting out with them again around midnight. It's like traveling with a bunch of reckless high school kids who have had too much to drink.

Mario is still driving. I accuse him once more of not taking me to Padua but roaming the countryside searching for police stations and Fascist barracks to attack. He laughs and points to a sign that says Treviso 4 KM. And I'm shocked as he enters the old walled city full of bombed out buildings, moving through the rubble to the center of town

91

with its canals and cathedrals and palazzos. Porticos line the streets along with houses decorated with Venetian-looking frescoes. No one is around. Little traffic and few lights. We pass a police station on a square, and I expect Mario to stop and the whole gang to jump out and storm the place. But he sails right past, and there's not a peep from anybody in back lying under a tarpaulin.

"*Poliziotti*," I whisper.

"*Tedeschi*," he says, pointing across the piazza.

I turn to the right and notice a group of army vehicles parked over there, an armored car, trucks, jeep-like cars, even wrapped up artillery pieces. A couple of guards stand by them.

"No *buono*," I say.

"*Buono, buono*,' Mario laughs softly. I almost expect him to honk the horn as we roll over the cobblestones. And he does give a muffled peep just before entering a narrow street.

"Shush," I whisper. He laughs and then speeds up, and in a few minutes we're on the open road again headed for Padua. Or I hope the hell we are. I can't get over these kids out joyriding through this dark, flat land with nothing on their minds but having a good time killing and burning and blowing up anybody in a Kraut or police uniform.

Chapter 11

We stop at a farmhouse just after daybreak, and Mario arranges with the owner, Victor Gamberini, for us to rest in the barn for a few hours. He introduces me as an American pilot, and I show the family my cap in the knapsack. They give us a tremendous breakfast, eggs, sausage, toast, coffee. The first solid meal I've has since I left Maria Pasellis's house. And while we're eating, the short, ruddy-faced farmer with the distinguished-looking white hair tells us there are *molti Tedeschi* in the area. We should be careful. Also *molti partigani*. They bring reprisals because of parachute drops and raids. Men, women and children have been killed. No *buoni partigani*.

Mario insists that he and his group are not partisans. They're only taking me to Padua. Nobody has to worry. But the little father acts nervous all morning, bothered by the weapons he sees the kids carrying around. He keeps dropping by the barn to see if we're leaving. He doesn't offer us lunch. And I hint to Mario that maybe we better *arrivederci subito*. I don't want these people on my conscience. He doesn't listen and talks about not being afraid of the *Tedeschi*. Let them come. His men can handle them. It's funny watching the kids clean their guns, wrestle with each other, stalk around scaring peasants, boasting to neighboring children about attacks on police stations and Fascist barracks. It brings back in contrast what I was doing at almost their age, playing football, having snowball fights with a gang on the next block, dating and going to movies. And before I know it we're staying all day and sleeping in the barn and surrounding sheds.

We end up staying for two days. I spend the time wandering around watching teams of drooling white oxen lumbering over the soil dragging wooden plows, the drivers switching them and yelling. Observe how two men fertilize an olive grove. They march back and forth along the rows of gnarled trees in single file spilling rusty liquid out of a cask suspended from poles resting on their shoulders. A shovel held by the one in the rear guides the stream. Someone says its urine collected from the oxen.

The big festive occasion is the slaughter of a hog the third morning. After one man kills it with a hammer blow on the head, two others string up the animal by its hind feet from a crossbar, drain the blood by severing the veins on the neck, scrub the carcass with hot water until the flesh is smooth and pink. Then a stocky peasant from a nearby farm steps forward like an impresario, swarthy, drooping mustache, impassive. He brandishes a long black-handled knife he has just finished sharpening on a stone. He measures the body in front of him, lifts his instrument like a scalpel, and proceeds with one quick stroke to slit it open from tail to head. Fat like sudsy pudding bulges out along with spurts of blood. The smell is nauseous. An assistant removes sacks that look like link sausages and places them on a board. Next comes a brown liver, bundles of knotted intestines with purple, blue, and rose veins, a gall bladder in the shape of an elongated drop of water, and finally the ragged heart. All that's left is the empty hulk. Everyone watches quiet, curious, detached as if they've seen this many times before yet still are somehow fascinated with the ritual.

"*Tedeschi, Tedeschi!*" a small girl runs into the yard breaking up the concentration of the group. The men gape at each other frozen. The women run toward the house, the children after them. Mario and his gang rush to the barn and sheds for their weapons. He returns to me.

"*Battaglione,*" he says calmly. For a kid he's a cool customer.

"No, no, *fuggiamo.*" I point to the fields beyond the farm. A bunch of vehicles are roaring toward us. It sounds like a whole army is on the move. I run to fetch my knapsack and Sten gun. Off in the distance clouds of dust rise closer and closer. I wave for Mario's gang to follow me. They stand rooted to the spot waiting for their leader to speak. He erupts in a frenzy of efficiency, ordering his men to arrange themselves in a semicircle so they can ambush the invaders the moment they storm into the complex of buildings. He wants some on roofs, some in the house, others in the barn and sheds. He hands out extra rifles to the peasants who had dropped over to witness the butchering of the hog. At first they refuse them. They look frightened. Then reluctantly they accept the weapons resigned to their fate. I ask him where I should position myself. He motions toward a rise just beyond the olive grove. I shake my head.

"No, no, *Capitano,*" he pushes me away, leveling a pistol at my breast and threatening to shoot. I take off fast and duck behind the hill that looks down on the farm. The motorcade roars into the area. Five or six vehicles, at least fifteen to twenty men. They surround the buildings, get out, and edge forward warily, their weapons at ready. It's strange being up here watching them. The suspense grows tighter and tighter. A single shot rings out, then another and another. A Kraut machine gun on an armored car opens up as it crawls into the yard. A Molotov Cocktail hits the metal plate and explodes. The firing intensifies. And I think, Jesus, that crazy kid is going to win this thing. He's got everybody so well concealed. He seems to be picking off the Krauts one by one. I sneak down the slope towards the battle through the tall grass, sliding along on my belly, Sten in hand. A truck blows up. I stop. Machine guns rattle away. Occasionally a bazooka-like boom breaks over the crackle of rifle fire.

I should be with them instead of lying out here listening, watching. But I don't move waiting for everything to die down. It does for a moment, then bursts out again in a furious exchange of shots. The automatics of the Krauts against the single pings of the kids sniping away. I curse the day I ever hooked up with them and their blood-thirsty fun. Practically pissing in my pants expecting the Krauts to come after me when they discover I'm here. My fingers grip the trigger of the Sten. The first ones I see emerging from the olive glove and surging up the hill I'm going to shoot.

The firing fades out. Motors crank up. Swirls of dust fill the air. No more explosions. I inch forward down the slope to the grove with the green leaves shining in the stark sunlight. When I hear nothing, I stand up and study the scene. Burned out vehicles lie in the yard, including the one we rode here in, a jeep, a truck, a disabled armored car. Nearby are dead chickens and goats. No one is around. Not a sound. It seems eerie for a farm to be so abandoned-looking in the middle of a bright day with the land everywhere appearing so fresh and fertile. Off to the right a brown dog is sniffing the carcasses of two oxen fallen on their sides and still bleeding like great white whales beached.

Gradually, I make my way to the edge of the trees and enter the cluster of buildings. Some of Mario's gang lie face down in the dirt, their hands still clutching their rifles along with a few peasants who witnessed the hog evisceration including the impresario himself, flies buzzing around them. No bodies of Germans. Those hurt or killed must have been taken away. Blood is everywhere. So are spent cartridges and broken glass. I notice stone walls chipped by bullets and punctured by shell holes. The stench of cordite, burned rubber, and flesh turns my stomach.

I head toward the main house. The front door has been ripped off. Inside furniture, dishes, holy pictures are scattered and broken everywhere. Two peasants sprawl on the kitchen floor, their guts spilling out as if they had been dogs run over by a car. No sign of the *Gamberinis*.

I walk back to the yard to search for Mario. Footsteps pad behind me. Swinging around with the Sten cocked, I stare into the faces of the family, the white-haired father, the stout mother, the two wide-eyed girls. They look like ghosts.

95

"*Capitano, Capitano*," they whisper stumbling toward me. I lower the gun and run over to hug each one. They tell me in excited sign language and broken English how they hid in the  basement of the house. Some of their neighbors were taken away. The boys were all killed. The screaming was horrible. "*Molti Tedeschi, morti, morti.*"

"Mario too?" I say.

"*Si,*" Victor mumbles pointing to the barn. Over the door the little fat-faced Il Duce hangs from a hook in his throat, his body blood-soaked and mud-spattered. His eyes bulge out of his head, his tongue dangles. A gash splits his face. Like a gargoyle in the flesh that's been hammered and gouged. No shoes or socks, the thick toes dangling motionless in the sunlight.

I look at the red stained ground beneath him, gulp and walk away to put my head against the house. Tears come uncontrollably. My body shakes and heaves. I vomit.

"*Niente, Capitno,*" the stubby father says behind me. "*Niente.*"

I confront him. His shoulders slump. Tears glisten in his eyes and his wife's. The girls gaze at the corpses frightened. He goes into the barn and outbuildings and comes back, motioning with his palms up. Nothing is left except dead chickens, pigs, and goats. They even took the carcass and the innards of the butchered hog. No food in the house, no vegetables, meat, bread, eggs.

He doesn't know what they will eat now.

"*Parti*, no?" I say.

"*Si, si, parti, parti*" He gestures toward the field where I had been hiding.

"Padua?"

"*Si*, Padua." A sullen impatience grows on his face, a suppressed anger in his voice. Who can blame him? The only guilty one is standing there alive. So I shake hands, quickly kiss his wife and daughters on the cheek, try to express my sorrow, my regret for everything that has happened. Feeling like the major after the drop the countess assured would go on without any dire consequences. How the old man will ever clean up this mess, get rid of the bodies, feed his family, Christ, I don't know. The place lies so still and stark like a battlefield after the fighting. And I think of the Coconut Grove fire Maggie and I witnessed in Boston two years ago the night following the Boston College-Holy Cross football game. We had just come out of the Beachcomber and heard the sirens and went to view the massive blaze. Bodies were sticking out of metal-framed windows impaled on the glass while a priest was administering the last rites and a man was using an acetylene torch to free them. Corpses littered the garage floor of the Film Exchange

Transfer Company at the rear of the Club on Shawmet Street. Maggie said later three of the dead girls were Wellesley freshmen with blind dates.

A terrible thing all right, not just the killing but to come here like this with these kids and ruin people's lives. And just before leaving, I glance up once more at Mario dangling from the hook over the barn door. You can't write poetry about that. Not even Dante could I bet. Yet somehow the mutilated body brings back those perverted souls stuck forever in his *Inferno*.

I leave the dead and the barely living and tramp across a field. It's mid afternoon. The sun is still hot. Peasants are kneeling in the dirt planting or digging up turnips and potatoes. Oxen are plowing away. In the far distance looms a cluster of stone houses, smoke coming out of some of them. People gaze at me as I walk by, but no one speaks, and I don't wave or say a word. I just plunge ahead until I reach a road. Then I start hiking down it toward the east. A church bell rings. Around a bend appears a statute of the Virgin Mary set in the blue niche of a stone wall and surrounded by flowers. I cross myself the way Maggie does and plug on.

At dusk I pass a couple of two-storied houses, goats tied up in front, the ground floor windows open. Inside a family is sitting at a wooden table eating and talking, moving their hands and heads and enjoying themselves shoveling in the food. Four kids and their parents and a grandmother. Pots and pans hang on blackened walls. I shift the Sten to my left shoulder and smile in at them at an angle. They smile back. The goats stop chomping away, lifting their bearded faces and staring at me. I wonder how I'm ever going to reach Padua, no food, no guide, not much ammo. The Krauts will eventually find out I was with Mario and his gang and be hot on my tail by tomorrow.

I spend the night in an abandoned shed. The next morning I stroll into a village and buy a loaf of bread and some salami and cheese, using my meager Italian and a lot of sign language. No police or Germans around. Hardly anyone is up yet except a couple of storekeepers, some emaciated mutts, a few farmers, and a priest. He's a young guy in black, tall, thin, chiseled chin, stern-looking. He reminds me of a second lieutenant. I follow him down the street and into the square. He heads for the church.

"Padre, Padre," I call out in a hushed voice upon entering with him. He marches toward the altar and turns as my words echo.

"*Americano pilota.*" He turns but his expression doesn't change right away, the dark smooth face confronting me, the black habit and hair blending together. His eyes are so small they give out almost no light.

"*Capeesh?*"

"*Si.*"

"*Inglese?*"

"*Poco.*"

"I need to go to Padua. You help me?"

"*Americano, Gamberini fattoria?*"

"*Si.*"I bow my head, take a step back.

"*Atroce, atroce.*" He raises his voice. His eyes open wider, and I wait for him to berate me.

"I know, I know. At least the *Gamberinis* are still alive."

"*E tu.*"

"Yeah, me too. Can you help me?" He shrugs his shoulders. "Any *Tedeschi* around here?"

"*Spia della polizia.*"

"Plenty of them, huh? You know them?"

"*Si,*" he says wearily, still not acting too friendly, hesitating, then beckoning me to follow him behind the altar. I do and he stops in the half-light and points to a trapdoor in the ceiling. He goes off and fetches a ladder and climbs up and opens it. Then he comes down.

"You stay here. They no look for you. I bring food. You stay, no noise."

"*Grazie, Grazie.* Can you get me *auto* and find someone to drive me to Padua?"

"*Possibile.* No young men anymore. Just old men. Very *difficile* find *auto*. No petrol. You wait. Maybe *domani*, maybe week. You safe here." He goes off again for a minute and returns with a candle and some matches along with bread, cheese, and salami. For someone acting so generous he acts awfully nervous.

"*Nome?*"

"Tony."

"Tony?" He frowns.

"Short for Anthony. You know you pray to St. Anthony when you lose something."

"Ah, *si, si.*" He is Francis and shakes my hand, grins grudgingly. The front door opens. Footsteps shuffle on the stones. Voices mumble. "You go up now. *Santa Messa.* I come back. *Buono.*" I climb the ladder with the things he's given me plus my own stuff, almost losing my balance.

"*Grazie, Padre.*" At the top I put everything down and light the candle and step up into the darkness. He closes the opening and takes

98

away the ladder, and I think, boy, wouldn't Maggie love seeing me hiding up here listening to prayers and sermons and reading from scripture. Not that she's any Catholic wearing her faith on her sleeve, but she attends church every Sunday, never misses a holy day, never eats meat on Friday, goes to Confession. Though she does use birth-control.

Only women seem to be below muttering away. Maybe relatives of those the Krauts killed have come to light candles for the souls of the dead. I sit down on the boards and feast on the food. Now what I need is some water and a pan to piss in. Wouldn't that be something, pee on the floor and have the water drip through the cracks to the altar. Goddamn, why am I always dreaming up junk like that? Must be the Dante in me.

This country has everything all right. Here's a place I could write a poem about. A good spot for a radio too. I point the candle at the rough rafters and flooring. The storage space is big enough to string up an aerial. It would be tough for a DF to spot the signal.

A long dull morning, a bell tolling right over my head startling me. After the priest finishes his droning through the Mass and the women cease their mumbling, a creepy silence settles in. I extinguish the candle and stretch out on the floor to sleep, using the knapsack as a pillow and my coat as a blanket. But I can't doze off for some reason. At every door opening, every footstep I jerk up, reach for the Sten, only to relax a little when the noises fade away. It must be noon. The bell tolls again right over my head. The sounds down in the piazza increase. People are shouting. Motors zoom closer and closer, their thunder rebounding against the buildings. I grab my gun.

Then everything is quiet again. There's just the normal hum of voices. The village appears almost deserted. Maybe it's siesta time. The great Italian somnolence has begun. Gosh, I can't ever remember lying down on the middle of the day. The only person I know who does that is Dad. He comes home from the State Office Building for lunch, and after a sandwich and tea settles in the red chair in the library and snores through *The Romance of Helen Trent* at twelve-thirty on the Philco. Then he gets up, and it's back to the office.

The front door of the church bangs open. A clatter rings out from the stones. Harsh tones cut the air. A German is speaking in Italian, and the priest is answering in a voice barely audible. There's a lot of angry murmuring and stomping of feet.

I tighten the grip on the Sten, kneel and face the trap door. Voices are almost under me. The leader snaps out a couple of words. So do some others. The priest protests, but he sounds pretty weak. A hand smacks a table and metal clangs to the floor, maybe the chalice and candlesticks. He responds like a child confronting an angry parent.

Christ, I feel for him. And I wait for the Germans to move to the back of the church and discover the ladder. Planning what I'll do if they come up here after me. Shoot as many of the bastards as I can? Surrender? Pray like hell? I don't know, I don't know what's going to happen.

The waiting is killing me, the damn suspense. I stiffen. The booted men march off to the nave and the front door. Their clicking resounds as if they're goose stepping. I can even hear them in the piazza heading toward their vehicles, those heels hammering away on the pavement. Then they roar off, leaving a vacuum, a deadly silence. Not even a dog barks. I hold my position, a finger frozen on the trigger. It could be a trick. That board could pop up at any minute, and there they would be firing into the darkness at me. My imagination of disaster.

"*Americano*," the priest whispers right below the trapdoor, "*Tedeschi!*"

"*Si, si,*" I say, walking over and lifting the board and peering down at him in the twilight. He's staring up at me, his face screwed up, his body stiff."Someone say they see you come in church. The *Tedeschi* question me. If they threaten people, I must tell them you here. They do terrible things."

"You want me to go?"

"*Si, Americano.* They find you, burn church."

"And kill you?"

"*Possibile.*"

"Want me to walk out of here in broad daylight and give myself up?"

"*Notte.* I find somebody help you."

"With a car?"

"You go to Padua, *quaranta chilometri,*"

"Can you trust anyone here?"

"*Si*, Angela LeDolce."

"A girl?"

"*Signorina.* She has *bicicletta.*"

"You mean you want me to ride away on a damn bike?"

"*Tandem.*"

"Nobody would stop us?"

"No, no. *Notte.* She has card from her brother to identify you."

"When?"

"We wait for *Tedeschi* go. She see you *notte.*"

"*Parla inglese*?"

"*Poco.*"

"Okay, Padre, I guess it's the best thing. I don't want anyone killed on my account."

"Sad, *Americano, é molto triste.*"

"Those kids and farmers at the Gamberini's. There must have been a dozen or more killed. And all partly because of me."

"The war, *Tedeschi,*" he sighs.

"You have water and a pan? I'm thirsty and I have to go *toilette.* Okay?"

"*Si,* I bring it and Angela. *Partigiana.*"

"*Buono, buono.*" The front door opens. Voices creak away in the quiet of the old church. He hurries off to meet his parishioners, and I close the opening and tiptoe back to my knapsack and lie down.

Riding out of town on a bicycle with a girl named Angela LeDolce. It's crazy. Except in the Dolomites I remember the partisans used girls for couriers. Here, though, who knows what they're used for. I know what they'd be used for in Bari. Pedaling a tandem between the sheets. Some fun. Those days are gone for good. And I've got to get the hell out of here. I can't sit in this attic the rest of the war listening to Mass being said two and three times a day, that bell banging in my ears, thinking of what happened out at the farm. I'd go mad, stark raving mad like Prince Myshkin at the end of Dostoyevsky's *The Idiot.*

Chapter 12

She's different from what I expected, older, taller, fairer, blue eyes, light brown hair, almost blonde. More German than Italian, at least in looks, but all native when she walks wiggling her hips. A white blouse and a short flowered skirt that shows off her long legs and sandals. Not sexy or teasing or anything like that. Not shy either. Just damn pretty. I can't make her out. Except she's eager to help me, brings a potty to pee in, wants to know all about America and hates the Nazis. They killed her uncle and cousin and some good friends. She's heard of a partisan brigade at Ravenna that's led by Americans. It shouldn't take us long to reach there, three or four days. And I resemble a little her brother who died last month of TB. She has his identification card. He was born in 1917, a good year because the birthrate was low then and few were drafted from that group. So I don't have to worry about being suspected of avoiding service. Besides, she'll tell anybody who asks that I'm deaf and dumb and can't be questioned.

"Do you think I'm that old?" I say in a hushed voice. She squints at me though the dwindling candlelight, her nose wrinkling.

"Not when you smile. Only when you look serious."

"*Tedeschi* still around?"

"We no go, wait for them to leave. They search for you. Think you know about *partigiani*. You parachute, no? Have radio?"

"Up north around Belluno. *Molti* partisans. Communists. No radio. Only gun and Dante." I show her both. "You communist?"

"*Si*." She takes a Red scarf out of her bag and grins.

"I was with a Russian colonel who's been fighting on the Eastern front. He's now with the partisans up north. A real tough guy."

"*Buono*."

"*Buono* nothing. I was lucky enough to get away from the bastard and the Garibaldini. Sometimes they can be worse than the *Tedeschi*." She scowls. I tell her the story about Marko's treatment of me. She sits there with her legs crossed watching me, alternately groaning and grinning, twitching and still. What a long torso. She reminds me of a tennis player. The blue eyes pierce me like pins. And she's terribly tense like she's strung up tight and the strings could snap any time and fly all over the attic.

"*Buono* here. You see *buono comunisti*."

102

"You have a bike for me? The *prete* said I could get away with you on a bike."

"*Si*, I ride. You like. Easy go Ravenna. Few hills. Much water. Bridges, canals, rivers. I know places we stay. *Molti paesani*. You like them, they like you."

"Communist?"

"*Si,* everybody communist."

"And will I like you?"

"*Mi*? *Sorella*, you *fratello*." She bends over the guttering candle and kisses me on the cheek, then draws back. Sort of like Maggie. Only she's no chipmunk. More like a doe or a gazelle. I pull her to me and kiss her on the lips. She twists free.

"You like me too much. No *buono*."

"Boyfriend? *Amante*?"

"He in love with war now." She laughs. "*L' afffare della Guerra.* I help defeat *Tedeshi*."

"Yeah, but I bet you love him."

"*Si,* he with *partigani* Bologna. I no see him long time."

"No other guys my age around?"

"Everybody in war but *nonni, bambini, signore, sacerdoti.* I go. *Domani* we leave." She stands up. I rise with her. Our faces practically touch in the dark over the candle flame. I lean over and kiss her again on the lips, lightly this time. She doesn't move.

"*Buono*?" I say.

"*Si*." I put my arms around her, draw her into me. She stiffens. The longer my mouth lingers on hers the softer she becomes. Without any warning she thrusts her tongue between my lips, hugs me tight, her breasts pressing against my chest. The good old boy hardens downs there, rubs against her inner thigh. She squirms away breathing heavily and reaches out and pinches the bulge in my pants, titters. I start to embrace her again, and she retreats toward the trap door. I lose her for a moment in the blackness, just her outline visible.

"You come back?"

"*Si, notte.*"

"We can…"

"*Impossibile.*"

"Nothing's impossible in this country. I've found that out all right."

"*Si, impossibile.*"

"You mean you…"

"*Domani*," she whispers. Her voice is low, deep, and intimate. The closeness strokes me in all the sensitive places.

She lifts the trapdoor and climbs down the ladder to the dusky space below. The church is still except for a few creaks. Only the flickering of the Vigil candles reduces the darkness. I wonder where the priest is.

"*Domani*," she says again in that hushed voice. I leave the board up until I hear a  door close and her footsteps fade away. Then I put  it down and return to my place,  sit down and imagine she's still here talking and gesturing across from me, both of us becoming more familiar. Pee in the pot she brought. If only I can trust her. If only she can help me get away from this place and doesn't turn out to be another countess. I can't stay holed up much longer in this musty storage room.

The next day it's the same thing. The bell wakes me at dawn. The priest comes with water to drink and rolls and pasta as well as water and soap to wash my face and body. Takes away the urine in the pan. I listen to Mass going on below, the women muttering, smelling incense from the thurible. The long afternoon stretches endlessly as I lie by the candlelight waiting for Angela and rereading this canto in the *Inferno* about wailing cranes, doves, and Francesca and her lover  putting down this  book about Lancelot and begin kissing like crazy while Dante seems full of grief and pity realizing what's going  to happens to her in the end.  And I'm thinking of Maggie and she reading Keats and Shelley to me one night at her house and I telling her about their lives but no sex.

After the Angelus she comes up with my supper, cheese and spaghetti, minestrone and wine plus a pot. And we eat with the single flame between us. I ask her to stay all night and talk, tell me about her life. She leans over and pecks me, squeezes my hand, laughs. More relaxed than the last time but still a little uneasy.

"You afraid of the dark?" I say.

"People watch the church now, *poliziotti*, *Fascisti*, *Tedeschi*. No *buono*. *Noi attento*."

"They're still around, huh?"

"They look for you *ovunque.*"

"Anybody question you?"

"*Si*."

"Give you *lire*?"

"No *lire*. No *buono*."

"Anybody been shot, tortured, taken away?"

"Only the people at Gamberinis. No one here."

"Gosh, Angela, I've got to go *sud*, report what's been happening to me and my mission. The officer in charge was killed by Germans. A lot of men are in danger. I'm about the only one left."

"Secret mission? You tell me?"

"I can't. How about tomorrow night? Can't we leave then?"

"I talk to *prete*"

"He with the partisans?"

"*Sympatico poco.* Afraid what they do if they find you here."

"Oh, my God, I don't want anyone else killed because of me. Enough have been already. You *capeech*? Gloomy, pessimistic."

"*Noi* go *domani. Va bene*?"

We embrace again before she drops out of sight. Not so much like brother and sister. Her body pressing against mine gets me so terribly worked up I can hardly let go. She's wearing perfume for the first time. She slips out of my arms, giggles, and glides through the trapdoor and down the ladder to the floor below and vanishes. I shuffle back to the candle, stretch out, and think about jerking off. Pee in the pot she brought.

The trouble is she reminds me so damn much of Maggie who's shorter with shoulder length brown hair and freckles and is always laughing. Except Angela feels sexier, not as brainy, more serious. You could just look at Maggie, a mass of nervous energy, and tell she's a Physics or Math major and her parents, Mary and Steve O' Dell, are probably doctors or professors. Actually, they're chemists that work for DuPont in Wilmington, Delaware and love concerts and operas and don't like me, a good-for-nothing poet. I'll never forget going with them to Seilier's in Wellesley for dinner and the two of them staring at me the whole time, one tall and one short and not saying a word and Maggie talking a blue streak.

I hear a truck in the square and a lot of violent talking that separates into German commands and Italian shrieks. I grab the Sten and the knapsack, crawl over to the opening and drop down without the ladder, a little shaken up by the fall. I recover and hurry out to the altar and through the nave to the front door, walking as softly as I can. Peek out.

A truck stands in the piazza with the motor running and headlights flooding the pavement. At the rear a group of Italians are waiting to board, two women in black and four men in dark coats and white shirts open at the neck. One of them is Angela wearing a coat and hat. Her hands are tied behind her back, and a Kraut is playfully poking a gun muzzle in her rear end while another guy and an officer watch. She spits at them and curses. The officer slaps her. She flinches but doesn't cry out.

I open the heavy door wider, slip down the steps and to the right, keeping in the shadows, crouching low, my finger on the trigger of the Sten. Slowly, reluctantly the Italians enter the rear of the truck with the canvas top. Only Angela is left. I draw closer. The Krauts stand around touching her hair, breasts, ass, laughing, joking. She looks sullen staring at the stones. The officer talks to her in Italian, and she shakes her head. She's as tall as he is and almost as severe-looking in her baggy black dress, brown coat and hat that contrast with his gray-green uniform. If they'd only toss her in back with the others, I'd let go with a blast. But the officer apparently wants her up front with him, and she stands rigid, refusing to budge. He tries to push her. She still doesn't move. He hits her across the face. She lets loose with another blast of curses. I edge nearer. The two soldiers grab her and struggle to drag her to the cab. She wiggles free and falls on the ground challenging them to pick her up.

Right away I crouch and let go with a burst, holding my finger tight and squeezing out the bullets. The officer drops, the other two Krauts run like hell. The truck begins to move. I race to the front and fire into the motor. Everything stops. The lights cut out. The driver bolts from the cab on the opposite side and beats it across the square behind the others.

I fire a few shots after them and run back to the rear where the wounded guy lies in a fetal position clutching himself, moaning. His uniform is soggy. I jerk my hand away from his body and rub it on my trousers. Blood. The wetness numbs me for a second. I pull Angela to her feet, untie her. She thanks me and leaps into the back of the truck where everybody is chattering, crying, stomping their feet on the boards. I yell we've got to hurry and get out of here. One after another they jump down with her help, and I sever the cords around their wrists, hug their hot bodies. The two women are weeping. The men turn to kicking and spitting at the Kraut still lying there moaning. One picks up his revolver and points it at him. I protest his firing it.

"*Parti, parti*," I call out, gazing at body the on the stones. I can't believe I shot him so fast. Like once I pulled the trigger I couldn't stop.

They scatter, and I stand staring at the dark form curled up in that crazy way groaning, wanting to do something to help him but knowing I've got to get out of there. Soon the whole place will be filled with Germans.

"*Avanti*," Angela says taking my hand, "*Subito. Tedeschi.*" I face her and she kisses me on the check."

"Bikes?"

"We hide. No *bicicletta*."

"In the church?"

"House. I know house. No *buono*."

And she pulls me toward an alley across from the stalled truck that looks like a tent set up in the empty piazza. I can't understand why nobody appears after all the commotion. Is the whole town scared out of its wits? Where are the Germans? The priest is the only one to show. He materializes out of a narrow passageway like some apparition.

"Sorry," I say to him.

"*Molto male, Americano.*"

"You mean for the whole town?"

"Take people away, *esecuzioni.*"

"Did you want me to let them have Angela for God's sake?"

"No, no, you do right."

"Don't worry. We're not going back to the church."

"*Buono.* Angela help you. They will be looking for her. You go *subito.*"

"Thanks for everything," I say reaching for his hand and shaking it as firmly as I can. His grip is limp. He sighs. "Someday I'll be back and help you out any way I can." He embraces me rather stiffly, hugs Angela, kisses her on the cheek. She tells him in Italian to take care of her parents and to do all he can to prevent anything from happening to them. She will return. He should inform the Germans that the American has gone. Nobody in the town knows him, nobody hides him. I stress if they harm anyone, they will be punished after the war.

"*Si*, I tell them, " he says. "I warn you once, Angela, remember, not join *partigiani*. No *buono*. All this killing, not bring peace, only more killing."

"It kept her alive," I break in.

"*Si*," Angela says. "I go with *Americano*. He *amico*. He needs me."

"Your *mamma*, your *papà.*"

"I come back help them. Now *morte ai Tedeschi*." There's an abrupt lift in her voice. She grabs my hand, and we start running down the alley. I glance over my shoulder. The priest stands at the entrance to the square, only the shape of his cassock visible like some great bat perched and ready to fly off.

"*Dove?*" I say.

"Padua, Ferrara, Ravenna. No road. No *bicicletta*. Take long time. No one stop us. We find *Americani*. They take you *sud.*"

"*Va bene, va bene*," I say almost breathless. We reach the country, and she slows down to a trot as we cross a field and head for a cluster of farmhouses. Behind us the town stands solid on a slight rise like a dark, low-lying rock, the campanile looming above the huddled buildings. Lighted vehicles are moving toward it in a hurry. The noise of their engines barely reaches us.

"*Tedeschi*," she points.

"Will they look for us over here?"

". *Dovunque.* We no stop. We walk all night, find a place to stay during the day. We safe. You stay with me, no? *Buono guida.*"

"Gosh, yes, Angela. What do you think after what's happened? I've only got you now to depend on to get me out of up here and go to the coast, Ravenna, Cervia."

"It is *molti chilometri, molti notti.*"

"You sure we can find places to stay?"

"We find them. I know."

"And *mangia*?"

"I find food. We stay in the country. No towns, cities. You have gun?"

"Only my Sten and not much ammo left."

"I too." She pulls a small revolver from inside her bra. It fits in the palm of her hand. "They no see when they search me."

"You a good shot?"

"*Si.*" She sticks the muzzle in my ribs and laughs. And I think of Maggie tickling me with her slide rule during a walk around Lake Waban at Wellesley.

We tramp on past farmhouses and empty villas, over canals and railroad tracks. There are few lights. It's flat land and dry. I can imagine what it's like when the rain comes. Clumps of chestnut and beech and polar trees dot the countryside. After a couple of hours we reach a stone hut off by itself. Angela goes in and lights a candle with matches I brought from the church in my knapsack. The place is bare except for some straw. There are no windows. The floor is dirt. We lie down side by side on the soft earth without saying a word. I reach over and touch her hand. She touches mine. We don't move.

"This the house you promised me?" I say. She laughs. "*Buona notte.*"

"*Buona notte*, Tony." She chuckles, and I put a hand on her breast and press down lightly. Not for long though. I'm asleep in a minute, and the next thing I know the sun is pouring through the entrance and Angela is gone. Not a trace of her. The light is dazzling. I hear voices far off, get up, go out and look around. Everywhere lush fields and little farms, vineyards and small trees and past them a red-brick *campanile*. In the distance loom oil refineries and factories and beyond towers and domes and brown roofs. We must be near Venice. She's probably gone there to hide. Deserting me after I saved her life, and she told me all those things about my trusting her. The bitch! I go back in the hut and plop down on the dirt and stew over how I'll ever get to Ravenna. Wasn't that where Dante ended his days? Oh, for a Virgil to lead me through this murky

108

maze. First no radio, then not much ammo, now no guide. Alone. But not the usual poet crying in the wilderness. I simply don't know where the hell I am or where the hell I'm going. And once I open my mouth I'll give myself away. And that will be that. I'll never get out of this inferno.

Damn her! Goddamn her! She leads me away from her hometown to prevent reprisals, to escape being shot herself, then deserts me after I saved her neck. Who in the hell can you trust up here anyway? Either they're like Bill or Mario committed and killed off, or like Marko and the countess double-crossing you. At least she left some bread and cheese for breakfast.

I think about vamoosing but decide to wait until night. Better to be lost than captured. So I'm gathering my stuff at twilight and getting set to shove off when a figure blocks the entrance. I glance up with my Sten at the ready.

"*Buonasera*," a voice rings out. Angela confronts me now wearing a beret and a leather jacket, wool shirt, trousers, heavy flat shoes.

"What the hell?" I burst out. "Where did you get that getup?"

"I see a friend, Antonio Bardini, in Mestre."

"*Partigiano?*"

"S*i*. Then she gives me in rough English his biography. Arrested 1935 for anti-Fascist work, escapes and goes to France to edit *Il Populo*. He fights in the Garibaldi Brigade in Spain in 1936. He is hurt at Guadalajara. When he leaves the country, he becomes a prisoner in France and is rescued by the Maquis. Last winter he is in Rome, no *partigiano*."

"He gets around all right, doesn't he? What's he doing now?"

"With the *partigiani* again but no fight. Bad heart. He plans raids, writes for *diario segreto*. See, he give me this. He tells me I need it." She holds up a 9mm sub-machine gun and laughs. "Two *pistole*. I help you, no?"

"Did you tell him about me?"

"*Niente*. Just say I go to Ravenna and be with my *amante*. We go, *va bene*?"

"Did he give you any food?"

"*Si*." She pats the bag over her shoulder.

"Hear anything?"

"They look for us, *Fascisti, Tedeschi ovunque*."

"What about your town."

"Two people are shot in the piazza. The *prete* tried to stop it, and they take him away. *Possibile morto*. I not hear about *mamma, papà*."

"Think we'll make it with everybody after us?"

109

"No roads, cities, talk to people. *Attento*."

"Angela, why are you doing this? Tell me straight, will you?"

"I like you, Tony. I like *Americano*. I hate *Tedeschi*, *Fascisti*. They kill *famiglia*, *amici*. *Vendetta*."

"How do you know you like me that much? Gosh, we've only been together a short time, hardly any at all. You've never told me much about yourself. I've never told you much about myself."

"I sleep with you."

"Not like that."

"How do you know? You never wake up. You *russare*." She makes a noise in her nose and laughs.

"Don't tell me I did something in my sleep I don't remember."

"No, *niente*. We *fratello*, *sorella*, no? *Buono*. In war everybody *fratello*, *sorella*, *prete*, *suora*. We go."

It's a long night walking over fields boarded by rows of poplars or willows, down dirt roads, past small brick houses under a low black sky. Once in a while we pass a Palladian-styled villa. Only stopping to eat and drink a cup of wine, talk, pee, shit. She tells me about her father. He fought in the Ethiopian War in 1935-1936 and was wounded in the leg. He was a cook. About her boyfriend, Giulio Alberti, an engineering student in Turin and now in Bologna fighting with the partisans. Maybe after she takes me to Ravenna she will join him. She cannot go back to her town until after the war and maybe not even then either if her mother and father are dead.

"You going to marry him?"

"*Possibile*."

"Work for the communists?"

"Ah, *si*. You?"

"I'm a poet. I write poetry." She laughs.

"You make *molti lire* writing poetry?"

"Who knows? Maybe."

"*Poeti* no kill *Tedeschi*."

"What do they do, write poems about them?"

"*Sognare*, no kill."

"Dreaming? You can do both, can't you? You wouldn't be here today if I hadn't shown up in the piazza."

"*Possibile*. Dream."

"You have the typical romantic idea of poets."

"They have romantic idea of themselves."

"You think I do?"

"You no *poeta*. You want to be."

110

"I write poems. Want to hear one?" She nods. I recite the sonnet on passing through the Strait of Gibraltar that I did for a French agent out of Algiers. It ends: 'We sail by the Rock in the wine-dark sea / Drunk with innocence, haunted by history.'"

"Where do you publish *poesia*?"

"A military secret."

"You joking with me. Who say you *poeta*?"

"Who says you're a communist?"

"I have card, hat, song?" She starts to sing and laughs. "All you have is *versi*."

"You're more romantic than I am."

"Ah, *si*. You have Shakespeare. I have Lenin. We see who wins the war." And I think of Maggie with her Einstein.

At dawn we spot Padua ahead, a mass of buildings and a few dim lights. All around us are cottages of workers who belong to the big estates. Angela says we will walk west of the city and climb into the Euganean Hills. *Bella campagna*. She will sneak in during the day to visit friends. There are *molti partigiani*.

We find another abandoned shed, sleep awhile, and then she takes off for town at noon. Her comrades live near the university, which she calls Bo." She hopes to see them at the Caffe Pedrocchi near the Piazza Cavour. It is the largest in Europe. She gives me her 9mm sub-machine gun and tells me if she's not back by eight o'clock to head for the hills and Ferrara without her. She will try to bring me a radio. I tell her what kind. She shakes her head.

She doesn't come back until nine, and once more I'm ready to take off without her and start looking for signs to Ferrara thirty kilometers away. She runs toward our little shed breathing hard, waving her hands, crying out in a low voice, "Tony, Tony, *parti, parti!*"

She crashes into me, and we embrace at the doorway. Her body is sweaty, her clothes wet.

"They follow me," she says hardly able to speak.

"You mean…"

"I leave Enrico, see this man in Fiat. He behind me past the station. I go different way, fool him. He stay behind. I no lose him."

"He recognize you?"

"*Possibile. Polizia* suspect Enrico and follow his friends. *Possibile* one a *spia*. Padua headquarters for the *Tedeschi* Military Command of the Veneto Region."

"So you think he followed you here. Why the hell did you go in there anyway? You're taking too many chances, Angela. We'll never make it if you do dumb things like that. I'll never reach Ravenna, Cervia, find a boat.

"I find *Americani* for you. They help you."

"Where?"

"Below Ravenna in the pine woods, Pineta di Classe. *Molti poeti. Molti partigiani.* A Garibaldi Brigade led by Lupo. Maybe it's the 29th they say is near there." I never hear of him. Enrico say he *buono* communist."

"Any radio?"

"No. *Parti. Va bene?*"

I give her back her gun, gather up mine and my knapsack and we start out. A couple of cars approach at a high speed, and we dive in a ditch. They shoot past. She says they are from the Black Brigade and mutters something low and hard in Italian. I ask her what it is, and she refuses to translate. Then she replies, *"Figli di puttane."* It hits me suddenly, and I say the expression sounds a lot rougher in English: Sons of..." She laughs.

We jump up and continue on until another car appears, and once more we have to drop into a ditch. On our feet again we leave the road and tramp across a field toward the hills. Padua fades away on the left.

"We lose them?" I say after an hour of silent hiking.

*"Possibile."*

"Ravenna?"

"Enrico says *grossa brigata. Molti armi.* Lupo *eroe. Tedeschi* afraid."

"Scared of the partisans, huh? Will we make it?"

*"Si,* we make it." She grabs my hand and laughs. The gesture reminds me again of Maggie. And I wonder where she is tonight. Probably in the 8th Street apartment near the Village Barn she wrote about and working on a secret government project. She could end the war before I do and prove that physicists really make things happen while poets only imagine they do.

I turn and look at Angela matching me stride for stride. Her submachine gun hanging off her shoulder, her beret resting on the side of her head, jacket unbuttoned, shirt opened at the neck. No Wellesley girl, that's for sure. Never heard of physics or Einstein. But somehow I feel content and secure with her, more content and secure than I've felt with anyone for a long time. She may not be a Virgil, a war hero, or a revolutionist who fought in Spain, just a sexy tomboy. But what a great girl to have as a guide through the circles of hell. If only she were Maggie.

112

Chapter 13

It takes us a week to reach Ferrara. Partly because we have to climb through the steep wooded slopes of the Euganean Hills southwest of Padua to avoid a German garrison at Monselice, a picturesque old town at the foot of the mountain topped by a castle. Partly because we spend twenty-four hours in a deserted villa south of Rovigo between the Adige and the Po river and finally make love on a canopied bed. It all happened so unexpectedly, so naturally. We wake up at three in the afternoon, turn over facing each other, and do it without even speaking, without even removing everything. She doesn't cry out or moan or get emotionally hot and start spouting mush after the orgasm, only looks up at me flushed and peaceful. And I don't debate with myself the way I did with Maggie back in Washington at the Willard, coming out of the bathroom in my mustard-colored shorts and seeing her naked for the first time, both of us tittering and uncertain what to do next or how to do it but determined to go through with the act of love before maybe never facing each other again. I open my eyes and feel my thing sticking up in the air through my drawers. Angela notices and laughs, puts a hand on it, tickles the tip. And we're off feeling the holy hell out of each other, kissing, sucking, caressing, and not thinking about rubbers or diaphragms or withdrawal before the climax. Bodies moving up and down, up and down faster and faster, her legs around me tighter and tighter until the bubble bursts and we sink into each other breast upon breast. I slide off and we lie there side by side gazing up at the roses on the white ceiling.

"You know Shelley wrote a poem about the hills we just went through. About how rotten he felt and how great the atmosphere was. You read him and you think you're bad off, kid. Then you read Dante and you think how bad off the world is and how you've had it pretty good after all compared to the way things could be compared to his life if what he's writing could be partly autobiographical. Shelley never would have made it through hell even with Milton as his guide. Gosh, I'm tired." She gazes at me puzzled by my long-winded rambling.

"We stay, no?" She raises up and leans over and kisses me on the lips, puts a hand on old Pete, who has gone limp. "Everything *buono*."

"So far going good. When we get to Ferrara I'm not so sure."

"No one follow. We lose them. You like Arquà Petrarca?"

113

"He's great. Nobody will ever put up a bust and a pink marble sarcophagus in Albany honoring me when I die, you can bet on that. I should have stuck to love sonnets."

"I make love, not read. Too much poetry make you sad. You have no fun. You know what you say?"

"Fuck?"

"*Si, si*, flunk."

I start to get up to go to the bathroom down the hall, look at again at the Po delta country stretching far away under the low gray sky, the canals, the green fields full of vines, the rows of poplars. Once back she reaches over and pulls me down beside her, strokes me all over. And, Jesus, I'm stiff again in no time. She guides my hand to the target and I'm once more riding a cock-horse to Banbury Cross, galloping faster and faster, and she's laughing and bouncing with me. A lot looser than Maggie, but I can't stop thinking of her and imagining she's with me. And, boy, does Angela know where to touch and how to build the pressure, harden the little guy, open her legs, suck me in deep. These Italian women! They're fantastic.

Dusk is falling and we're still in bed, not hungry, not eager to stir, just lying there lazy-like staring up at the ceiling not saying a word, both naked. Her sinewy legs stretching sometimes around me, sometimes under me, and sometimes on top of me. Touching her skin so smooth and warm and soft. I can't get over how different she is lying beside me. I keep moving a hand over her breasts and belly and between her legs, and she purrs for a while, then giggles like a little girl. The more we do it the more eager she becomes until one time she breaks out in a wild cry and shouts, "*Subito, subito*" as if she were urging me to hurry up, the *Tedeschi* are coming. After a burst of energy and the climax there's a moment of silence and utter relaxation.

I tell myself we can't keep this up, and I shouldn't be doing it. Besides, I think I hear somebody outside snooping around. It could be the one she said followed her in Padua. I start for my gun. Every time I do I feel her on top of me, squeezing and tickling, probing, pinching with those long fingers, and we're at it again rolling around in the big bed, both of us panting away.

We cease at midnight, drained, my mind a blank. I look over at Angela asleep, arms at her side, legs straight out. Funny, how much she reminds me of a German girl, the hair, the chin, the hips. Everything firm and angular. Yet when making love everything supple, round, and sensual.

I wake up with a start and listen. Someone is definitely outside. I hear footsteps and crouch down, move to the window to peek out.

114

There's only the flat featureless landscape stretching to the horizon, low buildings, few lights. I spot a couple of ghost-like figures gliding among the few trees in the yard. All the doors and windows downstairs locked. But we broke in through a side door. They could use it too. I come back to the bed and lightly touch Angela,

"They're out there."

"*Tedeschi*?"

"Maybe. No cars or trucks. A couple of bodies moving. Could be some guys looking for a place to stay."

She leaps up and scurries around for her clothes. I do the same. We grab our guns.

"Go downstairs?" I say.

"No, we wait."

"Think they're the only ones who followed you in Padua?"

"*Possibile*. When I tell Enrico I go to Ravenna, somebody hear and he come to Rovigo and ask if anybody see us and they tell him we go to a villa."

"Want to fight it out with them?"

"Better than running away, no?"

"Hiding is better."

"Under the bed?" She pokes me and laughs.

"I can't be captured. I know too much, and it could affect a lot of people. We can't take any chances, Angela. I've got to get to the front somewhere, sneak through, report to OSS headquarters."

"Give myself up, they leave?"

"No, good. Never do that. Christ, no!"

"Go downstairs and face them, shoot them."

"There could be too many. That would be suicide." She shakes her head and I explain.

"We stay here too long. No *buono*, Tony."

"You regret what we do?"

"No regret, no *buono*. No stop to make love in war. Only *cagna* do that." I put an arm around her. She shrugs it off. "No *buono*, Tony, no *buono*."

"You can always stop to make love no matter what's happening."

"*Poesia*, too."

"That's right. You don't have to give up the essential things just because there's a war going on."

"I give *molto*." She stares right through me. I can feel her eyes focusing on my face through the darkness, her breathing close.

She pulls me forward, and we creep down the stairs. A door creaks. We halt, stay still. I tell her to check the rear, I'll do the front.

Find out how many men there are and where they're positioned. We separate and then meet in the hall. She notes she saw three shapes among the trees. I did too. We could be facing at least six, probably more. Too many to shoot it out with.

"I tell them *arrrendiamo*. They not know you here. They come, you shoot."

"After the surrender, yeah, kill six or seven just like that. No, they'd get you first. The best thing is to go back upstairs, jump out of a window we unlock when we hear them coming up and shoot it out with a couple of guys below. It's only a short distance to the ground."

"I hurt my leg, lose my gun. We go to closet by *bagno*. They find us, we fight, they no find us, we safe."

It sounds crazy but I agree. So we go back upstairs, grab our stuff, lock ourselves in the shallow, narrow room at the end of the hall by the bathroom and wait. The space is barely big enough for the two of us and stinks like an outhouse.

They stomp up as soon as we're settled, coming in the same door we did. I count three different pairs of footsteps. They tramp from room to room with flashlights shouting in Italian, arguing, banging doors. At last they stand outside our hiding place, shake the knob. We inch back against the wall shoulder to shoulder, guns ready. *"Niente,"* someone yells. He stops yanking the knob and kicking at the door. A couple of others join him with flashlights. They hammer and tug. The lock almost gives way. A few more pulls and bangs, and they'll have us. The hinges even strain. We crouch down waiting, our bodies wedged into each other. Then the invaders walk down the hall. I listen for the different footsteps retreating. Angela stands up and moves forward, puts her hand on the handle. The air is suffocating, putrid. A strange noise erupts from her throat. She's going to be sick. I put a hand over her mouth, hold her. She wriggles free of my grip and edges forward again.

"One is still here," I whisper into her ear. 'He's waiting to see if we're hiding." She freezes, not even breathing for a second. In the hall a floorboard creaks, downstairs a door closes. Voices grow dim. The house is quiet.

Fifteen, twenty minutes pass. It's getting harder and harder to swallow in the stinking, stagnant air, harder and harder to remain motionless, not even crooking a finger. Angela is stiff as a board leaning on me. The man in the hall stirs, takes a deep breath. His pants rustle. I can picture him in his uniform poking around, harkening to every noise, sweating, his gun poised. After an hour he tiptoes down the stairs. We relax, drawing away from the door.

*"Parti?"* she says in a tremulous voice.

"In a few minutes". Looks like we're free." And we are because when we sneak out of the closet and feel our way downstairs, they're gone. All we have to do now is leave the grounds before daylight. Which might not be so easy. They won't give up the search for us that quickly. They could still be out there.

We delay an hour, then grope our way to the back door we entered, crack it open, and squeeze outside to stand against the wall. I toss a stick. The sound magnifies and a couple of men come running from the trees. They stand there like dark figures with guns at ready. I watch them hunt for the source of the noise and move to the left, calling in hushed voices to each other. I try it again, this time tossing a stick to the right. Several others come running, but they don't communicate this time. So when they disappear, we take off between the two groups not worrying about who else might be around. And it's clear all the way to a ditch. We plop down on our stomachs and peer out over the top as if we were in a trench. No one in sight.

"*Buono, buono,*" Angela says, kissing me on the cheek.

"I bet they'll be back."

"Ferrara, Ravenna? *Possibile. Attento.*"

"No more stopping at empty villas, huh?" She hits me. "What the hell was that for? You're the one who started it." She puts a hand on my crotch. It's bulging again, but I'm not thinking sex. I'm thinking about those bastards out there waiting for us. Like the time I was just a kid horseback riding at Camp Timber in Maine one summer, and my pony rears up and almost throws me and I hang on to the knob of the western saddle for dear life and for the first time in my life have a hard-on.

"No, no," she scolds. "I no start anything. You do." She tickles me on the ribs.

"Hey, it's not that now, its nerves. *Capeesh?*"

"*Pazzo, pazzo.*" She quips. And I agree, but that's the way things are with me sometimes, crazy, always crazy.

We stand up and start out across the flat watery landscape toward Ferrara, keeping off main roads, cutting through fields, avoiding dumpy-looking farmhouses with their chickens and birds, oxen and pigs. A dull dreary country, straight lines of willows dividing the land into strips. Short poles jutting out from stunted trunks supporting vines that string out over the plain. Beyond lie endless rice fields stretching away under the night sky. I recall the delta country I passed through on the way to basic training at North Camp Fort Hood, Texas, the muddy water, the iron bridges, those lonely-looking towns. But it wasn't as monotonous and desolate as this place. The Po is no Mississippi. Huck never would have made it floating down this river. Maybe an Acheron or a Styx when the Allies start to cross it with Charon ferrying the dead. Only Dante could find his way through such a mournful region, and I bet even he would have a rough time.

We walk at least ten miles before the sun comes up, and another two or three before it gets bright and we have to dive in a ditch again. Angela insists they haven't given up searching for us. She's certain the next attempt to grab us will be at Ferrara. Meanwhile we find a small barn and sleep dressed side by side in the old straw. No love making. We're both too tense and too worn out, and I keep thinking of Maggie. Unable to sleep I'm hearing animals and peasants moving outside along with suspicious sounding vehicles. But none come close. Once a farmer looks in, and I wake Angela and she talks to him. We're brother and sister going home to Ferrara. We've been to Venice visiting our grandmother. I play deaf and dumb. The old man leaves us, and we lie there for a while unable to close our eyes. More and more I'm beginning to have doubts about reaching the front and the British or the Americans. OSS has probably given me up for dead anyway. At least if I do kick off around here I have great company. Petrarch up in the Euganean Hills, Dante over at Ravenna. I tell that to Angela. She laughs.

"You forget Tasso at Ferrara, Ariosta at Reggio Emilia. That's all you think about, poets. Not think about war, what happens to people after it. We liberate them from *Inglesi e Americani.*"

"*Viva la Russia.*"

"*Sí. Italia Comunista buono.*"

We wake early, eat some bread and cheese, start up again in the darkness. To take my mind off everything I concentrate on the poets who once prowled these shabby medieval towns, haunted this moody, monotonous land of canals and vines, sugar-beets and rice fields, swamps and marshes. Like places in Dante. What a godforsaken corner of Italy. Hard to imagine so many writers living and dying here away from Rome and Florence and Venice. I wonder what they ever saw in this place.

"You *silenzio,*" Angela says."

"Listening."

"Nobody follow. I bring you to *Americani.* Trust Angela. She *buona signorina.*"

"Do you trust me?"

"*Si, sempre.*" She hugs me. I hug her back. We're on the outskirts of a village. No one is around. The brick buildings look abandoned. Some windows are broken, doors missing, trash littering the stones. The *campanile* stands against the night sky like the trunk of a dead tree. We decide to walk through instead of going around. Halfway to the end of the main street, I stop, I don't know why. There's no noise, no light. Just a feeling something's not quite right. I duck in a doorway and yank Angela in with me.

"You see something, hear someone?"

"I feel something, sense someone."

"What?"

"A trap."

"*Non capisco*." I explain.

Figures are coming toward us from both ends of the street huddled, shadowy figures vaguely visible against the buildings. They're moving slowly, steadily. I try the door behind me. It's locked. I call in a whisper for someone to let us in. No response.

"Surrender?" I say.

"No, no. I show you." She slides down the wall four or five doorways, waits, then starts firing, the bullets spitting furiously from her 9mm sub-machine gun. She stops and slips back to me in a hurry. The men advancing from the closer end of the street pass by a few feet away and kneel down. She tugs on my sleeve and quietly pulls me toward an alley. Just as we're about to dart down it, one of the stalking figures turns and fires at us. I raise my Sten to answer back. She pushes it away and shoves me forward.

"Run, run. I stay."

"You're nuts. They'll kill you."

"I faster. You see." And I think, Christ, not another Mario. She pokes her gun in my gut, and I beat it out of there. She hugs the wall and lets loose with a couple of rounds. The noise rebounds off the buildings, bullets zinging everywhere. The whole village seems about to blow.

I hit the soggy field and she catches up yelling, S*ubito, subito!*" Guns are rattling behind us, lights flashing, footsteps pounding. She passes me with those long legs and strong shoulders pumping. I call out that I've got to stop. *Fatica.* I drop on my stomach, crawl over the bank of a canal. She jumps down beside me and we glance back toward the houses. Just beyond them a group of men are firing widely in our direction, waving lights, shouting.

"They come after us?" I say.

"They on the road. They afraid *partigiani* get them. They think *molti* down here, no?"

She is right. They stick to the road, content to yell and shout away in safety, spraying spotlights over the field. Nobody comes after us. And soon everything is quiet again.

"A close call," I say. "We never should have gone in there. It was stupid. They must have been following us after we left the villa. And we thought we got away."

"*Spia*." She spits. "*Cacca*."

"Who do you think they want the worst?"

We climb up the canal bank and gaze around. No sign of soldiers or trucks.

"You have secret," she says. "You kill officer. I help you. They no like *Americani*."

"I wish I could take you *sud* with me."

"No, no, Tony. *Niente.* I follow like dog. They think *prostituta*. Here I fight. *Soldato*. I make things *buono*."

"You mean you want to paint the town Red?"

"*Non capisco*."

"Make a new heaven and a new earth. A big Red new world."

"Ah, *si, si*. A better world for the people who work in the sugar-beet and rice fields. You see how they live. Like slaves in your country. We go."

She starts out across the field. I stand there a minute watching her, the long strides, the square shoulders, the head erect, the machine gun hanging off her shoulder. To take such a gutsy girl down south and then to the States would be great. But I can't give Maggie up. In love with two at the same time. It's been like having sex with both of them, one I'm going to marry if I get out of here, the other I have to eventually leave yet wishing I didn't have to. We get along so well. And I bet if I put the pressure on maybe after the war Angela would come home with me. But it can't be. Another Francesca. Same church, different pew.

I run to catch up, kiss her on the back of the neck, squeeze her hand, saying over and over again, "*Grazie, grazie*."

"You *buono soldato*," she says walking beside me.

"How about *buono amante*?" She laughs.

"Only Italians are *buono amante*."

"I'm learning."

"*Si*, you are <u>buono</u> *studente*." And we swing along gaining momentum under the black delta sky. A cool rain begins falling. I'm weary as hell. Yet somehow I seem to be getting my second wind the way I used to do on those hot dusty ten mile marches down in Texas. Only it's not so easy. My legs aren't as tired as my brain. This country can drain you. There's too damn much of everything, war, love, religion, history, art.

"Have you ever had a better *studente*?"

"School not over yet. A long way to go."

120

"Some school you teach in."

"You no like?"

"I have a feeling I'm going to flunk."

"*Non capisco.*"

"*Fallo.*"

"*Fallo?*" She titters.

"What's so funny?" She touches me in the crotch and says, "No *fallo. Molto buono.*

I don't quite get the point but laugh anyway. There's something about being with her that just makes me feel keyed up and ready to hit the road running no matter how weary I am.

Chapter 14

The next night after crossing the Po we see the blacked out buildings of Ferrara on the horizon. An air raid is in progress, searchlights sweeping the sky, bombers darting in and out of them, tracers flashing like lights in a pinball machine. Explosions rip through the night one after another. The earth shakes under us. A lot closer than the attack on Naples I watched from the barracks part of the OSS palace above Caserta when I first came to the country and had a real balcony seat for the show.

We locate an empty hut, settle in, and Angela insists to reach Ravenna we have to have help. We'll never make it on our own. We'll need a car or truck and a few partisans along for protection. Too many *Tedeschi, polizia, spie.* So she's visiting some *amici* in the city the way she did at Padua. She promises to be more careful this time.

"You sure it's safe? We're closer to the front now. They'll be more *Tedeschi*. And a curfew after that raid. Be looking for you, too, for both of us."

"I *attenta.* I know the city. Not worry, Tony. My country. I *buona signorina* ." She kisses me on the lips. "You *buono* guy. We have *buono* time, no?"

"Not a good *soldato*?"

"All *soldati* are *buoni*."

She disappears out the door and cuts across the field toward a row of rundown brick houses near a sugar refinery. And I go back and stretch out on the floor listening for voices, footsteps, engines. I fall asleep. And the first thing I hear waking up is children nearby playing soccer, laughing, yelling. It seems years since I've heard kids carrying on like that. All those I've seen down in Naples and Bari seemed to be engaged in selling and begging, bartering and pimping. What a mixed up childhood I would have had living here. Where would I have gone to college and what authors would I have read? No Thoreau and Whitman, Wolfe and Eliot, that's for sure. Instead plenty of Petrarch and Dante. I bet I would have memorized a lot of lines from the *Divine Comedy*, especially those in canto five devoted to Francesca and her lover.

She doesn't come back at twilight. Not at midnight. I'm running short on bread and cheese. The wine is gone. I try to sleep again. In the morning she's still missing. I gather it must be Sunday since church bells are ringing more frequently, and I don't hear much traffic. The rain is beating down hard. Somehow I associate Sunday with dull days, nothing to do but attend the eleven o'clock service at St. Andrews with Mother, listen to Mr. Friendly talk about women who spend too time with their knees under the bridge table while his wife sits in the front pew timing the sermon and worrying about the roast in the oven. How remote all that seems now, how empty and yet how when I get back home, if I ever do, it will be the only reality there is, and this will be the remote, unreal stuff, what's going on in my inferno and in Dante's.

In the afternoon I venture out to find food and wine. Nothing is open, few people are around. And those that appear look at me not just as a stranger but as a homeless person. And I'm back in the dirty hovel waiting for another night and Angela's return. Thumbing through the *Inferno* by candlelight, I hit on Dante riding in a boat through a swamp toward Dis, the city of Lucifer and the flaming tombs. When he arrives, the Furies threaten to have Medusa turn him and Virgil to stone. The poor guy could be thinking he'll never get through hell now and return to the world without his guide. Too true, old mole. You can't be a good poet without a master leading the way. I don't have a soul, do I? Only Angela, but where is she?

Slowly the idea grows that she won't be coming back. They've seized her. She took one too many chances. Or else she's given me up as a hopeless cause and joined a partisan brigade. Tired of leading me around by the nose and being chased by Germans. Besides, I'm only an American to her, not Tony Defreest from Albany, New York, not part of her life.

At three o'clock in the morning I hear footsteps splashing in the puddles outside. The rain is beating down harder and harder. It's colder too, the floor feeling damper. Could this be it? I grab my Sten, blow out the candle, and retreat to a corner waiting for the door to open.

"*Ciao, Americano*," a voice whispers. I don't answer.

"*Americano, amico.*" I keep quiet, suspecting a trick.

"Lupo, Garibaldi brigade, Pineta di Classe, Ravenna, Angela."

"*Va bene. Parli inglese?*"

"*Si.*" A bulky finger blocks the doorway, stamps his feet, and enters. He shines a flash around the interior and finds me. He smiles. "Tony?"

"That's me. *Momento.*" I relight the candle on the dirt floor and scrutinize him. He's tall and bearded with brown eyes and a thick neck. He's wearing a leather jacket and cap, rough dark trousers, heavy shoes. I take him for a workman or a truck driver. He has the reticence of a big man about him, a softness that contracts with the course features and the rugged shoulders. Older than most of the partisans I've met. He says his name is Buffo and he's from Ferrara.

"*Dove*, Angela?" I mutter. He stops smiling and stares at me.

"*Tedeschi*. She walks in Via delle Volte, old part of town. They take her. She not coming back."

"*Polizia*?"

"SS."

"Oh, my God!"

"We see them take her. *Male, paesano*."

"So she's in prison. And they're probably interrogating her, aren't they, putting the screws on?" I look at him. He stares straight through me.

"*Si*. They ask about you."

"Me?"

"They want you, not her."

"How do you know that?"

"We have *spie*. They work for SS."

"They're torturing her?"

"*Si*, if she not talk."

"Has she yet?"

"We find out *subito*."

"I better get out of here, huh? If she breaks down and tells where I am, they'll be after me pretty quick."

"Angela no talk. She is *forte, molta forte*."

"There's no way you can rescue her? You can't attack the prison with your men?"

"*Molti morti*."

"Then she's doomed. They'll kill her just the way they did the major up at Belluno. Hanged him from a steam pipe because he wouldn't talk, made it look like a heart attack."

"No *morta*. They say she go free if you give up. They know you with her."

"Me? Give myself up to the SS?"

"*Si, paesano*."

"But then..." I look away into a dusky corner. "You want me to..."

"I come see. Angela tell me where you are, what you do, where you go. We talk long time before they take her. She love you *molto*. She say you love her."

"You sure they would free her?"

"*Si*."

124

"But I can't. Then I'd be the one they torture. They'd force me to tell them a lot of stuff I know. A lot of people would lose their lives. I'm in OSS, on a secret mission. *Capeesh?*"

"*Si, capisco.* They say if you love her, you will give yourself up to save her."

"No, no, it has nothing to do with love. You can't mix the two things like that. Impossible. I can't save her under those conditions. Too late. I've got to report to my headquarters."

"You save yourself, *Americano.*"

"I'm not thinking of myself, damn it, I'm thinking of the war and the oath I took when I joined the army and OSS, the secret stuff I know that could be used by the enemy, codes, missions. drop areas, plans. I can't betray anybody. You've got to rescue her, damn it. The *partigiani* do it?"

"*Impossibile.*" He gazes sternly at me over the flame.

"What about something else? Isn't there anything you could promise them? You won't attack for a couple of weeks, not blow up bridges, detrail trains, Things like that."

"They want you. They know who you are, what you do. They know you from American Intelligence and have *informazione.*"

"Yeah, I bet they know all about me by now. The bastards!" And I remember the major and his mission to Bolzano and wonder if the countess talked to save her skin. "Sorry, I can't do that." I study him. "*Capeesh*, Buffo? I know too much about the partisans and missions. A lot of your men could lose their lives if I talked. You too."

"Angela die if you not help her."

"But there's a war going on. You have to think of that, not just Angela. Your friends have to realize what my giving myself up might mean for them."

"They not know you. They only know Angela. *Trieste, paesano.* You no help? You pay them *molti lire* they let you go. *Americani* rich."

"What are you going to do if I refuse, deliver me anyway? Is that why you came here? Take me prisoner, exchange me for her?"

"Some say bring you to *Tedeschi.* You not one of them. They love Angela. She *partigiana.*"

"What if they knew I carry a secret that could end the war in Italy, and if the *Tedeschi* found out about it they could prevent that from happening?"

"You have a secret to end the war *Italia?*"

"I've been carrying it around for weeks. My major was killed because he wouldn't reveal it. Now I've got to get back to *Americani*, tell them what's going on. If I don't the whole plan could blow up. The war will go on, thousands of people could die." The sweat is pouring out of me despite the cold damp air. "Angela *non capisco*. I bet any money she wouldn't want me to give myself up and destroy everything. I'm sure she wouldn't. She's a good soldier, a good communist. She knows the war is bigger than she is."

"*Molto prezioso*." Buffo says softly.

"I suppose you could put it that way. She is valuable. This is not just about Italy but the whole war."

"The whole war?" He frowns.

"It would have worldwide repercussions."

"*Non capisco*."

"That's what might happen." His small eyes pin me down. The great bearded head looks enormous in the flickering light of the hut.

"You don't believe me, do you?" He doesn't respond, only stands there staring, his features hardening in the candlelight. "If I had a radio and could send a message to the Allies, they'd explain everything. Maybe they'd even send money to ransom Angela."

"*Io vado*." He makes a move, still glaring at me. I'm still holding the Sten ready to pull the trigger and blow him out of here.

"I'm sorry, but I can't help her, Buffo. I wish I could. Believe me. She saved my life."

"*Io vada*," he repeats still concentrating on me.

"You mean I better beat it before the SS shows up. You make a deal with them, tell them where I am?"

"*Niente*."

"You guys don't care if I reach the Allies Lines or not, do you?"

"We care for Angela."

"So do I if you want to know, more than anything. But nothing can be done for her. She took too many chances."

"*Io vado sud*. Angela *morta, morta*."

"They could be bluffing."

"*Non capisco*."

"They could be lying to you, pretending. They know what will happen to them after the war if they kill her. They could be tried for war crimes."

"They no *capisco*."

"They better. You tell them I'll report them if they touch her. I'll get their names too." He remains impassive. It's hard to know if he understands or if he's just being obstinate. Neither of us speak for a moment. "Well, I've got to leave. If you're going to give me away at least let me have a couple of hours head start."

He spits and says, "*Figlio di puttana! Subito, subito!*"

126

"You really believe they'll kill her?"

"What they do. *Execute.*"

I stuff the little food I have left in the knapsack along with some *lire*, ammo, and the Dante, the Sten at my side, put on my hat. He watches me.

"I'm sorry, Buffo. It's a terrible thing. I love Angela *molto*. I wish I could do something for her. She took a terrible risk bringing me this far."

"You go Ravenna?"

"I hope to. It'll be hard without her. But I'll make it somehow."

He doesn't move or reach for a weapon. His expression is blank. There's no point in asking if he'd propose an exchange like this to his friends, their lives for Angela, or if he were in my shoes he'd do it. He just hangs there scowling.

I slip past him and walk out into the cold rain still falling. He doesn't stop me. I glance back through the open doorway. He's still standing over the candle staring at me. Nobody is around.

So I jog toward a row of brick cottages and then head for the main road. Once out of sight of the hut I circle back behind it and wait for him to take off. He sticks inside for a while. I can hear him stirring. Soon two men appear, and the three of them start jabbering away in loud voices. I can't make out exactly what they're saying. Only it seems to deal with me. I hear over and over again, "*Morte ai Americano*" in the same tone I used to hear the partisans up north say, "*Morte ai Fascisti.*" The confab breaks up, and they stomp out into the night headed toward the road. Friends may come and go, but enemies keep piling up.

I return to the hut to dry off, gobble up the little bread and cheese left, think of Angela alone and scared in some cell with the threat of torture and death hovering over her. What she must be enduring on account of me. I debate what to do next. Go north and cross up the bastards. Head south through the Apennines. Or make for Ravenna and join the partisans and the OSS mission that is supposed to be there. Hoping like hell nobody will come after me or give me away and the SS can't find me. Back to poetry and peace. Long time no see, old friends.

I wait until it's almost light. I start out walking toward the row of cottages and the road, hiding the gun under my coat as best I can. The rain has stopped. A wagon pulled by a mule creaks and splashes along, a lantern swinging between the rear wheels. Baskets and boxes are piled up in back. The driver sways as if he's asleep sitting up.

"Ravenna, Ravenna!" I cry out, trotting alongside him.

" Ferrara," he mumbles.

"*Si, buono.*" He stops and I jump on the seat beside him.

127

"*Fucile!*" he says, pointing to my Sten sticking out. "*Partigiano?*"

"*Americano pilota.*" I make a plane noise ending with imitation gun fire and a crash.

"Ah, *buono, buono. Partigiani no buono.*"

"Yeah, they bring *Tedeschi, polizia.*"

"*Sí, sí.*" He's a short, skinny old man in a heavy coat and a fur cap. His little hands can scarcely hold the reins. The mule stumbles along like a toy winding down. No one else is on the road. Only a few houses have lights. It's a misty, chilly morning. Headlights approach, and I shove the Sten under the seat and sit up.

"*Polizia?*"

"No." And he tells me there are many soldiers in the city. None here. I better hide among the baskets and boxes in back. He's carrying a lot of grapes, mushrooms, chestnuts, and apples to market. The smell is sweet, earthy, fresh and damp. It makes me hungry. I climb back among them with the gun and cover myself up as much as possible. He turns around and says, "*Buono, buono.*"

As we enter Ferrara along Viale Cavour, the sky lightens. I can just make out a piazza, a castle with moats, gates, and drawbridges, a *duomo*, a *palazzo* with an arcade and a courtyard, one with a marble front and balcony. Everything looks ancient and ghostly in the nebulous light. I feel as if I'm back in the Middle Ages except for bombed-out buildings and a pile of rubble in the streets. A military truck rolls by. On the corner stands a Kraut with a rifle.

"Ravenna?" I whisper up at the old man.

"*Sí, avanti.*" The wheels scrape over the pavement. The wagon bumps and rocks along. I stay down, hoping like hell nobody wants to check the produce. No sound of a commanding voice yet. No boots or guns either. I bury my head in the floorboards. Just another potato with the dirt washed off as Frost said about his poems.

The Kraut yells something at the old man. He stops and protests. The soldier laughs. Then I hear him reaching back among the baskets and the soldier calling out, "*Grazie, grazie, Nonno,* as he hands over some fruit. Gosh, he has the voice of a teenager. And the wagon starts up, the clicking of the mule's feet, the rattling of the wheels, the creaking of the boards. I look back between crates and see the lonely figure with a rifle and one of those low-fitting helmets chewing on an apple.

The driver halts once again at the edge of the city and does the same thing. Only its lighter and there are two soldiers. They stand close to the wagon. I peer practically into their boyish fat German faces and can hardly believe they don't see me. The mule stumbles forward, and they shout, "*Grazie, grazie, Signor. Domani sigaretta, prostituta.*" He chuckles.

By the time we're out in the country everything looks brighter. He stops and calls back in a quiet voice that this is the road to Ravenna. I should wait for another ride. *Arrivederci*. I hop off with my stuff, thrust a couple of *lire* at him, and he turns around and disappears. I dart in between two buildings. Traffic is picking up, huge charcoal-burning trucks with stoves on the back, military vehicles, bicycles, wagons, people tramping along on the side. Two tubby kids waddle by. I hiss at them and they come behind the barn-like warehouse.

"*Americano pilota,*" I say. "Ravenna. *Cavalcata.* Go for a spin. And I imitate with my hands and my mouth what I want. They giggle. I take out a few *lire* and promise each one more if they help me. They explain that their father drives a truck. He could take me. It's a furniture van, and I could hide in the back under some blankets. They'll go find him. He's riding around selling wares. I should stay here until they return. So off they trot, those chubby dark faces lit up, their arms swinging, so different from Mario's gang. And I sit down against the back wall of the building worried about waiting. They could bring the police and earn a big reward. I stand up and walk away in the field, spot a ditch, and lie down to watch for their return, listening to the traffic, my heart beating.

Two hours pass, and I'm about to give up the vigil and beat it when I hear a truck stop in front of the building and the two kids start shouting for me. I don't answer, almost sure it's a trap. Go out, and there they are looking disappointed, standing there yelling their heads off for *Americano*. No doubt they told their father they had found a downed American pilot and dragged him away from his business. Now he's gone. And *papà* will be madder than hell at them.

"*Ciao,*" I wave at the kids. They romp toward me like two roly-poly puppies, throwing up their hands and smiling. A stout man wearing glasses plods behind them. With his enormous pot belly and double chin, he reminds me of that man-mountain Sicilian I met on the troopship coming over, only not so dark and sad-faced. He said he was supposed to work for OSS in Sicily, claimed he knew Lucky Luciano, the gangster. I could well believe it from the way he talked.

I walk over to fatso with the kids chattering around me, shake hands, and tell him I need to go to Ravenna. *Americani, partigiani* there. They help me go south to the Allies.

"Boom, boom," he says as I act out my plane being shot down and parachuting to earth. He breaks out in a belly laugh, jiggling all over, introduces himself as Luigi Venturi. He's the first jolly Italian I've met.

129

He sees planes coming over all the time, hundreds of them. They hit Ferrara, *morte, morte*. Trucks, tanks, cars wrecked. Do I drop bombs? No, only take pictures of the damage. Aerial photographer. Demonstrate. Then I announce I'm also a poet.

"*Poeta?*"

"*Si.*" I rattle off a couple of sonnets, hamming it up to stress the rhythm and the rimes. He laughs along with his sons at my gestures and facial expressions. It's good to be back with happy people.

We walk to the truck. His wife is sitting in the cab nursing one baby at her breast and calming another one squirming on her lap. By the looks of her she could be pregnant again. She's even more massive than her husband.

"You have big family all right. *Numeroso?*"

"*Molti bambini.* No *buono*, huh?"

"That's right. *Uno.*"

He takes me to the back, lowers the tailgate, and I climb in with his sons. It's crammed full all right. Furniture is piled high, a lot of second hand beat up chairs and small tables and rickety beds. Clothes, too, baskets of food, bottles of wine, books, religious paintings, two bicycles, toys. Even a mutt is tied up and yipping.

"You moving?" I turn to him, acting out my meaning.

"*Sí, sí, dovunque.* No *casa, villa, solo carro.*" He shakes with laugher. And, God, if there isn't a little wood burning stove, some rugs and lamps, and a basket of fruit. But how could they all live in there? A couple of Kraut vehicles come roaring down the road toward us. I jump in among the household goods. They shoot by honking their horns.

"Ravenna," I call out to Luigi as he hooks up the tailgate. "*Molte lire.*"

"*Si, buono.*" He goes back to the driver's seat.

We move slowly at first, then faster and faster. We take a sharp turn to the left off the main road. And I yell at the kids, "*Dove, dove?*" They shrug their shoulders. I point the Sten at them both huddled in a corner.

"*Polizia?*"

"No, no." They crawl back in the shadows amid the jumble of furniture ready at any time to come tumbling in a heap on top of them. I order the taller one to knock on the cab window and tell their father to stop. I want to talk to him. If they don't I'll shoot.

They both pound on the glass and holler like crazy. The big rig halts, and I jump out and run to the front.

"Ravenna, Ravenna!" I shout pointing east. "You go *polizia, Tedeschi, no buono.* I'll shoot the shit out of you." And I aim the Sten at him, feeling lousy doing it. He seems like such a friendly guy who would never turn me over to the police.

His wife grimaces at the sight of the gun and freezes. And I almost expect to see the baby at her breast stop sucking and the big pink right tit shrivel up. But mamma goes on feeding the kid and stroking the head of the other fat-cheeked bambino in her lap.

"*Sí, Signor, Capitano, Pilota. Si*, Ravenna."

"I'll sit up here with you to make sure." And I cross over to the passenger side and climb in the cab, resting my gun on the floorboard. We are jammed in tight. Their garlicky breath is strong, their perspiration sour as a damp washcloth.

He turns around, goes back, and drives down a side road leading across a field.

"Where the hell are you taking me?" I shout.

"*Chiesa.*" I glare over at him past his wife still nursing and stroking. Her reddish arms are tremendous, the uncovered breast like a mound of blown up dough with a strawberry in the middle.

"The church, the priest? What is this? No, no, what do I need them for? They can't help me." He looks dumb. "Ravenna, Ravenna. I need to go to Ravenna. Are you turning me over to the polizia for a reward, *lire* for *Americano Bandito*?"

"No, no," he protests. "*Americano buono, molto buono, grazie, grazie.*"

He returns to the main highway, and once again we're pointed toward the Adriatic I hope. Kraut trucks and cars streak by. No checkpoints loom ahead. The only ominous sign is a black car sitting on the right shoulder with the hood raised. Two men stand alongside it holding up their hands. Luigi starts to slow down.

"No *arresto*," I say, raising my gun off the floor. "*Avanti, avanti!*" He accelerates and I relax my hand on the trigger.

## Chapter 15

One of them is Buffo, the tall bearded man who came to see me about Angela. He's signaling for us to stop. Luigi waves out the window. His wife is still nursing and smiles away. I bend over as we sail by, peeking at the black sedan to see how many there are inside. Only two others. They're in the back peering intently at the truck. No guns in sight.

After we've gone a couple of hundred feet, I turn around. The car is moving onto the pavement, hood down.

"*Rapido*," I say, pointing toward the vehicle racing toward us. "*Polizia?*"

"No, no *polizia. Piazzisti.*"

"Salesmen? Are you out of your mind? *Rapido, rapido*! They're after me. Didn't you see them trying to get you to stop?"

I lift the Sten to my lap with the barrel pointing across his wife's bulging stomach. He leans over the steering wheel gripping it tightly, pressing his foot down hard. And we shoot forward with a jolt. The truck shudders and rattles, the motor bucks and wheezes. "*Papà, papà,*" the kids are hollering and banging on the rear window. The mutt is yapping away. Furniture is sliding and falling and banging around. Pans are crashing into each other, glass breaking, chairs and tables knocking together. It sounds like a bunch of drunken sailors brawling. Mamma next to me doesn't change her expression, doesn't even stir except to shift the baby on her breast and to comfort the one on her lap. Her husband sneaks a glance at them and then at me. He mutters to himself, acting helpless as if he's holding the whole thing together with his bare hands and can't do it much longer.

Corn and hemp fields spring up everywhere, marshlands and swamps in the distance. What a flat, damp, melancholy country. We fly through a couple of red-brick towns, dodging chickens and dogs crossing. At Argenta, halfway between Ferrara and Ravenna, there's a Kraut detachment, army vehicles parked on both sides of the roads and soldiers walking around. Luigi slows down driving by and grins at them, waves while telling me to hide my gun. Then it's out in the open again, the cement surface becoming a thin sliver through the muddy landscape stretching to the horizon.

The sedan hangs back, content to follow rather than overtake us. Occasionally, it spurts alongside, and the four men glance in at us before

132

dropping off. I crouch lower and lower, turning my head away, keeping the Sten out of sight. But I know it's futile. I'm sure they've spotted me. Still with all the military traffic they can't do anything except stick to our tail and wait for a chance to stop us somewhere when nobody is around.

And I'm thinking, what are you going to do now, Dante's fellow traveler? Sticking this family in the field of fire to save your skin. How many people have to risk death or die before you go home and write your poetry about them? Whizzing through this wretched world and watching these struggling souls taking it on the chin while you look on. But it's not just that anymore. It's this Sun Up mission to end the war in Italy and the Reds foaming at the rhetoric to take over the country. Somebody's got to tell Donovan the story, somebody's got to get through with the message and explain what's happening before it's too late.

The truck begins to vibrate worse than ever. The engine sputters. Luigi grimaces at me, shrugs his shoulders. He reduces speed. I don't say anything. The sedan is still hot after us. I could jump out and beat it across the field. But they'd come after me. Then how would I ever find the woods where Angela said a Garibaldi brigade is hiding? The traffic, most of it military, is increasing the nearer we come to the city.

"*Partigiani* hide?" I ask. "*Non capisco.*"

"*Sí, sí* Pineta de Classe." And he explains it's a forest south of the city. *Tedeschi* no go there. He will try to lose the car behind us when we reach Ravenna. He knows the streets *bene, bene*. But there are *molti soldati*. A Wehrmacht headquarters is nine kilometers north of the city at Villa Gamba. He's afraid, but no one will stop him. He drives through many times on his way down to Rimini, and everybody knows his truck. *Tedeschi* will take me for his *figlio*. He grins at the idea. So does his wife still nursing away and comforting the other baby. Boy, the only salvation of this country is *bambini* and more *bambini*.

His happy expression gives me the willies. Once inside the city he can stop anywhere and turn me over to the police and get a reward. I shouldn't trust him. Yet what the hell am I going to do? I've got to put my faith in somebody. He doesn't seem to be a bastard out for the *lire* he could get for turning me in.

We reach the outskirts. There's not much damage, nothing like I've seen elsewhere in North Africa and in southern Italy, mainly at Bizerte and the port of Naples. We rattle down an avenue, switch to Via Cavour, turn off it, and meander around town, through squares, one called Byron, and down a street where he points out the poet's house, a shabby heavy stone building that resembles an arsenal. Past red-brick churches, one octagonal with barrel-shaped, detached bell towers. Buildings that look like mausoleums seem to be all over the place. The city of the dead all right. Even the air has a sepulchral sort of stillness. The people match the atmosphere. What dour faces. They remind me of Dante's dismal mob of crazies. We pass a pile of rubble from a bombed-out house, a gutted building, one with a chalked slogan on a broken wall, "*Gesu' Benedici La Nostra Cittá.*" It's sad to see fresh ruins among so much ancient architecture.

We lose the black sedan leaving the Piazza Victor Emanuele with its two columns topped by statues in front of an arcaded town hall and rumble past a damaged church. Next to it is a small yellowish stone one with a dome, San Francesco. He says Dante is buried there and asks if I've ever heard of him. I mention that I found a copy of the *Divine Comedy* in North Africa and have been reading it ever since. Or trying to. My Italian is not too good and half the time I'm not certain what's going on. And I think, gosh, an ignorant guy like him knowing about Byron and Dante. In the States I bet you won't find many truck drivers who ever heard of Whitman and Frost.

At last we're headed south out of town on Corso Giuseppe Garibaldi and after about three miles sail past a huge brick church in barren country near a sugar-beet factory. It has one of those rounded towers alongside. He says it's a *moschea, molta bella.*" Then we go several more miles, across a railroad track and a canal. The sign points the way to the Pineta di Classe. There it is ahead, a clump of umbrella pines and scrub oaks and underbrush all by itself out in the middle of nowhere. The marshes and the Adriatic can't be too far off. You can smell them, feel the moist wind blowing. He stops at some locks.

"*Partigiani?*" I say.

"*Si, si,* " he mutters. And off we go.

His wife is no longer nursing, just sitting there placidly with her two *bambini* as if she were an overweight Madonna. No noise from the mutt and the kids. We're the only vehicle in the vicinity. Late afternoon and the sun has gone down, low gray clouds drifting in from the sea, darkness creeping in. A lot different from Bari and the Dolomites. No doubt about that. I wonder what Dante ever saw in this place except for background scenery in the *Inferno*. Or Byron. Hard to imagine him horseback riding here with his young countess in the cool of the evening and the choir of nightingales and crickets singing away. Talk about a wasteland. This is really "death by water."

I want to leave and don't. At least in the truck it's safe. And I sort of hate to say goodbye to the Venturi family even though they look impatient for me to go. I hand over some *lire* to Luigi, about the last I

134

have. He grabs the bills and thanks me. And I tell him I wish I had more. He saved my life. Now all I need to do is find the partisans and the Americans and hire a boat and sail to Rimini or go down to Ancona depending on where the Krauts are. I can see he doesn't understand. Anyway, "*Grazie, grazie*," I toss at him like a bouquet, lean over and kiss mamma and the *bambini*, shake the father's hand. Then I jump out and stand in the road as they take off. The boys are kneeling in back staring at me over the tailgate, the mutt between them yipping away. They remind me of two fat frogs ready to jump. I wave. They wave back.

"Well, Dante," I address the salt air, "Here I am in your world at last. Where they exiled you and you spent your last days. Where do we go from here, you old displaced person? Wishing you were back in Firenze?

A car motor sounds in the distance. I duck into the trees and wait. It's the black sedan with the four partisans. They slow up. Apparently, they spotted the truck leaving the area and were wondering what's going on. They ride into the woods. And I rush to hide among the pines, crossing canals and creeks. A great place for a partisan hideout. I keep moving. The light grows weaker and weaker. No signs of life anywhere. Not even a far-away noise of any kind, just a bird or two and the swishing of the breeze among the branches.

Night comes slower here close to the coast. I stop to eat a little bread and cheese I brought from Ferrara. Thirsty but wary of the water Luigi warned me about. Well, I figure if there's nobody around at least I can keep moving, taking time out for a pee till I come to the sea and a village somewhere. It's not like being up in the Dolomites awed by giant peaks and bottomless abysses. Only somehow it feels lonelier and more depressing. I can imagine Dante sitting in the middle of these gloomy shades thinking or writing about his demons and dreaming of his Beatrice back in his hometown or up in paradise. It's bad enough brooding about the major and Angela. But if your mind is filled with grim experiences and bizarre visions like people walking around with their heads on backwards so their asses are advancing toward you, gosh, I guess, you'd either go mad or write great poetry. Or get the hell out of there in a hurry, go see a psychiatrist.

I wander through the dark forest lost but feeling safe for the time being. A light glimmers ahead through the trees. I steal toward it, hear voices. A camp clearing, a fire glowing, shadowy figures milling around. There's a cabin and candlelight in the windows. I hesitate before barging ahead. Those men who've been following me in the sedan could be there talking to the partisans Angela told me about. But I can't worry about them now. I've got to reach the Allies somehow. And water is my only escape route.

So I approach the guard and call out, "*Amico, amico. Americano, Americano.*" His gun clicks. He shouts. There's a stirring in the camp, men talking, running. I move toward him and the fire, shuffling cautiously. He pokes the muzzle of his rifle into my gut. I put up my hands, the Sten hanging off my shoulder. Someone grabs it. I turn to protest. A group of partisans surround me jabbering away, pointing their guns.

"The 29th Garibaldi Brigade?" I call out," *Capitano* Lupo?" A cheer goes up at the mention of his name. "*Viva Comunismo!*" I whip out a Red scarf and a Red star that I had been keeping as souvenirs of the life up north and wave them. Another cheer erupts.

A heavy-set muscular man with a flowing black mustache, an Eisenhower jacket, combat boots, a .45 on his webbed belt, struts out of the cabin followed by Buffo, the tall bearded man I remembered from Ferrara and his companions I spotted on the Ravenna Road. There's the same kind of swagger about the chunky guy with the cigar I noticed in the partisan leaders up north. The difference is he's not so solemn and kind of casual and happy-go lucky. Yet he unnerves me with his breeziness, his fakey friendliness.

"*Ciao,*" he sings out. "I Lupo. You *Americano?*"

"*Ciao.* Sergeant Anthony Defreest, OSS. Everybody calls me Tony. *Parlare inglese?*"

"*Poco* Italiano?"

"*Molto poco.*" He laughs.

Angela's friend steps forward and shouts at me, thrusting his finger into my face. He rattles off something to Lupo who listens and studies me frowning.

"Have you come to take me back to Ferrara, exchange me for Angela LeDolce?" He nods. "You can't let them do that. It's insane. I'm just as sorry as they are about what happened to her. But I've got to go south, report to the Allies. I'm on a secret mission to end the war here. Everything depends on my information. *Capeesh?*"

"*Sì.*" He becomes more serious now, scowling, stiffening.

"Where are the Americans Angela told me were here?"

"*Parti.*"

"Where did they go? They coming back?" He shrugs his shoulders. "You don't know where they went. Nothing? What is this? What's going on?"

"They come back sometime, maybe two, three weeks."

"Did they take the radio?"

"No, we have radio. No operator to send message to Bari. No planes come." He glances up at the sky. "*Niente.*"

"How many Americans were here?"

"*Capitano* Monetti, *Tenente* Rialdo, <u>*Serg*</u>*ente* Bamberini."

"And they just left like that and didn't tell you where they were going, what they were going to do? That's kind of funny."

"Secret mission they say. OSS. No talk. You operate radio?"

"That's what I am, a radio operator."

"Ah, *buono*, I keep you. You no go to Allies or back to Ferrara. You help Lupo. You like? *Va bene*?" He laughs.

"You mean that's my choice, work the radio for you or go with these guys back to Ferrara and the SS."

"*Si,* come, I show you." He takes me into the large cabin where weapons and ammo boxes line the wall. It's a damn arsenal. And, Jesus, they want more. I can't get over the fact there's no SO team around. They just took off and left all this stuff. It's weird. I can almost feel their presence in the room as I view the parachute boots, the parkas, the canteens, the containers full of plastic explosives, the carbines and Thompson sub-machine guns. It doesn't add up. Enough for a whole battalion. I turn around after inspecting the equipment.

Everybody is staring at me through the candlelight. Lupo is in the center flanked by the bearded guy and his friends on the right and on the left a group of partisans in a motley collection of Italian, American, and British uniforms.

"Did you shoot them?" I say in a low voice that I can hardly hear myself. The light is unsteady. Shadows waver on the walls.

"No, no," Lupo laughs in that hollow hearty way of his. "*Possibile* they go Venezia, Udine, Gorizia. No shoot them, *Sergente. Americani buoni, molto buoni*." He smiles.

"Why do you need more drops? Gosh, you've got enough junk to take on the Krauts."

"*Tedeschi* strong. They attack us. We need *molti* guns, food, medical supplies. You help, no? You operate radio for Lupo?"

"But I told you I've got to go south to the Allies. I can't stay here. This isn't my mission. They will suspect something is wrong. I better start out tonight. Okay?" I gaze around in the dusky room. The men are still focusing on me. Nobody has a gun out, but I can sense everybody has one handy.

"No go *sud, Sergente*. You stay. Everything *buono*." Lupo takes the .45 out of the holster and points it at me.

"You planning to get rid of me just because I won't request supplies?"

"Buffo say you spy for *Tedeschi*. You bring Angela LeDolce to Ferrara. They capture her."

"That's a crock of shit. She was helping me to come here so I could find the Americans and get a boat and go south. You can't hold me."

"Nobody know what we do in Pineta di Classe. Nobody talk. Dante with his poetry, Byron a member of the *Carbonari*. *Buono salvo*? No *segreto*."

"Yeah, 'the woods are lovely, dark and deep,'" I mumble.

"*Non capisco*"

"Never mind. I have to leave, that's all." I hesitate, facing the men. They're waiting for me to make a move. Lupo shouts out a command, and a partisan leaps forward and grabs me, ties my hands behind my back. Everything happens so fast I hardly realize what's going on except I'm standing by a stone fireplace surrounded by a bunch of armed maniacs wearing Red bandanas and Red stars. Most of them are older than the guys up north, in their thirties and forties. They hate the Krauts all right, but worse maybe they hate not taking over Italy when the war is over and Mussolini at Lake Garda lies rotting in his grave, his Italian Social Republic defunct.

Lupo grins, lowers his gun, and orders the partisan to untie me as I breathe easier.

"Okay, okay, you win. I'll operate your damn radio."

"How I know you not spy like Buffo say?"

"A poet. Poets don't spy. I write codes for OSS missions. They're everywhere in Italy. For you too."

"*Si, si*, I read your poem for Pineapple. Funny and sad. You use it for code no?"

"With double transposition?"

"*Si, si, va vene*. I see operator code." He barks out an order. And one of the partisans races over to a metal box and takes out several sheets of paper and brings them to Lupo. He reads the lines of the sonnet silently to himself, his lips moving.

"'The time has come...'" he recites haltingly. "'To say goodbye to home, / To put long distance between it and death.'" And I think, gosh, those lines hit the nail on the head all right, though I kind of wonder what they really meant when I wrote them. They just sounded poetic I guess.

"*Buono*, you *poeta*. I teach at Rimini, Dante, Ariosto, Leopardi. I know *molti versi*. They make good music when you say them to *signorina*." He laughs.

138

"And when you send messages with them to General Clark and General Eisenhower, Churchill and Roosevelt, they sound even sweeter."

"You write poems for them to code and decode with?"

"That's right. I'm their code maker. You do anything to me, and the Allies will come after you fast. I promise you they will. The Fifth and Eight Armies aren't too far away either, don't forget."

He stares off in the distance, his mouth fixed.

"I no harm *poeta*."

"Or hand him over to *Tedeschi*."

"No do that. You know *segreti*?"

"The secrets of the gods," I quip. He mocks a laugh.

"You immortal, *Sergente*" he chuckles.

"I hope so."

"We see." He raises his .45 again and aims it at my stomach, the safety off. The whole room invisibly draws back, sucks in air. I stiffen, my mouth goes dry all of a sudden. A couple of drops streak down my legs. He pulls the trigger and I go limp, then numb. There's only a click. He smiles.

"*Nausea?*"

"No," I sigh, holding myself from shaking in his presence. "Just a little weak. I haven't eaten much today."

"You have white hair."

"White hair?" I grab the top of my head, pull out a strand. Everybody laughs. Some practical joke. He doesn't resemble any teacher I ever had, the beard, the flat nose, the black eyes, the thick neck. I bow my head.

"No shoot you today, *Sergente*. You send message to Bari. You ask for drop. You tell them you send message for Lupo."

"Then I go? You'll find me a boat, give me a guide?"

"At Cervia, *si, molti barca*?"

"How far is it?"

"Not far. Now you stay. I go and talk to people. You eat, sleep, *molto contento*."

"How long will you be gone?"

"I not know. I come back and you call Bari."

"Then you'll release me, take me to Cervia?" He pauses a moment, reflective, grinning wider and wider.

"*America* they say you famous poet?"

"Robert Frost does. Ever heard of him?"

"*Si*, I hear."

139

"I went to school where he teaches, Dartmouth College. I had classes with him. He considers me a famous poet. I won a prize he judged."

"And you write *poesia* for President Roosevelt, Churchill?"

"Generals too, Clark Alexander, Eisenhower."

"Okay, *possibile*."

"What does that mean?"

"We no shoot *Americano adesso.* You *simpatico.* I come back and we talk, make everything fine. *Amico* no? We fight *Tedesci* like I do with *Capitano* Monetti." He comes over and hugs me. And I can't figure him out. Is he going to release me or is he going to keep me here tied to the radio for the duration? Another Burrasco. Thank God, Marko's not around.

He leaves with a group of men. A partisan staying goes off and brings me a cold piece of beef and chunks of dark bread and a bottle of wine. They're not only older than those up north but tougher. Hardened veterans who've been at this business longer. Scraggly beards, knives, hand grenades on their belts. No gray long-peaked caps either that give the guys up in the mountains such a dashing air. I sit and chew on my midnight meal. Outside men are singing and chatting, joking and drinking. There's a pleasant, normal air about the place yet underneath the surface a sinister sort of secrecy I associate with the missing members of the mission and the stockpile of weapons and the two-faced leader.

I try to sleep on some prickly straw but keep listening for Lupo's return and the clicking and shuffling outside. If he did eliminate the Americans, why would he stop with me after I send a few messages? I could blow the whistle on him. Unless he believed that baloney about my poetry and thinks I can get him drops. Hell, maybe a sonnet will save my neck again. So far one's never failed. Like pure magic. Yet he doesn't seem to be the kind of person who would buy my story without questioning at least part of it.

At dawn I wake with a start and hear men stirring in the yard. Everybody else is asleep. I get up and tiptoe to the window. It's a breezy gray morning. Five partisans with rifles are standing on the other side of a dead fire talking to Lupo, reminding me of a similar situation. He's waving around his .45. Could the Krauts be coming? I drift back to my straw bunk and sit up, feet on the floor, head in my hands and wait. Or could it be something else I don't want to think about?

The men in the cabin begin to stir. No one pays any attention to me. They still view me as a stranger they can't quite trust. Maybe it's the civilian clothes. Lupo barges in smoking a cigar, the pistol in his holster. He's brisk and cheery as if he had had a woman last night and was feeling full of himself.

"Sorry, *Americano poeta*, we shoot you today. Angela LeDolce *condannata a morte*. We hear this morning. Everybody sad, angry. Buffo say you do it."

"Me? Angela dead. Christ, that's terrible! I had nothing to do with it. Nothing I swear. Nothing. How could I? I never betrayed her. I would have done anything in the world to save her except give myself up. I loved her. She loved me. What is this? Those guys from Ferrara just want to take it out on somebody. Could it be their fault she was caught?"

"You say a prayer for her. For you too."

I don't look up at him standing there motionless and my remembering Angela and those few rough, tender days we had together walking, making love, talking about poetry and communism. Remembering, too, all she did for me, so spirited and selfless. Like Maggie in a way, but stronger, more passionate. Like Bill, too, she gave everything and wanted nothing but to live with intensity for her mission and the communists and their belief in a better world that I'm beginning to find out isn't so great after all.

"A prayer for me?"

"*Finito, Americano poeta, finito.*" He yells out an order and two men appear and yank me to my feet.

"No, no, I'll operate your damn radio." I shrug them off. "I'll stay. Give me a chance. Let me make it up."

"Better this way, *Sergente*." He grins. The cigar is making me nauseous the way Dad's did on those drives to Hanover and Camp Timber on Long Lake in Maine when I was a teenager.

Outside a chilling rain is falling, the day growing darker instead of lighter, the sea breeze stronger. I dress, put on shoes, a coat and hat. They take me beyond the camp area to a clearing and plant me in the center, tie my hands behind my back. I look up. Thick branches of umbrella pines loom above me dripping wet, drops falling on my face. Five men stand fifteen feet away, rifles poised. Lupo stands to one side chomping on that cigar and looking kind of bemused. Not again the Dostoyevsky execution scene. Have these guys been reading too much of him lately?

It's something I guess I should be getting used to by now after reading Dante and racing around in the Dolomites with him. But he always has a rock to hide behind or a bridge to cross or Virgil to take his hand and lead him out of danger. After all the dead can do no harm, only look ugly and fierce at him, tell their sad and grim stories. And he knows he's going to meet Beatrice eventually after he gets to the bottom of the pit and at the top of the mountain. And despite my luck up north my chances seem zero right now for going anywhere, just down deeper, not up higher.

"You have anything to tell us, *Sergente*, before I give the order. You have a word to say to your *papà, mamma, signorina*?"

"No, nothing."

"I read your Pineapple. Very sad. You have sad view of the world, *Americano*. And your country rich, happy. Nobody hungry, lots of *lire. Buono, molto buono*."

"I inherited it from my Presbyterian grandfather. The old fire and brimstone type. You're guilty unless you're predestined to go to heaven." Since he's Catholic , I can see that's all gibberish to him, so there's no point in saying my mother tried to rescue me from that kind of rigid religion by bringing me up Episcopalian, but it never really took.

"You want blindfold? Turn around and face the trees?" I don't respond. "This a good place for you to end. Be immortal like Dante."

"What the hell are you doing this for anyway? Some kind of revenge, retribution?"

"I sorry we have no nightingale to sing for you. They all die in the war."

The men cock their rifles. I stare straight at them, trying to believe I'm dreaming or they're playing a game. Nothing is for real. Like that phony act with the .45. But what if he's serious this time? The guy's a madman, I'm convinced, a complete madman. I can't get out of my mind the fact he could have done away with the three Americans here. Like this too.

"*Pronto, Sergente*?" My knees buckle a little, my throat constricts. I feel numb, aware only of the rifles pointing at me and the pines dripping, the smell of the damp earth.

"*Pronto*?" Lupo bellows one more time. I don't say anything. What could I say at this moment anyway? I don't even think about praying. I just stare at the ground. Nothing happens. Not a sound, not even a click. The wind rushes through the high branches. The morning becomes lighter. I wiggle my hands tied behind my back. I'm shivering and sweating at the same time.

One, two, three, four seconds pass. I count them. Christ, why don't they shoot? Why don't they get it over with? Why do they keep me dangling here like this?

"*Va bene, Sergente*," Lupo shouts, "now I know you *poeta*. We no shoot. *Domani possibile*, or the day after if you no send my message on the radio. But today *salvo*. You stay with us. We hear Angela shoot guard and escape. *Tedeschi* after her. And I remember the little pistol

142

hidden in her bra, remarking no one will look there. Thank God, she's free. That's what she was born to be, but I hope no Francesca. Oh, Angela, I'll always love you wherever you are.

I lift my head slowly and gape at him, remembering after Dostoyevsky's phony execution how he kneeled and thanked the Czar for saving his life and sending him to Siberia for ten years, which he wrote about in *The House of the Dead,* his *Inferno.* Should I thank Lupo?

He's grinning away. The son of a bitch! So are the five men with the rifles, reminding me of those guys in Nell Dugan's boarding house up in Hanover. Not the traditional Dartmouth type drinking, partying at Green Key and Winter Carnival, going to football games. Keeping too much to myself. Should be shot. The next thing worse than dying I'm convinced is being an outcast. At least I held everything in. I didn't break down. Kept my composure and for once in my life my mouth shut.

Lupo runs over and embraces me. At first I'm still in a daze. He unties me, and I stand there free for a moment shaking, my legs wobbly, my mouth tasting funny.

"*Viva Americano poeta,*" he yells and props me up. The firing squad standing in the misty rain echoes him, their voices soaring through the columned old pines that once looked down on Dante and Byron and how many nameless poets who never wrote a living line but sweated like hell trying to. They fire their guns into the air. The vibrations shake the ground and the trees, rattle me down to my toes as I imagine their bullets are headed right for me.

## Chapter 16

"So now what are you going to do with me?" I say to Lupo as the firing squad breaks up.

"Eat, sleep, do message. We get *molti* guns. *Possibile* we give you to *Tedeschi* and they give us prisoners. *Buono*, huh?" I glance at him through the cold rain coming down harder than ever. He's laughing. Goddamn, he's always laughing. The grimmer the idea the funnier. Maybe Italians have a different sense of humor.

"Depends on what you want," I say, "more bullets or more comrades."

"We get both, no?" He looks at me slyly but seriously, too, the way he does so much of the time.

"Where is the front now?"

"Fiumicino River. Near Cervia. Not far."

"Then the Allies have taken Rimini?"

"*Si*, they close, but not come to Ravenna till Christmas. Too much rain. No *buono* for tanks in Romagna. Too many rivers, canals, marshes. Too much mud. Always flooding the roads. A long war, *Sergente*, a long war."

"Are you waiting for the Eighth Army?"

"*Si*, we wait. When they move we take Ravenna. You stay and bring supplies with the radio. No send you to *Tedeschi*."

"You mean I'm staying here permanently. You won't release me. I've got important information for OSS I have to deliver in person as soon as I can."

"Everything important in war, no? But some things more important than other things. You rest now, then send message. I see you."

He stomps off, and I walk back to the cabin in the rain, use a rag to dry off. Drop on some straw in the back away from everybody, seeing in my mind the firing squad raising their rifles, Lupo poised to give the command, a thin smile playing over his face. I can't believe I'm still alive. I can't believe he'd try anything so stupid as that for a joke with the front only fifteen to twenty-five miles away. Or was it a joke? Were they telling me something? Gosh, is this whole business up here trying to tell me something about a lot of things, myself, war, poetry, Dante, Italy, the States, the world? If so I suppose I'll never know what it is for a long time. My whole life has been a series of delayed reaction bombs.

I sleep for hours it seems, and when I awake the rain is still beating down, rattling the tin roof like shots from a BB gun. Daylight is fading fast. The cabin is crowded. I borrow a candle and read a little more of the *Inferno*. This time it's about somebody asking the poet whether the Romagna is having war or peace. He should be here now with me. And he hears about  cities under tyrants battling it out. The more I travel with these two guys, the pilgrim and his guide, the more I see what's happening to Dante is happening to me. It's the same dark, old, dirty world for the three of us, plenty of blood and shit, torture and betrayal, sex and black marketeering, phonies and sad sacks. Why didn't someone tell me about this guy when I was reading Wolfe and Whitman and that crew?  He writes circles around them. Only Dostoevsky comes close with his "fantastic realism."  They should have known each other. Gloomy Dis is another St. Petersburg, and the Neva the river of blood.

I stand up and mingle with the partisans. A sour bunch all right, cleaning and disassembling their weapons, talking Marxism with somebody who could be the commissar of the brigade. He's tall and thin with glasses and a pointed beard. Another Trotsky look-alike. Nobody's laughing together. They kind of resemble the countryside, flat, bleak, and ghoulish. A couple of them are keeping their eyes on me. I can't shake the feeling that somehow Lupo did away with the SO team, though that seems impossible. Still those three guys haunt the place. Any moment I expect to stumble on some of their personal affects.

I eat pasta and corn meal and minestrone for supper. Afterwards I edge over toward the door, gaze out at the rain rapping on the roof. Lupo comes in and tells me he has a message to send in the morning. He's still laughing about the way I acted in front of the firing squad. Yeah, I guess I behaved like a scared clown.

"*Si*, you *buffo*, *Sergente*. We laugh. *Viva poeta*. You like us, we like you. Everything *va bene*." He pats me on the shoulder and swaggers out of the cabin.

The partisans retire early. I stake out a place near the door. A guard stands beside it. Another one is outside. Three or four more patrol the perimeter of the camp. There are no lights. The air damp, cold, stagnant. Too many bodies crammed into too small a space. Too much snoring. And too many gaseous odors.

"*Paesano, sigarette?*" The man next to me on the straw touches me. I hold one out for him,

"*Grazie*," he says, sitting up and moving closer, a vague shape in the almost total blackness. Groping, I hand it to him and fumble around to light a match. He leans toward me to catch the flame. He's younger than the others, thinner face, no beard, shorter, big eyes and nose.

"Emilio, raincoat? Signaling what I want, whispering, "*Toletta, subito, subito*." I grunt a couple of times.

"Ah, *si, si*" he whispers back, chuckling. And he reaches over to fetch his poncho and cap to give me. When his back is turned, I grab in the straw for his Sten and hide it and the knapsack on my other side. In no time I'm standing up with his rain gear on and grab my stuff and the weapon I took and slip them on my shoulders under the poncho. He says I resemble his brother Francesco.

"*Grazie, grazie*," I mutter and hand him a pack of cigarettes, the last of a dozen or more I brought with me to give to partisans. He reaches up and shakes my hand. I move toward the guard at the door. A candle hangs on the wall, very dim. I keep my head down and turn away from the flame.

"Emilio," he greets me, and I make a grunting noise, adding "*cacca*." He laughs. And I'm through the door in a flash without a question or a search. Even the guards outside don't challenge me, calling out, "*Ciao*, Emilio, *ciao*." I walk casually toward the edge of the camp. Once beyond I speed up being as quiet as I can. The rain has stopped, but the trees are still dripping. The wind is blowing pretty hard. Puddles are everywhere. I slop through the mud making a racket splashing. I expect footsteps behind me. There aren't any. All I have to worry about for the moment are Krauts and crossing swollen streams and what's going to happen to Emilio when Lupo discovers he stupidly let me escape. But I can't let his fate slow me up any more than I could Giorgio's. The bigger the conscience the better the target. But I've got to find someone to guide me through the lines now that the sea route is impossible.

I tramp out of the woods at dawn and spot a farmhouse across the road, knock, and barge in on a little skinny man and his skinnier and older-looking wife shivering around a fireplace having a breakfast of bread and cheese. They tell me I'll never get to the coast or through the lines. Too many *soldati*. The front is not far off. I believe them. I'm not in the house more than a couple of minutes when artillery sounds in the distance. A convoy of trucks and ammo carriers zoom by followed by a column of Panzer tanks that shake the brick walls. It's really frightening seeing them so close, the helmets and the great coats, the black leather jackets, the swastikas on the vehicles. An officer stops to ask questions of the nervous little guy, Alberto Martino, and he gives clear directions and then comes back to the bedroom where I'm hiding to tell me *Tedeschi* are preparing a big attack. My only chance is to cross the lines in the mountains between Bologna and Firenze. The country is wild and foggy. I might never make it, but I've got to try. He will take me to the area tomorrow, pass me off as his son. He has papers for his *figlio* who has gone off to join the *partigiani* at Modena. He looks like me.

I can't believe he's doing all this for a complete stranger. Risking his life. But he insists. He knows someone who can help me reach Firenze. I argue I might better stay here until the 8th Army breaks through to the Po Valley, which shouldn't be too long, should it? He says no, they will never reach the Po until spring. Too much rain, too many casualties. He heard the Allies lost *molti soldati*. And if I stay in his house the *Tedeschi* might search it and find me and then he and his wife could be shot. He's a dim-eyed dark man with fits of tremendous animation followed by fits of stubborn solitariness that convinces me I should leave him and his wife alone. They're old and don't have much. And, damn it, haven't I done enough damage to people's lives up here during the past couple of months? His wife hardly smiles or speaks, even more glum than he is, only brightening up at the mention of her son, who could be dead.

I'm amazed at how people survive in this desolate country. The loneliness of the faintly lighted house standing by itself on the edge of a marsh. Crude wooden furniture, a few holy pictures, snapshots of their son on the homemade wooden table across from the fireplace. It makes me think of a frontier cabin out west a century ago with Indians lurking everywhere.

The next morning after breakfast the fidgety old man hitches up his mule, throws a few sacks of grain and rice and sugar-beets into the wagon, and we start crawling toward the Apennines. It's another soggy day, misty, water on the roads, streams spilling their banks and flooding fields. Off in the distance guns are thudding away muffled by the heavy air. German trucks and motorcycles and staff cars splash by. No one stops us inching along. In fact, soldiers even wave, smile, and holler as they pass. Some of them are younger than I am. You wonder what they thought about when they got drafted. Whether they had a choice of different programs like V-12. I bet none of them were interviewed for intelligence work in Abwehr the way I was at Dartmouth for OSS and then given the choice of an overseas assignment not to mention the choice of writing poetry for codes.

We don't talk. He sits in front holding the reins, and I sprawl in the back on the sacks watching the traffic and the hills growing nearer and nearer, feeling the air getting colder and colder, hearing the explosions becoming louder and louder. For the first time I'm beginning to realize what it's like having a war going on in your own backyard

147

fought by people from outside your country and none of it mattering to them or to you in the long run. Worrying about things being hit by a shell followed by having enough to eat and losing all your possessions and your family. The big wide picture, then the intimate small one.

The first night we stop at a rundown farmhouse in the foothills belonging to the Vitalises, every one of them overweight from the two kids to the parents and the grandmother. And that's strange because they have almost nothing to eat except soup and bread and a little cheese, some pasta. What a somber group. Hardly anyone talks or smiles. They just sit around with their wine and gawk and listen to the old man mumble about *Tedeschi* he'd seen today. They act timid even though they know I'm an American.

Alberto explains I need to get to Firenze. I have important information to give the Allies. Is there anybody who could take me through the mountains safely? A long pause follows the announcement. The father gazes over at his twin boys, Pupo and Carlo. They look in their teens. They pop up and volunteer to act as guides. They claim to know a secret trail over some peaks and through a valley where there's no fighting and no *Tedeschi*. It's southeast of Bologna and not too far off. It may take a few days to reach the spot. I don't mind the time. I just want to arrive in one piece. And, gosh, the more I scan them, short, stout, and wearing glasses, the more I'm skeptical of the two leading me anywhere, certainly not through enemy lines. Yet it turns out they've done this before, escorted pilots, partisans, friends along their special route. Or they insist they have. But it's hard to believe them.

"*Quanto?*" I say. They glance at their father with those little pig eyes. He smiles at me, shrugs his shoulders. I pull out a handful of *lire* I didn't realize I had and give them to him. He nods with a "*grazie*," and the two boys come over and shake hands as if they're closing a deal. They mutter *domani* they'll take me in a wagon to the Soldarises below Route 9, then proceed on foot over the mountains to Firenze. Everything sounds so simple and matter-of-fact the way they explain it. Real pros. Not like Mario and his gang or the kids back in Albany. What's that quote from Melville: "All wars are boyish, and are fought by boys." Their initial boastfulness is gone. Or maybe it was just a put on. I'm convinced war is a kid's game anyway after you strip away the rhetoric. And that's why they love to play soldiers so much from five on.

The next day after saying goodbye to Alberto, we start out with Pupo, the talkative one handling the reins, and Carlo, the silent one, sitting beside him. I stretch out on a cluster of potato sacks in the back of the mule wagon. It's a long rough eight to nine hours. We reach Faenza on Route 9 around twilight, a walled town with an unfinished cathedral-like structure and a *piazza* surrounded by arcades with galleries above. Pupo jabbers about a famous ceramics museum and art gallery. I'm too busy watching out for Krauts to get very interested. Then we spend another couple of hours bumping through the darkness over muddy country roads until we reach a farmhouse. Inside are the Soldarises, a wild, brawling family if I ever met one. Five kids from babies to teenagers. They have a great time horsing around with each other. The supper is delicious, lots of wine and salad and cheese, a thick bean stew, fruit and pastry. We sing, play cards, even dance after the meal. The trouble is I can't sleep listening to the booming of the guns throughout the night and worrying about crossing the lines. The floor is rough and the blanket not much protection against the cold air when the fire dies out. Early the next morning we leave the wagon and mule and set out on foot. The firing seems less intense than yesterday, the temperature cooler, the fog denser, the hills steeper. I look around at the stark scrubby slopes and can't imagine how guys ever fight in country this rocky. No coral peaks turning different colors like in the Dolomites. No endless green fields either or big muddy deltas. The road is scarcely a road, only a vague path. And no picturesque Tyrolean villages with those wooden houses fitted with balconies. No ski lifts, quaint inns, hiking trails. Hills topped by grisly watch towers. A machine gunner in one of them could wipe out a battalion. Thank God, I'm not in the infantry and have to slug my way through this country.

The kids never talk about the terrain. Or about the war or the Germans. They waddle on like two fat ducks out of water. I ask where the hell we are and how much farther we have to go, but they don't answer. They seem to talk only to each other.

"*Tedeschi*," the shorter one, Carlo, shouts pointing ahead. Three Krauts are ambling on foot in our direction. They don't see us at first through the rainy mist. And I head for a couple of big rocks on the left to hide.

"No, no, *signor*," the kids whisper. "No *buono*."

I tell them I can't speak Italian well enough to pass as a native and don't have any identification papers. They'll surely stop us, ask questions, end up shooting me.

"*Non capisco*," Pupo says. I imitate the sound of a gun and pretend to be hit. They laugh and show me their old-fashioned pistols. They look as if they belong in World War I. I reach for the Sten under my poncho. They warn me to keep it out of sight. But we can't fool them. What's the big idea? What are they trying to do? They ignore my protest and let the Krauts advance. One is older and heavier, the other two my age and size. They're wearing rain gear and helmets and

149

carrying rifles. I have my poncho and cap. They smile. We smile back. They halt ten feet away and the older one cries out, "*Amici, amici*" as if he really meant it. We do the same, each of us keeping a hand out of sight, one of my fingers on the Sten, my voice lower than the kids'.

Pupo tells them we're on our way to see our grandmother in Brisighella. And I think, yeah, just like Little Red Riding Hood. They ask to see our identification. The kids say they're too young to have one and I'm not all there. They point to my head and shout, "*Pazzo, pazzo*." I act stupid, making a lot of funny faces, gesturing widely, sticking out my tongue. The bastards get a big kick out of my antics and tell us to go on. We slip by them quickly, and I'm breathing easier when instinctively I glance over my shoulder. One of the Krauts is turning around, raising his rifle, and firing at us. I spin around to face them and so do Pupo and Carlo. I fire back. The fat guy drops and the other two run as I ram home a couple of rounds. Did I kill him or is he just wounded? The kids yell obscenities and beat it the way I used to do on Halloween night getting away from some old geezer hollering at me for tipping over his garbage can. I race after them amazed at how fast they can travel over the rocky grounds and scramble up the slope. Just like goats.

"*Chilometri a* Firenze?" I shout out of breath.

"*Molti, molti*," Carlo mutters.

"*Dove?*"

They move toward the trees in the hills. They say we have a couple of hours before the *Tedeschi* come after us. I stop and look back for a second. The Krauts are disappearing in the rain with the black-rain-coated body that lay on the ground as if wrapped in a shroud. I can't get over how quickly if happened. A flick of a finger and the big man is down and then helped up and limping away or maybe dying. Why have I become so trigger happy?

They find a path and in no time we're in the woods and over a hill and into a hollow and up another steep grade past farmhouses, through villages consisting of a church and small houses and a cemetery. Streams are overflowing. All around us the noise of 105's and 88's firing and even once in a while the whistle and whoom of a mortar, the staccato of a machine gun. Nobody says anything. Pupo and Carlo plod on. I struggle to keep up, sick about the person I shot. The rain comes down so heavy at times the country seems darker and grimmer than hell with the gray soil and the limestone canyons and the thick prickly brush and thorny-looking towns the kids call *spinacristi*. Along the way we come upon a cultivated field, a vineyard, a grove of oak and chestnut trees and bushes with green leaves like spinach noodles. Poplars, too, and scrub oaks. The higher we climb the more barren the landscape. The

150

oaks give way to weeds and the weeds to mosses and bare rock. Dante must have been through here surveying the land for the location of some of his circles. The whole atmosphere reeks of the *Inferno* minus the sinister crazy characters that occupy hell.

Finally, at twilight we come to a stone farmhouse with a number of tiny windows and a terracotta tiled roof piled high with rocks. Next to it stands a stone barn larger than the house and a chicken coop with a big stove oven on top. Everywhere there are watering troughs chipped out of stone or cut out of logs, wagons with heavy wooden wheels, and vats for wine. The twins march up to the front door. Soon we're inside and being greeted effusively by two middle-aged parents and a bundle of kids, most of them short and light-skinned, fair-haired with blue-green eyes. Only one has swarthy skin and brown eyes. I look around and see a wood-burning stove and a built-in stone sink, religious pictures, crucifixes, and candles burning before statues. One of the kids has on a Tyrolean hat but no feather or Red star.

They're the Stefanises, and they act as if Pupo and Carlo are part of the family, warmly embracing them but staring coldly at me until the boys explain I'm an *Americano*. I respond with my meager Italian. We enjoy a great meal, fresh cheese and lots of wine, noodles with onions, stew, a chestnut pastry *mistocca*. I haven't eaten like this in a long time. And after a visit to the outhouse it's off to the bunk beds. Guns pound away in the distance like paddles beating rugs on a clothesline, only much louder. Another lively experience with Italian home life. And I think, Jesus, imagine coming here to the Gothic Line to find out what makes this country tick. Some relief from Dante all right. I haven't read him in days. Both a guide book, a list of enemies, and a diary that he's keeping of his journey first through hell, then up to purgatory, finally reaching paradise, the poet and the pilgrim acting as one. I'll be lucky to find my way through the first one!

We get up at daylight, and the mother, a bustling little woman with deep dark gypsy eyes, gives us bread and sausage, a raw egg, blessing effusively everything we eat. And we're off for Firenze, another day and night away according to the kids. As we march out of the yard, I look back and can't help wondering what will happen to the family if the war ever reaches them or they're caught aiding the enemy.

All morning and afternoon we crawl up and down slopes, tramp through fields and orchards, take paths through woods. Still no Krauts, only the thunder of artillery booming around us, trucks roaring down mountain roads. In a hollow a cluster of tents. Once we spot a line of soldiers strung out below and another time a convoy snaking along a narrow road. By evening we run into a second group of infantry and a

151

second motorized column. Deeper and deeper into the Gothic Line. The big guns should almost be on top of us. Any moment I expect a shell to explode overhead and the shrapnel to rip the tree tops and rain down.

"*Dove?*" I say. "*Dove?*"

They take me to an abandoned hut on the side of a steep hill. We'll wait there for the fog to cover the area. Then tomorrow night or the one after that we'll slip across the line five miles away. They know a place where there are no *soldati*. It's a stream with a thickly wooded bank. Easy to walk along without being seen. They have never met any *Tedeschi* there. Are they planning to go all the way to Firenze with me? They shake their heads.

"No Firenze?" I bark.

"No, no," Carlo mutters. "*Pericoloso.*"

"*No capisco?*"

They explain that after I leave the stream area I must cross the stand of trees all by myself. *Americani* on one side, *Tedeschi* on the hill above on the other.

"Safe?" I act out what I'm expecting when alone.

They stare at me over the candlelight, their fat faces enormous in the flame. Their eyes bulging through their glasses. They don't answer. Shrugging their shoulders, shaking their heads.

"You told me it was *salvo*," I shout remembering the word. "Now it's not, Goddamn it." They're still silent. And I jump up and point the Sten at them. I feel like pulling the trigger. They don't flinch. Carlo smiles faintly. I can't tell whether he's sneering or scared, faking or innocent. The two of them look so damn smug. I envy their confidence and their preparing to go back home and on the way pick up the wagon and hitch up the mule.

"*Lire*," I say, "I gave your *papà lire* to take me all the way to Firenze. And it was supposed to be *salvo*, no *Tedeschi*, a secret trail. What's going on?" Is this some kind of racket he's in? An underground railroad from north to south with the old man raking in the dough and you kids doing the dirty work?"

"*Papà*," Pupo whispers, watching my eyes. I hesitate, leveling the Sten gun at them. "*Papà*." They turn up their hands, act dumb.

"*Va bene*," I concede putting down the weapon and sighing. "You win. *Domani*. I guess I shouldn't expect any more than this from kids."

"*Non capisco*," Pupo mumbles.

I don't explain. What's the use? They earned their money getting me this far. It's my turn to see what I can do. Though Dante without a Virgil would be like a man without a country, family, or friend. He

152

wouldn't have a prayer. Only his poetry. But even with it I bet he'd have a hard time cracking this Gothic Line.

Chapter 17

Instead of continuing on to get where we're going  we wait two days for the fog to roll in and settle thick in the low places. And I pass the time with my Doomsday Book, reading first about these poor guys in the ninth section of the eight circle, one of them has his body ripped from the chin to the ass so entrails are dangling between his legs, another his hands and nose sliced off, another his throat pierced, another his ear missing. Reminders of Mario. Too gruesome to stick with very long. So I go back to the nice neutral guys in Limbo like Plato and Socrates, Euclid and Democritus and that bunch. At least they don't live in this sorry mess of a world. That's where I belong but not too far down in the circles, just in a relatively safe place. Not with those naked and muddy in a bog fighting each other with hands, head, chest, feet, even teeth. The fate of the angry and the wrathful.

On the second night we climb down the jagged slope to a stream and grope along the bank to what looks like an orchard of some kind. The trees appear -like old men straggling across the rocky landscape, branches twisted into grotesque shapes. The hill above is invisible. No doubt the Krauts are dug in up there with machine gun posts, mortars, and assault gun positions. Occasionally, they lob a shell toward the Allied lines and two or three boom back. The sounds are muffled. Flares fill the air and fall burning like Roman candles through the murky stuff.

Carlo and Pupo tell me to stay close to the ground and between them. There are no mines along this path.  How they know they don't explain. I kind of wonder whether they'll even stay a second after I set out. I bet if they guided someone here before, they never hung around to see if the guy was getting to where he was headed. Like the kids in Naples directing the G.I.s to cat houses but not waiting around to see if they reached their destination and got a good dose of clap.

Anyway, I shake their hands and say I'll look them up when the big push starts and their region is liberated. They hug me, kiss my cheek, and babble something that sounds like poetry. Italians have a way of making everything sound like poetry, even going to the bathroom. I wish I had a poem to give them to remember me by. But the only ones in my head are in use and in English. Imagine handing them "Fala" in Italian. Wouldn't that be something?

"No *Tedeschi*?" I point to the trees ahead.

154

"No, no," they whisper grinning. "*Arrivederci, Signor.*" They melt away in the soup, and I shuffle forward crouched over moving through it. My Sten gun ready, pointing towards the woods ahead.

Bent over I inch along, stumbling over roots, almost losing my balance crossing rocks, circling around tree trunks. One time coming upon what feels like a dead body but not stopping to confirm my suspicion. No noise anywhere except the dripping off  branches. No wires either or soft earth to indicate a mine. Maybe the kids knew what they were talking about after all. Except the possible corpse I touched that haunts me. In an open space I stop, gaze around. The fog is still too dense to see more than a few feet ahead.  Nearby there's the brushing of clothing, the creaking  of boots, a tiny jingle. I freeze. The sounds cease. I wait. Nothing. I start up, one foot first, then the other, tiptoeing along. Dead silence. The presence of someone close by works on me. Like being in a dark room with a threatening person. I hold my breath, swear I can detect breathing. Any second I expect a machine gun to go ra-ta-ta-ta, a guttural voice ordering me to halt. I want to run and get it over with, break out of this cramped position. As bad as being stuffed in a box grasping for air.

Shells from both sides lob overhead regularly, and I don't budge until the booms go off and there's a suspenseful interlude. I scratch forward a few feet and squat down still as a toad when the bombardment resumes. Listening for Krauts or G.I.s.  Because I sense definitely someone else is here. Not my imagination. The nearby noises seem to be growing louder and nearer. I can almost reach out and touch the mysterious figure looming close by.

It must be early in the morning. Another couple of hours and light will begin filtering down, the fog will thin out. If only I could gauge how much farther I have to go. Lots of limbs with eerie twists hovering above me, dangling, dripping, almost touching my head.  Like being in the wood of suicides in the *Inferno* except there is no wailing. I think of reaching up and breaking off a twig and hearing some poor bastard scream out. Goddamn, to be dredging up stuff like that at a time like this! But, boy, I sure feel like an old mole burrowing through the muck. There's something about this country and up in the Dolomites and around Ravenna, too, that prompts me to think of Dante on his lugubrious journey. Not just spooky like in Poe but downright dismal, the deep chasms, the smelly marshes and canals, these gnarled trees, this swirling mass of damp web-like air clinging to me, the rocky slopes, the soggy soil. If only I was positive about emerging from this mess of a mission alive and going on to higher and greater things, not staying permanently among the dead.

155

A machine gun opens up. I fall kerplunk on my stomach, feel bullets zinging overhead. Like back in basic training on the obstacle course at North Camp Hood. The firing ceases and I crawl forward in the mud, get up, take a few steps forward. Another burst and I bury my face again in the earth. Somebody knows where I am. Did those damn kids tip off the Krauts? No, they'd never do that. They're not the *scugnizzi* in Naples. Their father didn't seem the type, and they're doing this for him as well as for me.

A mortar pops off. I scrunch up. Shrapnel ticks down against the leaves. A near miss. I scramble ahead on my knees a few more yards. It can't be much farther to the American lines if there are any.

"*Halt*!" a voice booms out from behind with a foreign accent and I spin around. A gigantic obscure figure in a helmet and black boots looms out of the fog, a Schmeisser in hand. I can't see his face clearly, but know he's going to fire that thing right into my gut, and this is it. I stiffen. A mortar whooms close. He falls flat. I kick at his gun, turn and beat it like hell through the maze of trees, zigzagging around trunks not worrying about mines or shrapnel now. Just eager to get the hell out of there. His footsteps pound after me, his gun firing so fast it sounds like someone ripping paper across a dotted line. Others are jumping out of nowhere and shooting through the fog, bullets splintering branches, tearing at bark, spiting up dirt. And I'm knocking into branches and tripping over roots and breathing so hard my lungs are ready to burst. As if I'm reaching for the goal line and about to be tackled, pounding harder and harder into the turf, moving faster and faster, expecting any moment a blow in the back and everything going blank.

A cluster of trees appear out of the fog, and I burst into them shouting, "*Americano, Americano*!" No answer. The air is thicker than ever. I keep hitting my head against limbs, slipping on leaves, stepping into holes full of water stumbling forward, fighting my way through the brush. Bullets are slamming into trees, churning up the ground, scattering leaves. They can't follow me much farther I keep telling myself. The Fifth Army must be close by. The artillery bangs away, but no shells falling near me.

A silence settles over the place. Nothing moves anywhere. I duck behind a rock and listen. Footsteps die away. Gunfire fades. Where Goddamn it are the G.I.s? I thought surely I'd run into them by this time.

I trudge ahead not knowing where I am. Only feeling cold and wet, shivering despite the coat and poncho. Cursing Pupo and Carlo and their father. I can hardly hold the Sten. Panting so loud anybody nearby can hear me. My footsteps echo.

156

I have this fantasy that at any moment a G.I. will rush out of nowhere and take me to the rear, and I'll be sleeping in an OSS villa tonight far from this terror. But the fog and the blackness seen to grow only denser. So I plunge on afraid to call out anymore.

The outline of a hut appears a few feet ahead. I hold up, straining to hear voices, men stirring. There's no light, no one around. It must be abandoned. I edge closer, grope on the ground for a stick and toss it at the entrance. A scratch. The sound magnifies. The building could be booby trapped. I find the door open, push on it quickly and jump back. A rusty creaking breaks the stillness. Not a big place. Sort of like one of those *maglas* up on the Dolomites though not as well built.

A bullet zings overhead, then another and another. I hit the ground. Guns keep pinging away.

"*Americano, Americano,*" I cry out, recognizing a BAR firing.

"Identify yourself," a voice yells out.

"Tech Sergeant Anthony Defreest, 11099651, 2677 Detachment OSS." A tall figure stands in the doorway with an automatic in hand. I jump up and move toward him.

"Christ, a damn Eyeti, Mike!" he calls back into the hut. A light shines on me.

"No, no, I'm in civilian clothes. I've been behind the lines with the partisans. See my dog tags?" I pull up my poncho and yank them out from under my coat and shirt. "I need to go to Florence right away, see General Donovan of OSS."

"You one of those guys, too?" the big man says as we go inside with a candle burning. "The fuckers are turning up all over the place. Had a guy from your outfit yesterday, said he was in something called MO, moral operations. Sends POWS across the line. They go to the Kraut latrines and plant rumors to demoralize the bastards. Said MO used to send whores across with the hope they'd come back with information, but they never did. What a lot of crap."

"This is important. It could mean the end of the war in Italy."

"You're nuts. We'll be fighting here when I'm fifty and can't raise a finger, worn out screwing dagos and drinking vino."

A couple of other guys are there with rifles. They're all enlisted men. One shines a light on me, and I notice the 85th Division CD shoulder patch.

"Jesus, an Eyeti teenager," a corporal says, "What's he doing here, rounding up customers for his sister?"

"Where you from?" the bulky Master Sergeant barks.

"Albany, New York."

"And you're in this nutty outfit?"

157

"I parachuted a number of months ago in the Dolomites. I'm a radio operator."

"Send codes and stuff, huh?"

"That's right. Can you get me to Florence right away? I've got a lot of top secret information I need to deliver."

"Okay, Ryker, take him back to the old man. He'll get him a jeep."

"Ryker is a little guy, smaller than even I am. His M1 looks larger than he is.

"Seen any Krauts coming through the woods, Sergeant?"

"One chased me, then gave up."

"So that's what all that firing was about. The bastards won't come this far if they know what's good for them."

"Many civilians come through the lines?"

"Oh, yeah, a few homeless Eyties looking for food and a place to stay. The Krauts are planting more mines everywhere, patrolling around the clock. You're lucky to get through. We're expecting they'll be attacking us one of these days. They're really dug in on the hill. Wiped out a couple of our guys the other night. Didn't see any bodies, did you?"

"One I think. Nearly tripped me up."

"One of our guys or one of theirs?"

"I didn't stop to check."

"Just another stiff, huh?"

" I guess so."

"Get him out of here, Ryker."

I start off with the runt corporal. He's grunting and groaning and every couple of hundred yards squatting to take a crap, cursing the damn grapes he's been buying from the locals. His guts are killing him. He can hardly walk. He says he's been on the line twenty days straight. No hot food or change of clothing, hardly any sleep. His voice cracks. We come to a hollow. The fog is lifting slightly, the darkness thinning out. You can see sharp peaks and remnants of pillboxes and dugouts blasted from solid rock and surrounded by barb wire. The road is a quagmire. Artillery pieces and trucks litter the shoulder and ditches. Stone houses lie in ruins.

We enter a village that has been reduced to rubble. G.I.s are sitting around, not talking, staring at nothing. A Red Cross tent blocks a street. We come to the skeleton of a building that has lost the top floor and go in. A captain is at a field desk with a radio nearby. He's short with glasses, salt and pepper hair. Reminds me of a physics teacher I had in the Albany Boys' Academy. I tell him who I am. He's Captain Trask.

He questions me about the Kraut positions I've been through. His casualties in the past two days have been eight dead or missing. He wonders how much longer the company can take it even with the replacements trickling in.

"I betcha we look like the scarecrows to you, don't we, Sergeant?" He does seem kind of ravaged, the eyes deep in their sockets, the cheeks gaunt, a dirty beard. He says General Clark wants to get to Bologna before winter. Alexander wants to reach Vienna. Those guys are nuts. What do they think these kids are made of? I don't say anything. It's a different world down here. He asks if I would like to hang around for a couple of days and help out, though he doesn't have a uniform for me. But I've got a couple of extra MI's.

"I wish I could, but I've got to report to General Donovan."

"You report to a general? A sergeant?"

"He's head of OSS."

"Seen any action?"

"A lot of partisans killed, civilians too, women, kids. It's a Dante world up there."

"Who's he? No different from a G.I. I bet. Put a uniform on a guy, and he think it's his duty get it in the balls and not come back home. Put a shirt and tie on him and he thinks how terrible if anything happens to him when he goes to work and doesn't come back, pity the poor wife and kids. Kill any Krauts?

"Maybe a couple."

"Working with the partisans, huh?"

"All the time. They're doing a great job."

"Not around here they ain't. These Eyeties, Sergeant, don't give a shit who wins the war. They just want shoes and cigarettes. You ought to see them loot the Krauts they find, strip'em down to the underwear. Doesn't matter as long as they've got something they can wear or sell."

"Not the people I've met, a great bunch. Most would give you their shoes, socks, and underwear plus a good meal and a place to sleep. Scum are everywhere, even in our country. And those up here are having it tough right now. I better be going."

"Yeah, you better before I stick an M1 in your hand. None of this cloak and dagger baloney. I suppose now you'll spend the rest of the war in Florence admiring David's balls."

"I'd rather look at Madonna's tits." He laughs.

"Okay, Sergeant, get this horny kid a driver and write him up a ticket to go to OSS in Florence."

"Company D, 2677 Regiment," I shout out. The sergeant scribbles away on paper at another field desk, hands the sheet to me, and I follow him out to the *piazza* and the motor pool.

"Hey, Patterson," a G.I. yells from a weapons carrier, "does the Eyeti have a sister?"

"No, but I've got a brother," I call over to him.

"Screw you, buster."

"You guys been here a long time, huh?" I turn to the tall sergeant who grunts he's from Arkansas.

"Over a month. Looks like we've found us a home, don't it?"

"Lost a lot of men?"

"I heard the division's lost a hundred or more in the last twenty days. We're doing our job. Clark can't complain."

It's starting to rain again, though the fog has lifted. He finds me a driver and a jeep, checks me out, and I'm off down the road away from the big guns reverberating through the mountains, the razor-back slopes, the shot up vehicles abandoned in fields, the stumps of shattered buildings. Every now and then I see the body of a German soldier and an Italian civilian lying by the side of the road and wonder how long they've been there. At first the sight shocks me, then somehow it blends in with everything else from the ruins and the mire and the pieces of discarded equipment to the dreary morning.

We drive slowly, sometimes spinning wheels in ruts, sometimes detouring around a shell hole or over a pontoon bridge, a stretch of road blocked off because of mines, meeting more and more G.I.s until it seems a lot of the army is strung out back here--- Red Cross tents, a replacement center,, a mule corral, a Signal Corps and a Combat Engineer camp. The conglomeration is overwhelming. So few guys seem to be at the front. It's like OSS where most of the action takes place in the Dolomites and the Romagna knocking off Germans and Fascists and being knocked off.

Inside Florence the driver stops at Fifth Army Headquarters to find out where OSS is located. He comes out, jumps behind the wheel, and we zip through the city on our way south toward Siena, into the busy Piazza della Signoria , past the Ponte Vecchio with all those shops. Cross the Arno above it on a pontoon bridge and go by the Pitti Palace and a garden. A little farther on turn right and wind up at a steep incline between low stone walls. The fields to the left are full of peasants at work. Soon we're high enough so you can view the city below with the famous Duomo in the center and the Apennines in the dim distance. On surrounding hills to the east are avenues of cypress leading up to palace-like white villas, I can't get over how cultivated and built up everything is. A long way from doomed Ravenna where Dante ended his days. He must have hated like hell to leave his home town. Old men wave to us. Boys in black suites and girls in white smocks walk along the dirt road singing, carrying books, wooden lunch boxes, flowers, acting carefree. I never saw kids in the States romp off to school like that. Everywhere are olive trees and grapevines, oxen pulling plows or wagons. The rain has stopped, the sun is trying to sneak through the clouds.

We come to a brick castle with battlements, a tower, and a high wall. Just like in the movies. I can't believe it. Only a moat and drawbridge are missing. The entrance is through a gate and down an avenue bordered by gleaming white toga statues and Caesar-like busts on pedestals. Olive green tents squat behind them on each side. A few dogs are running loose. We pull up at an arched wooden doorway, and I'm almost afraid to get out and go in and face the lords of OSS. Nothing like I thought it would be, back from a mission loaded with exciting secret information. The star of the hour. Now maybe the punk of the place.

The driver zooms off and leaves me stranded. A voice calls my name. I look up, and there is Moe Jacobs I worked with at the Message Center in Washington and Algiers standing in a third-story window waving, a shell hole right under him. I wave back smiling. It's beginning to feel more like homecoming. I bend down and ring a bell mounted beside me just for fun, the kind you see in the center of a small American town used for alerting there's a fire or a celebration going on.

Inside the huge hall I gaze at a fireplace with a coat of arms, a high-ceilinged windowless room on the left filled with a long table and King Arthur-like chairs, a smaller, similar one across the way with a white tablecloth and silverware, no doubt for the officers. Boy, OSS always picks remote, regal places for their headquarters like that moldy old palace above Caserta and the villa in Parc d' Hydre above Algiers overlooking the harbor. I guess they love to live in the grand style.

"Who are you and what are you doing here?" a tall, starchy-looking captain approaches. "Civilians aren't allowed. This is United States Government Property."

"Sergeant Anthony Defreest, sir." I salute. "Back from the Orange Mission. I had to ditch my uniform to get through the lines."

"Defreest!" he gapes at me. "Defreest! Good God, the general is upstairs talking about you!"

"About me? He's here, he's in Florence? I thought…"

"That's right."

161

"Gosh, that's great. I've got to see him. Tell him what happened, what's going on up there. Give him some terrific information that could end the war in Italy.

"I'm sure he would like to hear from you. We all would. Marko came out a couple of days ago and gave us his version."

"He here?"

"Down in Caserta filing his report."

"You're..."

"Captain Baker, SO."

"Then you heard…"

"Oh, yeah, Sergeant, we've heard everything." He grimaces.

"From Marko?" He nods. "I bet he didn't tell the whole story of what happened to Major Rudd. The Russian colonel come out with him?"

"He's over with Tito they say. I think he told his story too." He glares at me.

"What's the matter?"

"I better take you upstairs to see the general and Colonel Glenn."

"I can't believe he's here. What luck."

"He's here all right. I wouldn't call it luck. As soon as he heard Marko arrived he hotfooted it from Washington. More like fuck."

"Why? What's up?"

"You. You're up."

"Me?"

"Up the creek without a paddle. On the verge of being court-martialed. The first one in OSS."

"Christ, not again!"

"Again?"

"That's all I've been doing up north, escaping from guys trying to blow my brains out because I wouldn't play ball with them, including Marko. He was going to court-martial me himself up there partisan style."

"Treason isn't exactly not playing ball, Sergeant."

"Treason? What are you talking about? I didn't give any secrets away, talk to any Nazis or Fascists. What is this anyway? I break my neck to come back here to explain what happened to the major and the mission he told me to cancel. And how Marko's friends practically handed him over to the Krauts. Talk about treason. Bill was tortured and hanged. He never got a chance to complete his mission."

"To blow the Brenner?"

"No, no, the other one. The big one."

"You mean...?"

162

"The end of the war in Italy."

"Let's go upstairs and face the general."

"Shouldn't I clean up first take off this poncho, leave the knapsack?"

"Yeah, better get rid of them." I do, my hat too.

I put them on a bench and ready myself for the appearance of a lifetime.

"Does everybody know about me? The guys in the Message Center?"

"Been a lot of rumors."

"I suppose they all must hate my guts."

"They're wondering what the hell you were doing up there."

I follow him up a wide curving staircase and down a corridor to an oak door. He knocks and enters, and I'm left standing outside speculating about what's going on inside, feeling dirty and small in this mammoth medieval museum. Down the hall there's even a suit of armor with a visor on a fake knight.

The captain comes out and tells me to go in. They're waiting. I stumble forward and find myself standing at the end of a long table with General Donovan at the head in khaki, silver stars on his shoulders, rows of ribbons across his chest. He's as silver-haired and red-cheeked as ever. His blouse appears immaculate. But he's not smiling the way he usually is. None of the officers look very friendly either. I salute, stand at attention and wait. The atmosphere becomes tense.

"This is quite a coincidence, Sergeant," he stares me straight in the eye. "We were just discussing you. Captain Marko has made some pretty serious charges against you. He claims you told the Germans where his camp was, and he lost a lot of men in a raid. Tripped up the major in the church at Cortina. Gave away codes to a Nazi official in Belluno, compromised a number of our drops. We've had to abandon all your sonnets by the way and go to one-time pads."

"Those are lies, sir. Honest, they are. I swear to God I never did anything like that. He's just trying to blame the failure of the Orange mission on me. Major Rudd was the greatest guy I ever knew. I'd never do anything to hurt him. That partisan who came in the church and took me out might have tripped him. Marko and his men didn't like him. Thought he was in league with the countess and the SS. Were any of the agents or missions I wrote codes for captured?"

"I'm afraid so. We've lost a couple in the past two weeks. Right, Colonel Glenn?" He turns to the soft-featured, slick-haired man beside him sitting up straight with shoulders squared. His uniform appears custom-made and freshly laundered. Definitely a West Pointer.

"That's right, sir. SI lost two, SO one."

"Not because of my sonnets. The Krauts never broke them. I never gave them away. You don't know what was going on up there, sir. None of you do. Those Garibaldi brigades are planning to take over the whole country after the war. Most I think are communists. They have weapons stashed away. They wiped out the Pineapple Mission at Ravenna. I know they did. I was there and talked to their leader of the brigade, Lupo, and he all but admitted it. He tried to get rid of me too. But I escaped." I falter for a moment, lose my train of thought, start to waver. "Look, sir, I've just come through the lines. I've been on the run for weeks. Everybody and his brother's been after me. I'm tired. I'll explain everything if you'll give me a chance to rest up."

"We abandoned the Pineapple Mission. Nobody was killed or missing. And we doubt you caused the major to be captured, and the partisans didn't trip up the major we think. The Gestapo had been tipped off about seeing him outside of Cortina. You better get some rest, Sergeant, something to eat, change your clothes. Then I want to talk to you before I leave tomorrow. This is a serious matter we're considering here, a breach of security, collaborating with the enemy. Captain Monetti and his men, by the way, are in Udine now. There was a disagreement. They didn't get along with the partisan leader. They're safe."

"I want to tell you about Major Rudd."

"Good. I need to hear your story. I was counting on him to change everything."

"Give my version of what happened. Marko's men could have saved Bill at Cortina. But like Marko they thought he was in league with the countess and that German professor involved in some anti-communist scheme, to prevent them from taking over the country. But he was only trying to do what you asked him to. And they were trailing Bill and me hoping to find out what we were up to. The last thing he said was to tell you to cancel the mission. The Krauts beat the hell out of him in that church. They really did. I couldn't do anything to help him. The partisans wouldn't let me."

Choking, I struggle to catch my breath. Tears blur my eyes. I can't hold them back. "He wrote a great letter to his father, gave it to a peasant to mail. Thanked him for a great life. He knew he'd never get out of those mountains alive. The Gestapo tortured him, hanged him from steam pipes when he wouldn't talk. That's what I heard."

"Some story, Sergeant," the general says. "You better get that rest now. It's been a long ordeal for you."

164

"I didn't betray you or OSS or anybody, sir. If anybody did it was Marko and that Russian Colonel."

"The major never should have let him go along. That was partly my mistake."

"Marko forced him to, sir. Claimed he was a partisan who fought on the Eastern Front and knew all about this kind of warfare."

"He's an NKVD agent sent here to spy on the organization we found out. Togliatti, head of the Communist Party, recommended him."

"I'm sure he was behind everything. Marko was always consulting him. The partisans were all licking his boots."

"That'll be enough for now, Sergeant," the general snaps. The officers around the table are glaring at me tight-lipped.

"Those two guys belong in the Ninth Circle cased in ice." They all look at me as if I was talking nonsense.

"Take him out, Captain." He stands up, his face flushed, his voice low and hard. The officer grabs me by the arm. I break free, face the room ready to tell them all what I've been through. They wait glaring at me.

I hang my head and shuffle out, hearing behind me the heavy silence of the door and the heavier silence of the brass.

Chapter 18

"I screwed that up, didn't I?" I say to the captain in the corridor.

"You better go down to Supply and get a uniform."

"A pretty sorry-looking Eyeti, huh?"

"You're dark like them all right."

"Not greasy enough, huh." I grimace.

He looks funny at me.

"I heard you're a poet."

"I was. I don't know what I am now. Do you think they'll court-martial me?"

"Either that or send you back to the army."

"Which is worse?" He laughs.

"Take your pick. Better get moving. Then report to the Message Center. You'll be sleeping down at the villa with Communications. Draw some blankets too."

He gets ready to return to his office down the hall.

"Do you believe I gave codes to the Krauts? I told them the location of Marko's camp. Christ, I was there when they attacked. I could have been killed or captured."

"A lot of evidence against you, Sergeant."

"Most of it from Marko. You a friend of his?"

"I know him."

"In the Spanish Civil War too? You with him and Frater and Martino?"

"What are you driving at, Sergeant?"

"You know what I'm driving at."

"You mean that bull you were throwing the general about the commies taking over the country. Nothing like that's going to happen." I study him, red-faced, sharp little eyes, blunt nose, thin lips.

"You been up there?" He shakes his head. "You ought to take a quick trip. Great Dante country. The Reds are in every circle but Limbo."

"You've been reading too much poetry. See you in court."

He laughs and walks off. I go down to the Supply Room on the ground floor next to the enlisted men's mess with my knapsack, leaving the poncho, draw clothing and bedding, even finding a uniform and Tec Sergeants stripes to pin on it. As I'm putting everything in a duffle bag and telling the sergeant where I've been, I find myself yearning for the freedom of the north and forgetting the dangers of the south. Gosh, I bet I'll never be on my own again like that, no forms to fill out, orders to

166

obey, officers to kick me around, just Krauts and Reds on my tail. Alone as I've ever been but then as desperate, too, ready to face my end. Could be caked in ice forever with Satan.

"How was it up there?" the sergeant says. He's an older guy with a beer belly. "I bet you got all the pussy you wanted and it didn't cost a *lire*." He grins.

"Oh, I had to pay all right. But not with *lire*."

"Jesus, I can hardly wait to get out of this country and see some real babes again. Not these broads walking around in burlap bags." A stout cleaning woman and a young girl pass by brooms in hand, black dresses with nothing underneath it appears, breasts bouncing. They're giggling. I wave.

Once more in uniform, I leave my bag in the downstairs hall and trek up to the Message Center on the third floor. It's a big room with a high ceiling and a wood floor. A board covered with wires hangs on the wall in the far right corner between narrow windows. Several radios sit on a table in front of it. Two operators with earphones are twisting the dials on their Hallicrafters, trying to make contact with a mission and every now and then clicking away with the Morse Code. Guys at desks are working with metal strip boards and one-time pads. Nobody's doing double transposition. A typist pecks away paraphrasing in-coming messages. The same busy silence I remember from Washington, Algiers, Caserta, and Bari. I think of the phrase "the treason of the clerks."

Only Moe is familiar. He glances up from a strip message he's working on and shuffles over to shake my hand, that smooth swarthy face breaking into a smile. As sleepy-looking and slow-moving as ever, the thick black hair combed straight back, the rumpled uniform. People used to mistake us for brothers, both dark and the same height. Only he's from New York where his father owns a dress shop on Fifth Avenue and I'm from Albany where my father works for the state. And he's Jewish and I'm Black Dutch. Gosh, I wish he had been with me up north. We would have had a great time hashing over Whitman and Eliot the way we did when we roomed together on F Street before I went to radio school at Camp C in Virginia and then up to Parc d' Hyrdra above Algiers before I took weapons and parachute training at Club des Pins near Sidi Ferruch. He had a whole library at the bottom of his duffle bag---Shakespeare's plays, *The Brothers Karamazov, Ulysses*.

We talk briefly about where I've been and how I got here, and he tells me what's been happening in the Oh-SO-Social wonderland. Lane has come from Washington to take charge of the Message Center in Caserta. More civilian women from Algiers are there now along with a few WACs. I'd go nuts being with them again. There's something about feeling guilty working with civilians so near the front. Too much like life back in the States. Funny, how you want being overseas to be entirely different from being in the States.

"I see you're using only pads now."

"They're faster."

"Safer too, huh?"

"That's what they say."

"Unlike my poems that can be broken because they're produced by a human being instead of a machine."

"There's even talk of doing away with strips and putting everything on one-time pads, scramblers, and big Berthas."

"The death of the poet. This war is going to end a lot of things. I suppose you've heard the rumors about me."

"I'm sorry, Tony."

"You believe them?"

"Hell, no."

"I bet any money that's why they shifted to pads."

"I miss reading your lines. You ought to have those sonnets published after the war. Call them 'Double Trouble.'"

"What did they do with them all?"

"Locked them up in a filing cabinet."

"To be used as evidence against me. Found guilty by my own poems. Did you hear they're planning to court-martial me? And not for dereliction of piss-can duty like that time in Algiers when nobody relieved me from guard duty and I went back to my tent, left my post, was threatened with a court-martial. I just came from a meeting with Donovan and the big boys. They're accusing me of cohabiting with the enemy."

"You shacked up with a Kraut?"

"They say I leaked my sonnets to them and betrayed a major by not helping him get away from the Gestapo, even was responsible for the Germans raiding a partisan camp."

"They can't do that after all you've been through."

"Your friends in SO are behind it I'm sure, Marko, Frater, and Martino. They fixed the major's wagon. He didn't have a chance. Afraid he'd mess up their plans for post-war Italy."

"So it was rough up there, huh?"

"I thought so until I came back here. This might be rougher."

"Come on, let's go up on the roof. I want to show you the sights. The view is terrific."

So he takes me through the tower, and we stand at the parapets and survey the scenery. The sun is shining. To the north the snow-tipped

168

Apennines, down in the valley Florence and the Arno and the great dome of the cathedral standing out, to the east castles and villas on hilltops with avenues of dark green cypress leading up to them. Everything so postcard picturesque, the green fields, the red roofs, the winding dirt roads. Dante, you should be living at this hour. And I break down and tell Moe the whole story, leaving out the love stuff and Bill's failed mission to see General Wolff. He interrupts to tell me you can see the flash from the artillery at night.

"They can't court-martial you, Tony," he says after I finish. "Don't worry. Never in a million years. They're just bluffing to make OSS seem more like the regular army."

"This is different, Moe."

"You mean the difference between dog and cat shit."

We laugh. It feels good being with him again, the only guy in the army I ever felt close to. He slouches in that familiar way of his, the dark hair and eyes, the full jowls and thick lips. I long to tell him all the private stuff I left out. How I fell in love with this great Italian girl who was captured because of me, maybe even tortured, rumored to have escaped. I wounded or maybe killed a couple of Krauts. I almost lost my life to a firing squad twice. I keep pretending at the same time we're talking as if we're still at Dartmouth discussing Shakespeare, Stevens, Frost, and the "Wasteland."

"I finished *The Brothers*," he says out of the blue."

"How about *Ulysses*?"

"Tough. Working on it. Taking Italian lessons from a poet in Florence. His name is Saba. He's from Trieste. He told me the people there are so bad off a piece of meat has to last a family a month. Everybody gets one lick a night."

"Wow! Hey, I saw the church where Dante's buried in Ravenna and stayed in this forest where they said he used to go to write. I've been reading the *Inferno*. Remember the copy of the *Divine Comedy* I found in the rubble of Bizerte the day we toured the city after we landed?"

"Good, huh?"

"More real than reality. There's this story about a father stuck in ice in the ninth circle, a traitor and denier of God, put in a cell with his sons and watching them starve to death and they offering themselves to him before they succumb and he's either dying of grief or going hungry and maybe taking a bite out of them. It turned my stomach. I skipped to the end to see how Dante and Virgil got out of the horror they were in. And I couldn't believe it. There they are walking away from hell and gazing up at the stars, ready to climb a mountain."

"Then parachuting into paradise." We laugh.

169

After lunch three SO guys questions me, Frater, Martino, and Baker. And I spill the whole story. But I can tell they don't believe me just as I wonder if the general believed me. Accusing me of being responsible for the raid on Marko's camp at Mount Pelmo. Claim I gave away codes to the Germans and had a deal going with the countess and her Nazi lover. They grill me hard about her and Bauer. I pretend I don't know anything about the business with General Wolff, the SS chief. Whatever I told them they'd twist to prove my guilt. So what's the use? It's as if they're trying to turn my own words against me, beat me over the head with my own poems. They keep coming back to the fact that if their men had used one-time pads instead of double transposition they might be alive today. I just say poetry never hurt anybody and mutter to myself, "'Who's injur'd by my love?'"

The same thing goes on in the SI Office. Except the two lieutenants interrogating me are a Wall Street lawyer and a psychologist from Yale. At first they want to know why a guy like me, a poet, would do something stupid like this, turn double agent. Was it for money, a woman, love of Hitler, afraid for my life? Did I think I was above patriotism and morality? Did I enjoy wounding those who trusted me? Talking about the Oedipus complex. The whole thing is silly Freudian stuff. I can see they've swallowed Marko's line without knowing fully what the major's true mission was. So I tell the Yale guy that he reminds me of the district attorney in *Crime and Punishment*. His face lights up. He asks me if I ever thought of myself as a murderer and starts writing furiously in a notebook. I tell him sometimes but not now. I feel more like a louse than a superman. Anyway, I'm too tired to confess to a crime today. Maybe tomorrow.

After an hour they release me. I have supper with Moe in the enlisted men's dining room with all those high-back chairs and the long table. Chicken and peas, French fries and greens with lots of olive oil, crispy pastry topped off by coffee. I picture the poor bastards up in the Apennines scrounging around for something to eat. Moe says wait till you taste the breakfast---pancakes and scrambles eggs, sausage and toast. Some nights there's even steak.

At twilight we walk along a dirt road to the villa, a low stone wall on each side and fields full of gnarled olive trees. Moe says the place used to be a convent. There's a legend about nuns hiding silver down the well when attacked by bandits. It's a two-story, ivy-covered house with bars on the first floor windows. We go upstairs to a sitting room where everybody stays. Birds and flowers decorate the ceiling, impressionistic paintings of nudes on the walls, pink cushioned round chairs, a pink pot-bellied stove, a sideboard full of German and Hebrew books. The

170

adjoining room has canopied beds. They're all taken. So I drop my bag by an empty cot and explore the building's sinuous passageways and tiny rooms. In the back there's a corkscrew staircase leading to a bathroom that has a chain toilet with a trapdoor but no water. Lights are dim. Downstairs is just as unfamiliar and exciting with a sunken kitchen full of pots hanging in neat rows on smoke-blackened stone walls, a dining room with a huge chandelier, a living room complete with piano and sheeted furniture, French doors that open onto a court that divides the villa.

We wander out back to the low-walled garden and sit on a stone bench, gaze at the lemon trees in boxes, the flower beds, the gravel paths. An iron gate with fancy grillwork opens onto an olive grove. Beyond lies an orchard, a field, and a grape arbor climbing to a ridge. Everything so quiet expect for a church bell ringing. The Ave Maria hush of old Tuscany at dusk. What a contrast with Naples and Bari. I could sit here for the rest of my days and write poetry. Poor Dante driven out of Florence to be buried in that murky corner of the country.

"A typical OSS mansion," I say. "And we're all guests of Wild Bill Gatsby. Any parties yet?"

"You mean orgies? No. Wait till the women come up. You know, Tony, sometimes I wonder if we'll ever have it so good again, even in civilian life. Working in a castle overlooking Florence coding message to secret agents."

"You maybe. I've got a court-martial facing me remember. Those guys grilled the hell out of me this afternoon. Looks bad, Moe. Under this good life a lot of worms are crawling around. I'm beginning to think I'm being set up just because I'm a poet."

"You didn't do anything, did you? You never gave away those codes? Told the Nazis about the partisan camp?"

"No, Christ, no, but somebody has to take the blame for the loss. A poet is more vulnerable than anybody else. You can accuse him of anything and get away with it. Talk about your double agents. He's the original one."

"I don't know about that, son," a quiet, firm voice steals up behind us out of the shadows. We turn and there's the general outlined against the house, the overseas cap, the silver hair and the two silver stars on each shoulder, the ribbons, the solid stubby frame. I almost imagine I see Gatsby's white suit coming at me out of his Long Island mansion. We jump up, salute, gulping down our words.

"I know some pretty reliable poets you can trust. Archibald Macleish, head of the Library of Congress and the Office of War Information."

171

"We were only talking, sir," I respond looking sheepish.

"About me, weren't you?"

"About me mostly and my court-martial."

"That's what I came down here to see you about."

"Well, I've got to go," Moe says and scurries off through the French doors, forgetting to salute. The general ambles over to the wrought iron white chairs on the terrace, sits down at the matching table, takes off his cap. I follow him.

"You haven't said anything to anyone about Bill's mission to Bolzano, have you, son?"

"Just a little, sir."

"You know what it was all about, don't you?"

"Sort of. The major didn't give me any details."

"Bill was going to contact General Wolff, head of the SS, about the surrender of all German troops in Italy, and he would use a radio and contact Caserta. Kesselring was in on it too. Nobody else knew on our side except Dulles in Bern and those Bill contacted. My idea originally. Even the president and the Joint Chiefs and Churchill didn't know about it at first. Hitler either. And if they had I probably would have been the one court-martialed." He laughs. "OSS would have been shut down. But you've got to take chances in this business, son, sometimes big ones. That's what it's all about. And I've taken my share I can tell you. This was my greatest gamble, bigger than my idea of exchanging intelligence with the NKVD that got killed by Hoover going to the President. Of course, Stalin would have blown his top, complained to Roosevelt. The German divisions here could be moved against his forces. The Italian commies would complain, not looking for the war in their country to end so soon. But it would have saved thousands of lives, prevented any chance of a Red take over in the north, finished the war in Europe a lot sooner. And I would have been forgiven in the end. What the hell happened anyway?"

I tell him about the countess and Bauer, his death, the major's differences with Marko and his capture at Cortina that could have been prevented. About Marko threatening to have me shot. I ask him if there isn't still a chance of going ahead with Sun Up using somebody else. He shakes his head.

"Am I going to be court-martialed?" I finally get up the courage to blurt out.

"No, I suspected something fishy all along. But I had to put up a front so nobody would suspect. Maybe Captain Marko should be reprimanded if he was indirectly responsible for the major's death by not having that partisan trying to save him, giving him the idea he was

172

betraying the Allies and the communists. Maybe my fault, too, setting up the mission. But I can't have any of this leak out. No way, son. The boys back in Washington, Hoover and Assistant Secretary of State Berle, would have my scalp. I've got a bad reputation for coddling communists as it is. And if they started an investigation I'd look pretty bad. But I don't care what a man believes, son, as long as he does a good job for me fighting this war. And Bill was giving his life for me."

"They've stopped using my poems, all together, haven't they?"

"Pads are faster. Even the president and I have one now. But he misses your Fala poem. It's going into his scrapbook."

"He really sent you messages with it?"

"A couple. I did too. Never divulge that to anyone, will you? One of them saved my job when General Strong over at G-2 almost persuaded the president to fire me and get rid of OSS. Thank God, he's gone from there now. I was at Detachment 101 in Burma when it happened. Sometimes I think I have more enemies in Washington and London than I do in Berlin and Tokyo."

"I won't, sir, don't worry. About the major's mission either."

"He was one of the bravest soldiers I've ever known. I'm putting him up for a posthumous Medal of Honor. You've done a lot for me, too, son. I won't forget it."

"What about Captain Marko?"

"He and the others are being shipped back to the States and transferred out of the organization. They've become hot potatoes."

"They getting medals?"

"I might have to give them the Legion of Merit just to prove to Congress they did fine work for us."

"What happens to me?"

"You'll be reassigned to the Message Center. I would like to recommend you for something but…"

"No, I didn't do anything up there but run like hell to stay alive."

"If all you told SI and SO today is true, you put on a Goddamn good show. And you brought back some solid information about German troop positions on the Gothic Line and the building of the Alpine Line. But I'm afraid you'll have to go unacknowledged."

"I'm used to that. Poets are only appreciated after they're dead anyway." I smile at him.

"I like that, son, like your spirit." He reaches over and pats me on the back, puts on his cap. Then he stands up, and I leap to my feet beside him. Not too much difference in height. "Poets I guess take more risks than most people, don't they?"

"That's funny, sir, because I joined OSS to avoid taking them."

"Be a code clerk sitting at a desk, huh? Like I can't stand my office in Washington. That's why I am always flying all over the world to see what's happening. Eisenhower really bawled me out for going in with the first wave on D-Day along with David Bruce, head of OSS's European operations. But we had our cyanide capsules just in case. You take one along with you up north?"

"Just my poems."

"Any lethal ones?"

"They all were if you swallowed them." He laughs heartily.

"Well, I better be off. My driver is waiting out front. Have a meeting with General Clark tonight. Send me your first book, won't you?"

"I'll dedicate it to you."

"Your Maecenas, huh? I appreciate that, son. Oh, one more thing, be careful." His tone changes. He focuses hard on me. "You know an awful lot."

"You mean…"

"I mean you know an awful lot about Bill's mission and the work of that Russian colonel, the NKVD agent."

"You think somebody might…?"

"Never can tell, son. The NKVD is everywhere. They don't like people knowing their business. The same goes for the Italian Communist Party. That's the toughest part of these missions, they don't end when you think they should. The repercussions stay with you for a long time. A new war is brewing, you know?"

"A new one?"

"With the Russians. It could be a long one. We'll just have to wait and see. When you get back to Washington, drop by my office and we'll talk about it and your poetry. You did a great job for us, a great job. In the meantime, keep your secrets to yourself."

He fades away, and I stand on the terrace looking out through the grillwork of the gate at the olive grove and the orchard slipping into the twilight.

I go inside searching for Moe. He's upstairs in his canopied bed dozing away, the big blue *Complete Works of Shakespeare* resting open on his stomach. I stand beside him. His eyes flick open, and he smiles that slow sleepy smile.

"What play are you reading?"

"*The Tempest.*"

"In a teapot, huh? Put you to sleep fast. Well, what do you think?"

"At least he knows who you are?"

"Good or bad?"

174

"Depends on what he knows about you and what you did up there?"

"He knows everything. Or almost everything. Guess I'll ask for a transfer back to the army."

"You're crazy, Tony?"

"I figure my chances might be better at the front than in some dark alley."

"What the hell are you talking about?"

"He intimated I know too much and certain people might want to silence me."

"OSS will never let you transfer. Suppose you were captured and grilled. You could give away a lot of valuable secrets."

"I never should have agreed to write those silly sonnets."

"They were a great idea. It's just we've got quicker and easier codes. Now you can write poems for yourself and get them published. You don't have to consider them confidential anymore."

"But I kind of liked doing that. All poetry is sort of confidential you know as well as useful and indispensable."

"Gives you a sense of power?"

"Stupid, isn't it? They weren't very good. Not original or anything. Nobody would ever read them much less publish them. They were just for sending messages."

"Go on, you wanted them to help win the war, change the world." He smiles at me with those big dark heavy-lidded eyes. "Think Shakespeare and Dante ever felt like that?"

"Probably not. Shakespeare was just writing for money and Dante wanted to get back at his enemies and save his soul and ours too through Beatrice and love." I gaze over his head into an empty corner of the room. "You hate to be a nothing, though, you know it, Moe."

"You mean a lowly code clerk? You'd like to be Shakespeare and Napoleon at the same time." He smiles that somnolent smile.

"I'd just like to write something that would last."

"Who wouldn't. Unfortunately, only a few can do that. You might turn out to be one of them. Better go to bed. You're on the eight o'clock shift same as in Washington. I just got the word."

"It's going to be hard getting used to the routine again."

"Not as hard as being at the front. Don't kid yourself. Now you can concentrate on your poetry for real, none of this double transposition puzzle stuff."

"I wish I could. I blew it up there, Moe. I really blew it."

"Blew what?"

"Doing something big like ending the war in Italy with my poetry."

"Dreams. They never work out."

"Yeah, my lousy sonnets. I guess in the end they were only that." I leave him laughing, thinking about how Maggie used to call me immature, idealistic, unsophisticated," an awful little boy." Guess I've grown up following Dante.

Chapter 19

Since Moe doesn't wake me for the eight o'clock shift, I don't get up until nine. Everybody is gone. I have the whole villa to myself. I climb the spiral staircase in back and pee in the toilet. The place stinks worse than an outhouse. And there's no paper. Then I head for the well house in front smothered by wisteria vines and turn a big wooden wheel until water pours out of the spigot into my helmet, remembering the nuns and their silver. I wash and shave a little, leaving most of the beard. It's a brilliant morning, crisp and clean. The sky as blue as a church window. Like nothing I have ever seen in Italy so far. Out on the road a couple of children in those black and white uniforms are walking to school with wooden lunch boxes and flowers. They must be late. I wave and they wave back. I saunter around to the walled garden, shuffle up and down the gravel paths, contemplate the olive grove and the lush grass under the bent old trees, recalling how I saw men watering them up north. Peasant women wrapped in rags kneeling in the fields digging up potatoes probably. An oxen team lumbering along pulling a wagon. Up on the ridge across the way stands a church and a line of poplars. Overhead a silver speck of a plane darts through the sky not seeming to move or make a noise.

Everything feels peaceful. Lizards crawl out of the stone wall. Clusters of chrysanthemums burst into sunlight. Grapes hang heavy on the vines. It's hard to believe a war is going on not far away. It's even harder to believe that when I leave this place and walk up to the castle somebody might take a pot shot at me.

I just want to stay alive to write poetry, that's all damn it! Why else did I join this crazy outfit? To come back after the war as a poet and get published, be recognized, surprise everyone, especially those jerks in that boarding house in Hanover who thought I was a fairy and a loser. But standing there racking my brain, nothing new is stirring. Only the mission sonnets I wrote pass through my mind one by one like the beads on Maggie's rosary, a voice saying as they slide by, "Hail to thee, blithe spirit." It's art that makes life after all, not the other way around like Wolfe and Whitman taught me. The hell with their barbaric yawps. But how to do it? Like Dante I suppose. But, gosh, he's pretty rough on people. Like a preacher sometimes but more like a magician on paper turning the violent, the fraudulent, and the traitors into creatures resembling their sins and crimes with a bunch of nutty characters real and imaginary.

Depressed yet happy at the same time despite what the general said about watching out for someone sneaking up and letting me have it. Such a mellow autumn day in melancholy old Italy. Cool green olive trees wave in the breeze, no leaves falling yet. Dante is strolling beside me talking my ear off and pointing to the white-topped peaks of the Apennines saying he wants me to climb them today, return to Ravenna. And I'm ready. Boy, am I. No more working in the Message Center as I did for a time in Washington, Algiers, Caserta, Bari, eating chicken and steak, reading Shakespeare and Dostoyevsky, sitting across the table from civilian women coding and decoding, becoming nostalgic watching them. One of the reasons why I volunteered for Orange in the first place was to go beyond the familiar and delve into the unknown.

I walk up the dirt road to the castle and enter the gate, stroll down the row of statues, busts, and tents. Moe waves once more from a Message Center window. It's going to be tough to say goodbye to him and leave all this. Anybody would think I was nuts. Then I've always been the Section Eight type. You can't be the sanest, bravest, happiest guy in the world and write good stuff. Your imagination starts churning and you never know what will turn up. After getting something to eat and drink in the kitchen, an egg, bacon, toast, coffee, I trudge up to the second floor. The colonel's office is at the end of the hall. The captain at the desk says Colonel Glenn is in Florence seeing the general off. What did I want him for? My pay? I have a lot coming. They're working on it. Be a few days before the exact amount has been figured out. How about a court-martial? That's been dropped. Nothing will appear on your record. The general's orders. What do you think of that? I'm grateful. But that's not why I came to see the colonel.

"I've come to say goodbye." He looks at me funny. He's a short, square-shaped guy with a thick black mustache, hard chin, stubby hands, and swarthy complexion. The name plate on the desk reads "*Capitan* Lazzari."

"Where do you think you're going, Sergeant? To the States?" He laughs.

"I can't tell you."

"Secret, huh?"

"Top secret."

"Dropping behind the lines again to see if you can louse up another mission? Did you really work with the Krauts, hand over those codes, gave away the location of a partisan camp? If you did and I was the general, I'd have you shot and the hell with any court-martial. Or maybe you're going AWOL."

"Would I tell you if I were? No, I've just got to go where I belong." And I walk out of the office, hesitate, thinking about Moe up in the Message Center. Then I shuffle toward the stairs.

"Hey, Sergeant, wait a minute." The captain runs after me. "What the fuck are you up to anyway? Gone loco or something? That mission affect your brain?"

"Tell the colonel I've gone off to the mountains to write poetry."

"Poetry? What mountains? What is this, some joke?"

"If it is, it's on me."

He grabs my arm, forces me to face him. "Come on, what's up? Losing your marbles?"

"You mean my mind. I had a pretty hard time up there, Captain."

"I heard you did. A lot of narrow escapes."

"One too many. Don't worry I'll be all right. Just need a little time away from everything."

"How about a pass into town?"

"I prefer a ride in the country."

"Why did you want to see the colonel for then? Know him?"

"In a way. He knows me and what I've been through and where I'm going."

"Where ever that is don't forget to come back by five. We don't want to send the Marines after you." He guffaws. "We're having steak tonight I hear."

"I won't."

I walk down the stairs to the great hall and the fireplace with the coat of arms. Somebody at dinner last night said the castle wasn't authentic. Just built to look that way to attract American tourists and filled with phony antiques. The perfect home for OSS.

Light out like Huck, that's what I've got to do. But this is Dante country, and there's not that much to light out to. Not like the States in those days when the West was wide open. I go to the Supply Room, draw a .45, a Sten, an M1 rifle, several rounds of ammo, a knife, and a couple of C-ration cans. I tell the sergeant it's for a mission up north with the partisans. He's skeptical but issues the stuff anyway. OSS never bothers with forms very much. Except sometimes these guys from the real army can be sticky. They don't understand what goes on in OSS and how different it is from the regular army.

I head for the motor pool and inform the sergeant in charge I'm driving over to see Major Derkins at the Fifth Detachment. He's reluctant to give me a jeep without written authorization. Motor pool guys are always stricter than Supply guys. They think they own the vehicles. So I ask him to call Captain Baker in SO, tell him I'm reporting on my mission to Major Derkins, the general's orders. He strides off and rings him up and comes back.

"Okay, enjoy the joy ride and the mission whatever it is. OSS has some weird ones."

"I never joy ride. Wish I could someday."

"Why all the firepower?"

"Just what I had on the last little outing I was on."

"I heard you had it rough. Lost your major, didn't you?"

"Almost my mind too."

"I don't see how you guys take that kind of life up there for long. I guess you have to have a sense of humor."

"Do you?"

"Funny as a porcupine sometimes. I bet the pussy's great."

"The best there is. Free as the birds and no VD."

I pick out a jeep, throw my stuff in, and settle behind the wheel. Moe comes running from the castle. I've never seen him move so fast. You can tell he's no athlete and likes the good life.

"Where are you going, Tony?"

"On another mission."

"With a .45, a Sten, and a rifle?"

"Headed for the front."

"Out of your mind? You can't do that."

"Why not? I know too much? I might be captured?"

"You just got back. You need to rest up. Hell, you've done your duty."

"I didn't finish a number of thing up there. Have to see a man about a mountain and what's on top. So long, Moe. Say goodbye to Shakespeare for me. I'm sorry I never got around to doing it his way, only Byron's and Dante's. They understood this kind of life and went for it."

I turn the switch, shift into first, jerk forward, and stall. I've always had a problem with the gears on these damn jeeps. Finally, I take off thinking of the statutes and busts, the tents and dogs running around in the courtyard. Then it's down the dirt road to the villa to grab my knapsack, run back to the jeep ready for the return to the *Inferno*.

After I'm ready to go a wizened little man accompanied by a dimple-faced boy blowing a Halloween horn greets me in the drive between the hedges. I get out of the jeep to talk to him. He says he's the owner and is in the olive oil business. All of a sudden he's gesticulating and spouting about how many *lire* he spends every month on food. Europe no good, dirty, ruined. America fine, beautiful, rich, *va bene*. Here you think what your grandfather did. In your country you think for

180

yourself. Oh, you have beautiful pictures. I love your *Life*, your *National Geographic*, the glass houses you see out of and no one sees you.

He's getting wound up with something in mind. The kid stares at me with that pimply fat face, tooting away on the horn.

"You like Rome, *molto storia*, New York no *storia*. *Libertà*. Oh, what happens if no America? English no good."

He asks me what I think of Russia. When I tell him a lot of people are afraid of her. He says he's just a working man. He doesn't have to worry like capitalists. He giggles. Then he starts talking about a friend who was in Berlin last year and saw Russian girls marching through the streets wearing large crosses. I tell him I have to leave. He wants dollars. Give *lire* for them. I shake my head. How about C-rations? I shake again. He shrugs his shoulders. The boy keeps peeping away on his tiny horn and gaping up at me.

"How much you sell jeep?" he says out of the blue. "With jeep you ride into the clouds."

"No can sell. Belongs to the army."

He acts disappointed but smiles away. I hand him a pack of cigarettes and give the kid a bag of licorice that I picked up at the PX.

"Time to be off for that ride in the clouds," I say. "Want to join me?" He shakes his head sadly. I jump in behind the wheel and shoot off to the city with the Apennines in the background. The guns are on the seat beside me. I wonder why he never made an offer for them.

It's a short trip down to the Siena-Florence highway, then to the Via Romana, cross a temporary bridge south of the Ponte Vecchio where there are a few shattered buildings. Art among the ruins, though the main city was hardly touched by war, just a few structures in the center hit. No doubt it was declared an open city. I ask an MP how to get to the front. He tells me to follow the convoy of trucks ahead. They're going north on Route 65 to the Second Corps. So I trail them to a *piazza* and the Arc de Triumph and then through the suburbs into the hills. The landscape becomes more and more familiar. After two hours of stop and go driving I turn off and bump along east to Firenzuola that looks as if it had suffered a lot of damage. No sign for the 85th Division yet, only one announcing we're approaching the front.

A MP stops me to ask for my orders. He's the squat, meaty fullback type with the black brassard and the white helmet and a .45 on his webbed belt. I tell him I don't have any orders. I'm from OSS. I'm sneaking through the lines tonight to rejoin a partisan brigade around Ravenna. I'm not supposed to carry identification, only dog tags.

"What are you, Sergeant, some kind of spy?" He squints at me while chewing tobacco.

"A radio operator. I brought some top secret information to OSS a couple of days ago, and I'm returning to pick up some more."

"What is this? You gonna drive that jeep right through the lines waving a white flag?"

"I'm leaving it for somebody to drive back to the castle."

"Castle? Who is your superior officer?"

"Colonel Glenn, Company D, 2677 Regiment, OSS. But he will deny he ever heard of me. It's all very top secret stuff that even he's not supposed to know about."

"Where did you come through the line a couple of days ago?"

"I don't know the name of the village. It was in the 85th Division sector. A Captain Trask was in command. I don't remember his regiment or battalion or company or anything like that." He walks over to consult with a couple of other MP's and then strolls back with a captain. He's a little guy with glasses and reminds me more of a clerk than a policeman.

"What the hell is this, Corporal?" he yells at the MP questioning me. His voice is deep and rough. "You're holding up traffic." He ambles over to my side of the jeep. "Who the fuck are you anyway, and what are you doing here?"

"Tech Sergeant, Anthony Defreest, sir, code name Dante, radio operator from Company D, 2677 Regiment, OSS, Fifth Army Detachment. I'm going through the lines to work with partisans in Ravenna."

"You mean you're selling those weapons you got on the black market?"

"There's no black market up there."

"Don't kid yourself. It's everywhere in this country. How do I know you're not going AWOL?"

"Through the enemy line in a jeep with guns?"

"You might be. Anything's possible in this war. I've seen a G.I. let himself be captured just so he could get away from the front. You say you're a radio operator?"

"Yes, sir. A code clerk. General Donovan's sending me back to my mission."

"Who's he? And where the fuck's the radio?"

"With the partisans. He's the head of OSS."

"And what's this Dante crap?"

"Code name. Everybody behind the lines has one."

"You a spy?"

"A poet in disguise." I smile at him.

"A poet? What is this, you pulling my leg? How old are you, Sergeant?"

182

"Twenty-two. From Albany, New York. I went to Dartmouth."

"Yeah, I heard this OSS outfit has some fruitcakes. Okay, go ahead. But you'll have a hell of a time getting through to the front and then through it."

"I know that. But I'll recognize where I came through the other day, know the guys there if they're still around."

"They might not be when you arrive. The Krauts launched a couple of heavy attacks in that sector last night. The casualties have been rolling down all day. Why don't you pick a quieter spot on the east coast? These mountains are fuckers. The worst fighting the Fifth Army's been in I hear, worse than Salerno, Cassino, Anzio, and Monte Altuzzo in the Giogo Pass. The bastards are really dug in."

"Yeah, I had a hard time coming here. But I've got to get back to Ravenna. You know, the place where Dante died."

"He did, huh? Well, don't you make the same mistake." He laughs. "He was a poet, wasn't he?"

"The greatest."

"I like Edgar Guest myself. Good luck, Sergeant Dante. Say hello to hell for me." He chuckles.

He steps aside, waves me through, and I zoom away. Howitzers are booming in the mountains, I can even hear faintly the chatter of a machine gun. I see a sign for the 85th Division and veer off and move along a dirt road past tanks and trucks and tents in a field, a mule pen, a Red Cross tent, the same conglomeration I saw the other day. The sky is darkening fast. It's colder up here. The steep bare rocky slopes press closer, look starker. Shattered farmhouses lie in rubble everywhere. No civilians around. Just soldiers walking by the side of the road or sitting in bombed out barns and churches, drinking from fountains in squares, the stones torn up. Their faces gaunt and gray. Those chugging along glancing at me with dead stares. I ask a corporal in combat boots, fatigues, carrying an M1 if he ever heard of Captain Trask.

"Yeah, he is up at Pike's Penis."

"What's that?"

"One of them shitty hills around here. I don't know the name of the place. They say he lost some of his company last night. You a replacement for the 338th? That's his regiment."

"No, just a friend."

"Then you better wait. He's being shelled to death. Nothing's getting through up there but mules."

"I've got to see him."

"You have a message for him or something?"

"Sort of."

"Then your next right. The mud's thicker than cow crap. Your jeep will never make it. Better walk. When you hear one of those 88's come screaming over, dive for a ditch or you're a goner."

It's starting to rain. The wheels are sinking deeper and deeper, spinning faster and faster. I move ahead slower and slower. A sergeant sitting in a weapons carrier I pass tells me it's two miles to the 338th. Be careful. Can't I hear?

I listen above the roar of the engine to the artillery banging away. But I keep hearing another sound, too, beating inside me. And I jam my foot down on the pedal, shift into low gear grinding my way forward. The jagged skeleton of buildings stand out against the grayness. Shells are landing closer. Explosions rip through the dull sky becoming a kind of turbid twilight. One screams over not far away. I grab the M1 and leap out and run for cover behind a pile of rocks. The next scores a direct hit, and the jeep blows up in a flash, the pieces flying into the air like splinters. I lie in the muck for a couple of minutes waiting for another one to sail over, gazing at the small fire. The smell of burning rubber filling the air.

Then everything is unnaturally quiet, and I stand up and go over and examine the blackened shell of a jeep. The knapsack with my Dante is in ashes, the Sten and ammo are missing along with the knife and C-rations. Still have my rifle and .45. Now I'll never get to the *Pugatorio* or a chance to reread any *Inferno* cantos. Oh, well, there's nothing like the first time. I stare at the remains for a minute, then hike the rest of the way up the hill to a clump of broken houses. The streets are deserted and clogged with rubble. Not a G.I. anywhere. Not even any vehicles in the square. No jeeps or weapons carriers or half-tracks.

I head for a church, the only structure still standing, though most of the roof is gone and parts of the walls. And if there isn't the crew I met the other day along with the sergeant from Arkansas and Captain Trask. Sitting at the altar out of the rain around a small fire with a number of G.I.s. They're all wearing helmets. The only one missing is Ryker, the little guy with the shits.

"Holy Christ, look who's back!" the sergeant yells out. He seems shrunken somehow, his shoulders hunched, his face wraith-like. "The kid from OSS."

"That's me," I answer walking toward them listening to my boots clicking and splashing on the stones. "I'm back. Who says you can't go home again?"

"Just in time to join the homeless," he bellows.

"You guys all that's left?"

"Out of a hundred and twenty," the captain notes. "Company B, 1st Battalion, 338th Regiment, 85th Division ceases to exist. We were supposed to be relieved this morning but nobody showed up. Got cold feet." He laughs. "What the fuck are you doing up here anyway? I thought you wanted to get out of the fighting?"

"Going back through the line to the partisans. Orders."

"You picked the wrong place. Everything is tighter here than a virgin's hole. You'll never make it."

"Got to try anyway."

"Just because some shit ass officer down in Florence told you to. They don't know what the fuck's going on up here."

"Stop the war."

They look at me stunned and then break into smiles.

"Holy Mother of God!" the sergeant says. "Another one gone off his rocker. If they don't get it in the balls, they get it between the ears."

"You got some secret weapon?" the captain says.

"I think so."

"A ray gun?"

"Poetry."

"Poetry?" They burst into laughter. I look startled at first and then laugh with them because it does sound funny. And I wonder why I said that. Even what I'm doing here at the front, ending up in this blasted old church with the rain forming puddles in the nave.

"I know it sounds crazy. But that's my job, communications."

"You mean going back across the lines to set up communications with somebody back here?"

"Going to try."

"Who you seeing?"

"That's confidential."

"Better forget it. Those woods you came through the other day have been mined solid. And we had to abandon them the shelling got so bad. You better join us, kid, when our replacements arrive, if they ever do."

"I don't know."

"I do," the captain says. "Let's hope there's no attack before then. We're down to a skeleton crew." He chuckles to himself, and when it sinks in everybody joins in the joke. What a dirty, smelly, depressed, beaten up bunch of guys!

"You really believe this poetry crap, don't you?"

"It's worked so far."

"How?"

185

"Can't tell you. Top Secret." They smile. I sit on the step near the fire to dry off and warm up.

"Jesus," he says "why would you want to leave Florence for this shit hole?"

"Nuts I guess, like all poets."

"Just wanted to say a prayer for us while paying a last visit to hell," the sergeant guffaws. "Or was it a poem?"

"That too. Hey, look." I point at a crucifix resting upside down against a beer can.

"Who did that?" the captain yells out. "Bad luck." The sergeant jumps up and rights it.

Completely dark now. We huddle closer to the fire fed mostly by wood from fallen beams, eat K-rations, drink out of canteen cups, stare at the rain pounding the stones. The damp chill is numbing. And the big guns resume firing all around us. Every time a shell explodes nearby the church shakes and I jump.

"You guys gonna stay here all night?" I ask.

"You got a better place for us to go?" the captain mutters.

"Down the hill."

"We have our orders."

"Even if the shelling drives you out of here?"

"Afraid so. That's the army for you, Sergeant. Course you're in this OSS outfit and can leave anytime you want. Got a heavy date in Florence with a good pair of tits?" He smiles at me.

"Maybe I better go down in the morning after all. I guess I'd never get through."

"Given up ending the war, huh?"

"For the time being."

What a rough night between the cold rain and the artillery, using the altar as a command post and letting it serve as a place where the wounded come on the way to the Red Cross tent nearby. One guy's leg is operated on without any anesthetic, another dies on a stretcher soon after two medics bring him in. His face is raw meat. Shrapnel had ripped his body to shreds, and he looks like a bloody rag of bones. Someone runs in and yells it's stopped raining. I go down to the nave and gaze up through the splintered rafters and see a couple of faraway lights flickering above me.

"Hey, the stars are out," I holler. Two G.I.s come running and glance up as if I had announced the Northern Lights were on display. The glimmering vanishes and low clouds hang over us again. Drizzling begins. And they slump back to the fire.

186

At daybreak I go down the hill with a couple of G.I.s from the church as a line of them trudge up to the town past us. Nobody says anything or looks too happy. Like two groups of prisoners passing each other on the way to different cell blocks. The sun is trying to come out, a ghost gliding behind a curtain of clouds. We stop at a replacement center, pile in a weapons carrier with a bunch of guys, and in no time we're our way down to Florence.

"Great to see you again, Longfellow," the driver who took me to OSS the other day shouts and I told him I wrote poetry. "You poets are lucky bastards living at that castle." I'm sitting beside him. Taking off we're all just waiting to see the great dome of the cathedral. "'Thank God, Florence,'" I mutter to myself.

"Yeah, but most of us don't live too long."

"But you live good. All those women and that drinking."

I sneak a look at him and then at the others behind me. They act as if they're not really seeing or hearing me, thinking no doubt how they have to come back in a week or two."

"Since you guys will be in Florence for a while, why don't we all get together sometime?" I burst out. They're silent for a moment. Still that resigned look. Nobody stirs.

"Sure, Longfellow," someone pops up in the rear, "Let's meet and have a ball. We'll take in the art museums and you do the cat houses." A few grin. Nobody laughs.

The weapons carrier stops in front of the Red Cross building, and I climb out, smiling around at the group, none of the guys meeting my farewell glance. And I don't even know their names. In a few weeks I won't even remember their faces. Not ships that pass in the night but the dead. I feel everything welling up inside me. My eyes water. They ride off down the street and disappear. Nobody says a word or waves.

I dash in the building, get in touch with OSS, wait two hours for transportation. And, gosh, if Moe doesn't show up in a jeep. He blows his horn a couple of times, and I run out and jump in the front seat and shake hands.

"Where the hell have you been, Tony?"

"I'm not sure. Somewhere at the front."

"Everybody said you'd gone AWOL."

"I thought about it. But I wanted one more look at Ravenna. They thinking about court-martialing me again?"

"I doubt it. Why did you come back?"

"I lost Dante. A shell hit the jeep. I decided I couldn't make it without him. Wanted to see you too."

"Me?"

187

"Yeah, you and your great books". He laughs with that deep rich voice of his.

"What has that got to do with it?"

"Everything."

We ride through the city and over the Arno onto a pontoon bridge. It's almost noon. The sun is high but hazy and a little weary it seems. The pavement has a worn look. The air cool but not yet crispy. Past the Pitti Palace and the terraced Boboli Gardens with their statues and fountains that Moe points out to me. I wondered what they were when I came by the other day. And despite the military traffic things begin to feel normal again.

"Well, I guess that's the end of Dante and the partisans," I say. "*Finito*."

We come to a side road and turn right up a hill.

"Don't kid yourself, Tony. They're always be there for you."

"'*Seguir virtute e conoscenza*,' huh?"

"So you've learned some Italian up north. Follow virtue and knowledge. I've learned some too."

"Mine from a partisan in Ravenna." He winks at me. "I wish you had been with me."

"I'm not."

As we climb between buildings and low stone fences heading into the country of villas and olive groves, I muse about sailing home someday in a troopship, past Sardinia and Spain and through the Strait of Gibraltar with Ettore and Giorgio, Mario and Bill, Angela and Moe, and all the guys from Company B. They're tired as hell but eager to light out, fed up with war and the Old World, now looking for the New. When they reach the Atlantic, they burst into a cheer. And after many days and nights, there it is, the great green mountain rising up out of the ocean just the way it does at the end of Ulysses' heroic last voyage with his crew as Dante points out, urging them not to be like animals but seek new worlds, strive for new knowledge, find new ways to live. The peak, dim through the mist, soars higher and higher, grows closer and closer. Everybody stands open-mouthed at the railing and stares up at the top and the stars.

"Well, here we are," Moe, says. Ahead looms the brick walls and parapets of the castle.

"Better than being drowned at sea."

"What do you mean, Tony?"

"Just thinking where I've been and what I've done."

"You've been through a lot all right. More than most of us."

"He got me back somehow. Maybe I'll go on with him after all."

188

"You mean..."

"Continue the journey, climb *Purgatorio* At least I'm out of the "dark wood."

## About the Author

John Kimmey, born in Albany, New York, a graduate of Dartmouth College, joined the army in 1943 and was recruited by OSS, the precursor of the CIA, to work in Communications, first in Washington and then in North Africa and Italy. His work in Washington dealt with OSS operations around the world, in North Africa with spies in Southern France, in Italy with spies in Rome and partisan groups in Northern Italy and the Balkans. He received a Ph.D.in English on the G.I. Bill at Columbia University after the war and has taught at the University of Virginia, VMI, and the University of South Carolina. His stories have appeared in a number of magazines, such as *North American Review, Confrontation, and Image.* His novels are *Mussolini's Gold* and *The Poet in the Code Room.* His nonfiction includes anthologies on tragedy, satire, modes of literature (five volumes), a guide to writing, and a critical anthology of short fiction. He has also published a book on Henry James, a monograph on 17th Century English poetry, and articles on 17th Century English poetry and American and Russian fiction. His memoir of a weekend in New York during the World Series was cited as notable in *Essays 2018.*